Bound by an ancient blood pact, Deidra MacKay is a reluctant witch who would do anything to give up her powers—until she meets a darkly handsome Scotsman who may give her reason to use them. . . .

Don't miss Jen Holling's

MY IMMORTAL PROTECTOR

"Holling crafts an enchanting and action-packed adventure/romance that will thrill readers. She secures her place as a writer of unique talent and a storyteller extraordinaire."

—*Romantic Times* (4.5 stars—HOT)

**My Immortal Protector and My Immortal Promise
are both available as eBooks**

**Praise for Jen Holling's "superb" (*Booklist*)
MacDonnell Bride series**

*My Wicked Highlander   My Devilish Scotsman
My Shadow Warrior*

"Medieval Scotland comes to life . . . each book is moving and . . . alluring characters, Holling . . . over evil. . . . No one shoul . . .

ALSO BY JEN HOLLING

MY
IMMORTAL
PROMISE

JEN
HOLLING

POCKET BOOKS

New York London Toronto Sydney

Pocket Books
A Division of Simon & Schuster, Inc.
1230 Avenue of the Americas
New York, NY 10020

This book is a work of fiction. Names, characters, places, and incidents either are products of the author's imagination or are used fictitiously. Any resemblance to actual events or locales or persons, living or dead, is entirely coincidental.

First Pocket Books paperback edition November 2008

POCKET and colophon are registered trademarks of Simon & Schuster, Inc.

For information about special discounts for bulk purchases, please contact Simon & Schuster Special Sales at 1-800-456-6798 or business@simonandschuster.com

Design by John Vairo Jr.
Illustration by Larry Rostant

Manufactured in the United States of America

10 9 8 7 6 5 4 3 2 1

ISBN-13: 978-1-4165-2586-8
ISBN-10:   1-4165-2586-6

MY
IMMORTAL
PROMISE

Prologue

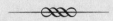

She was twenty-seven when she'd first acquired a taste for blood. A grown woman, past her prime, and good for little except hard work. And she did a great deal of that. She worked all day in the fields, cared for their animals, and in the cottage she cooked and washed and made certain they had light and fuel. Then *he* came home and worked her in bed. She usually made it through it all unscathed, provided she kept her mouth shut.

But sometimes she didn't, or more aptly, *couldn't*. Sometimes the devil inside of her made her say something. Like that long-ago night.

Gareth had been hungry. According to him, he'd just come in from the fields and, damn it, he was famished! Where was his dinner? Aedammair knew he'd been a few cottages down, drinking ale, but she hadn't commented. Not then, at least.

She had told him dinner wasn't ready. She'd had to patch a hole in the roof and had gotten a late start.

His dark brow lowered over red, veined eyes. He sat at her clean table, scattering crumbs all over it as he crammed her fresh-baked bannocks in his mouth. "Damn it, woman, I am short on temper tonight."

Her gazed traveled downward as she said, "That isna all yer short on."

She would have slapped her hand over her mouth had she not held a ladle in one and a turnip in the other.

Never mind that she had spoken the truth. Color burst in his cheeks, a red so deep it was almost purple. He looked as if he was ready to explode, and likely he was, as there was no disputing her statement.

And so that was how later that evening Aedammair found herself huddled on the floor of the cottage she shared with her husband, barely able to see out of two swollen eyes and unable to crawl to the bed because her body was so battered. She thought she had broken bones—ribs, arm, legs—but she was not sure.

She could not cry. She could do nothing but lay there and wish to die.

And then someone was there, in her cottage. A woman. Aedammair was ashamed and wished to hide, but could do nothing. Everyone knew he beat her, but no one had ever seen her like this. The woman touched Aedammair's face. She could barely see the woman through the watery red haze. She had dark hair and pale skin, but that was all Aedammair could discern.

"It was your man, wasn't it child?"

Aedammair couldn't nod, but she tried.

The woman made a sound of disbelief as she pushed a lock of red hair out of Aedammair's face. "Men are worthless, disgusting vermin. We do not need them."

Aedammair wished that were true. But she would

probably starve without Gareth. It was the Highlands; there was no work for a lone woman. No one would take her in if she left her husband. She wished she could kill him and find another man, but who would have her now? Her bones would probably heal crooked and her face would be scarred.

"I see you do not believe me," the woman said. "Would you like me to show you?"

Show her? "I . . . do n-not . . ." She couldn't get the rest out. Her face hurt too much and her teeth wobbled. The woman swam before her as tears filled her eyes. Her teeth. She'd always had good teeth.

"I ken, child. More than you know." Her hand stroked over Aedammair's hair. "You do not understand. But you will. When you wake tomorrow night, you will be a new woman, free of this pain and weakness. We will choose a new name for you. And then you will come back here and make your husband suffer as he has made you suffer. When that is over, you will come with me and we will live a new life, free of men and their base wants and needs. Would that please you?"

It sounded heavenly. Was that what it was? A place where she was free of this pain, free of Gareth? Where justice would finally prevail and Gareth would suffer all he had inflicted on her?

"Aye," she forced the word through her raw and bloodied lips.

"Good," the woman said, and there was a smile in her voice. "This will only hurt for a second, and then the pain will be gone forever."

Chapter 1

$\mathcal{D}$rake stood in the dark alley, gaze fixed on the village center, waiting. It was full dark. The night was quiet, cool, devoid of insects. His eyes had adjusted to the darkness, but without the moon it was still difficult to make out any details.

The witch should have escaped by now. Drake's gaze narrowed on the dark smudge of the thieves' hole, marked by a pole. Earlier that day the witch's hands had been nailed to the pole, but later he'd been ripped free and thrown down into the hole.

Drake had seen the cycle often enough in the past six months. It followed a similar pattern each time: the witch was captured, tortured into confession, and then waited in a hole or other prison to be executed. And through each one, Drake observed—an interested bystander, nothing more. On occasion he would plant suggestions if he thought it prudent, and he always made certain the witch had opportunity to escape eventually.

The escape was of vital importance, since he had to be captured by another village in order to start the whole process all over again.

They'd been through this dance a number of times and the pattern was always the same. Usually by now the witch had escaped and was slinking away into the night, with the occasional frantic stop to feed on a farm animal.

But tonight was different. Drake continued to wait in the darkness, his lips tight, his fists opening and closing rhythmically, debating whether to leave the safety of the darkness. He scanned the town square again. The windows of the houses surrounding the square remained black. He sprinted across the square, dropping to a crouch beside the thieves' hole. He surveyed the square again.

He leaned over the wood grating. "Luthias," he called in a loud whisper. "Luthias."

Nothing but silence. Drake sat back on his heels, listening and waiting, wondering if the witch had finally died.

A *baobhan sith* did not die easily; Drake knew this, so the silence puzzled him. True, the cycle of abuse had been ongoing for months, and any human man would have died long ago—or, at the very least, been permanently crippled from all that Luthias had endured. But Luthias was not a human man and had been through worse than the relatively tame bit of torture he'd been subjected to in this village. A dunking. The wheel. Some rocks on the chest. Nothing a *baobhan sith* couldn't recover from in a few hours.

"Luthias," Drake called again, his voice a harsh whisper. Still no answer.

Drake's chest constricted. If Luthias was dead, then

it was over. Drake could be finished with this duty he'd assigned himself.

And move on to the next one, the one he had been using Luthias to avoid.

Drake's head bowed. He stared sightlessly at the ground. He was tired, weary to his bones. His taste for vengeance had been satiated. If Luthias was not dead now, he would be tomorrow, when they burned him at the stake.

Drake stroked his beard. Had it not been for the dreaded task that followed, he would have loved to be finished with this one. It had been six months. Doubtless the thing that waited for him believed he did not intend to fulfill his promise at all. And that was not true. Drake MacKay honored his promises, even the ones that were misery to even contemplate.

It was time to go. He had done what was necessary to protect his family and punish the man who persecuted them.

But it was over now.

He secured the grate over the thieves' hole. He had unlatched it earlier so that Luthias could easily escape. Let him meet the village's sentence. It was in their hands now.

After another visual surveillance of the village, Drake returned to the safety of the dark alley. His horse was stabled close by. Now that he'd made the decision, he didn't want to waste another moment on Luthias.

He saddled his horse and led it out of the village. When he was clear of the last cottage, he mounted and rode into the night, bound for the far northern highlands and a promise overdue.

The island was exactly as Drake remembered it. Windswept, treeless, lonely. A lethargic bell clanged in the distance as a goat wandered through the tall grass. The clouds broke, and sunlight blinded him. He squinted as he crossed the island, following the sound. He remembered the last time he had made this same journey under very different circumstances. He had come here with murder on his mind. To take revenge on the *thing* responsible for his years of misery. Instead, the blood witch had saved the life of his friend.

This was not a woman who granted favors out of the kindness of her heart. In fact, technically, she wasn't a woman at all and probably didn't have a heart. She was a *baobhan sith*. A blood-sucking witch. And he owed her a life.

His life.

It wasn't worth much these days anyway.

He waded through the tall grasses to the top of the hill. A lush green valley, dotted with white puffs of sheep, spread out before him. The *baobhan sith*'s house nestled in the side of a hill, not immediately visible to the unobservant. It had a new door—no doubt thicker than the last one, which he had hacked through with an ax.

The door was locked from the inside, but he had expected no different. *Baobhan siths* were nocturnal creatures. They derived their power from the night or the moon—he didn't know which. Because of this they often hid themselves during the daylight hours.

He pounded on the door, not really expecting any response. When none came, he settled down beside the door, crossed his arms over his chest, and closed his eyes.

He slept fitfully, startling awake frequently, hand on dirk, wondering where he was. The moment he remembered, his body relaxed, his eyes turning to the door, still closed, then to the sky, gauging how long until the sun set. Then he shut his eyes and slept some more.

He dreamt, too. Strange, vivid dreams that seemed real and yet couldn't be. He saw the *baobhan sith* in his dreams, walking in shadows, just out sight. He would tell her to stop running and come out where he could see her, but she only faded further away.

The next time he woke it was in increments and with care. His eyes opened to the darkness. He didn't move as he waited for them to adjust to the gloom. It was night, but no stars or moon were visible. A thick fog had moved in from the water and hung around him, clammy. He suppressed a shiver.

He got to his feet, listening. Sheep bleated in the distance. He felt along the grass wall until he touched the door. It was open, just a crack. He pushed on it, and it creaked inward.

Muscles tensed and ready, he stepped into the house. The darkness was complete; not a single candle lit his way. He had a vague recollection of his last visit six months ago. There had been a table several feet to his right, and on it had been a fat, squat candle. He moved toward the table, hand outstretched until he touched it. His hands skimmed over the tabletop, searching for candle and flint.

Before he encountered anything, there was a scrape, then a spark. A halo of light spread across the table.

She sat at the table across from him, the flickering candle in front of her, her long, slender arm lowering the flint matches to the tabletop. The candlelight lit her hair so that it burned like fire, deep auburn and copper.

The sight of her there sent a jolt of energy through him. His hands curled into fists. She was so still, so quiet. He could discern nothing by her blank expression.

The silence stretched out interminably until Drake felt compelled to say, "Well. I'm here."

Her head tilted slightly to one side as she regarded him thoughtfully. Silken copper hair slid from her shoulder to fall behind her back. "It took you long enough."

He lifted a shoulder. "Aye, well . . ."

She looked away, disinterested. "You can go."

Drake frowned at the woman before him. She seemed different somehow. Previously she had been enigmatic, mysterious . . . now she just seemed bored.

"No," he said. "I made a promise, and my word is good."

She waved a pale hand in his direction. "Apparently." The emotionless line of her mouth curved minutely into something resembling a smile. "Your honor is noted, Drake MacKay. No one will speak ill of the solidarity of your word. I release you from your promise."

Drake had been dreading this moment, dreading coming to this island, and most of all, dreading the fulfillment of his promise. Her words should have been welcome. And there *was* a sigh of relief in his soul. But the larger part of him was annoyed.

She stared up at him, waiting. Her eyes were large and sultry, curtained with thick auburn lashes that seemed too heavy for her to hold up consistently, so they lowered, shadowing her eyes and making her thoughts elusive.

"I came a long way," he said. What was he doing? Arguing? My God—was he insane?

Apparently he was, because rather than run to the boat and row back to the mainland, thanking God for this reprieve, he was still here.

She seemed as puzzled by his strange behavior as he was. "I imagine you did. And if there had been some way to get word to you about this, well . . ." She lifted a palm and shrugged. "Well, I wouldn't have done it anyway, so never mind about that." The corners of her mouth pulled tight, and she exhaled. "You are released. Do not be a fool and question it."

His brows drew together as he regarded her. She was right. There was no sense in questioning such a gift. He was free. He inclined his head, not willing to thank her verbally. She held his gaze for a long moment. Then her gaze drifted away, disinterested.

Drake backed out of the house and closed the door. He stood outside, hesitant for some inexplicable reason. She seemed so odd. Not that he had known her well, but he had spent a fortnight in her company, and during that time she had been very different. Though insouciant and understated, she had still seemed *alive*. Witty and clever; conversant. He had not found her company objectionable.

The woman inside was a shell.

He turned away from the door. Whatever ailed her was not his concern. He was free, and that was all that mattered now.

He rowed back to the village, relief washing over him in slow waves. He had stopped thinking about a future. There had been no point. His future had been sealed when he had made the promise to the *baobhan sith*. But now the future opened before him again, full of possibilities. Where did he go from here?

The thought was such a profound one that he stopped rowing. His oars trailed through the water. Before the blood witch had saved his friend Stephen, he had lived his life seething with anger and misery over his wife's horrible death, needing someone to blame. And that someone had been the *baobhan sith*. But then she'd helped him, and though he hadn't forgiven her, he no longer felt compelled to revenge himself on her.

Luthias had been punished.

The blood witch had released him from his promise.

What now?

The sudden hollowness in his chest unnerved him. It seemed abnormal to view the years that stretched ahead of him with no interest.

He was no longer young, but neither was he an old man. He would find another woman, have sons. He'd lived practically as a monk since his wife had died. That needed to change.

He pulled at the oars with new vigor, letting the hard work dominate his thoughts. He kept at it until the bow hit the beach. He dragged the boat ashore and left it, trudging up the pebbled shore. No one paid attention to him. The fishermen were further down the coast where a narrow dock extended out into the water, readying their vessels to set sail. It was very early; the sun had not yet risen.

Shops and houses clustered just past the waterline. Drake had not rented a room, so he entered the tavern and dropped wearily onto a bench. The taverns never closed, since the fishermen came and went all night. The smell of bread and porridge filled the air. Within seconds a tall, lean woman stood over him with a tankard of ale and one thick brow arched. Drake tossed his coin on the table. She exchanged the ale for the coin and left him to his drink.

Drake drained the tankard and then a second. He wanted to drink away the troubling thoughts that plagued him about future and family. He had just started his third when he realized the men sitting at the table behind him discussed the *baobhan sith*. He paused, then slowly brought the tankard to his lips, shifting backward to eavesdrop better.

"She rejected the offering again," one of the men said, his voice deep and gruff.

"What does that mean? What does she want?" another man asked. This one sounded smaller, his voice thinner. He was frightened.

There was a brief silence. An exhalation. "Human blood," deep and gruff said ominously.

The silence drew out longer this time.

"So . . . what do we do?" a different one asked in a low, harsh whisper. "Do we send her a human?"

"Mayhap we should wait," the thin voice said anxiously. "Mayhap she doesn't care about us anymore."

"The last time we waited and prayed," the gruff voice said, "bad things happened. She killed entire herds of animals. Dried up the fishing. Preyed on humans. No." Drake imagined him shaking his head decisively. "No more. We have been at her mercy too long. I say we kill her."

There was a sharp intake of breath. "It canna be done. She canna be killed."

"*Everything* can be killed," gruff man drawled.

Drake's heart beat into the silence. He realized that he had stopped drinking and sat very still, head tilted toward the men. He took a drink of his ale and leaned forward on the table, rubbing the back of his head wearily.

His antics to appear as if he wasn't listening caused him to miss what was being said.

". . . told me the only way to kill one was to cut their heads off and burn them to ash."

"How do we manage that when she lives on an island? She knows who is coming and going. There is no surprising her."

"Then we have to outnumber her. And daytime is the best time."

Drake couldn't listen anymore. He stood and left

the tavern. He paced outside for a moment, his chest a knot, teeth clenched. They were going to kill her. And it sounded as if maybe they knew how. He raked a hand through his hair and stopped short, staring out to sea. It was too dark to make out but he saw it in his mind. A green place, populated with peaceful animals. A calm place, a safe haven, not the lair of a *baobhan sith*.

She wasn't his problem. She had released him from his promise, and if he had kept walking to the stables rather than stopping to have a drink, he would never have known any different.

But he *did* know. And he couldn't just ignore what he knew. He owed her. Being released from a promise was one thing, but deliberately allowing someone who had aided him to die . . . well, that was quite another.

He headed for the beach and the skiff he'd left resting on the pebbled sand. Urgency mixed with impatience in his gut. He had thought he was finally free of everything, ready to start fresh, and here he was, in the thick of it again. But no sense starting anew when there was unfinished business to resolve. Some part of him felt better with a task, a mission, something to distract him from thoughts of the future.

He shoved the skiff into the water and stepped in, rowing back toward the island and his promise.

Chapter 2

$\mathscr{H}$annah sat on the beach, waiting. The breeze off the water was chilly, but it didn't affect her. A cool breeze did not refresh her on a warm day, and cold, wet days did not make her uncomfortable. She did not shiver or sweat. Still, she intellectualized the temperature differences. Acknowledged them and then dismissed them.

She had been waiting for weeks now, but so far, nothing. She didn't always sit on the beach, but after her unexpected visitor she had grown restless. Where were they? Were they really so stupid and cowardly?

More than six months ago the nearby coastal village had experienced more excitement than they'd seen in years. Witches. Not just tales but real witches in their midst. Drake MacKay and his family.

Hannah was their resident witch, to whom they were accustomed. This pack of witches had brought witch-hunters and trials and then had dragged Hannah into it. Nothing had been the same since.

However, those witches had left and gone on with their lives. And Hannah was back in the position she had worked so hard to overcome. The villagers feared her again. They were whispering and blaming.

Her hand had been forced. She had to shift the balance back in her favor or find a new home. So she had gone to the mainland one night and appeared at Tam Guthrie's bedside. She had given him explicit instructions about how to kill a *baobhan sith*, and had even implied that God had chosen him for this exalted fate. Of course she had appeared in the guise of an old woman, wrapped in a cloak, her face smudged with dirt. She had also used the power of suggestion on Tam, a gift all blood witches possessed. Some humans were more susceptible than others. Tam was highly susceptible. He had lain in bed, his blankets wadded in fists under his chin, and blinked at her owlishly. She had given him the information and left. In retrospect, she supposed she should have made him repeat it back to her. After all, he had been drunk. He'd thought it was a dream, which was what she had intended, but an *important* dream. A portentous dream. A dream to act on. Now, she had begun to fear that he did not remember it at all. Or worse, thought her a malevolent visitation and therefore ignored it for fear of being fingered a witch himself.

She sighed, her mouth flattening into a bored line. Perhaps it was time for another dream in a different guise. The prospect held little interest. It just seemed another tiresome task and perhaps not even necessary. This generation of villagers talked a lot but did little else. Mayhap it was just time to move on.

Last night she had thought the moment had finally arrived. She'd awakened at dusk and had immediately sensed a presence on the island. She'd been prepared.

Perhaps a bit excited, too. Her adventure with the MacKays had reminded her how uneventful her life had become. She relished a diversion.

It had not been the villagers come to lynch her. It had been Drake MacKay.

Temperature she could not feel. But shock she could—all the way to her dead marrow.

She had never thought she would see him again.

It had been . . . unsettling. She had almost reevaluated the decision she had arrived at over the past few months. Until she had remembered who he was; that the passionate, intelligent man was only part of the picture. He was also reckless and vengeful. Deeply angry. Not a good candidate to become a *baobhan sith*. The kind of man who might abuse such power.

She went still, a distant sound drawing her from her thoughts. Her toes dug into the sand, an unfamiliar heaviness in her chest that she recognized as a building sigh. She released it, her shoulders lowering, but she didn't feel any better.

The faint dawn light couldn't penetrate the thick cloud of fog. But sound echoed. The sound she heard was the swish of oars cutting through water.

Someone was coming.

She stood, bare toes curling into the sand as she strained to see. Her eyesight was far better than a human's, but it couldn't penetrate fog. And the night was nearly gone anyway, taking with it all that made a *baobhan sith* special. She stood motionless, breath frozen in her chest, waiting for the craft to become visible. Was it Tam and the lynch mob? She should return to her house and lock the door until nightfall. But something held her there, compelled her to stay and see.

The shadow of it emerged first. A skiff with a lone rower. A lantern hung on the stern, swaying gently to the rhythm of the rowing.

She frowned. There was something familiar about the figure—the set of his shoulders, the line of his dark profile. The realization jarred through her.

Drake had returned.

She let out a breath, toes curling tighter into the beach, as if holding her steady. Why would he do that? Why would he come back when she had set him free?

Hannah could only stare, rooted to the beach. As if sensing her gaze boring into his back, he stopped rowing and twisted around.

Their gazes met through the haze, the memory of last night and the weight of a man's promise passing between their eyes as his skiff drifted on the current. A wave rolled under the skiff, raising it higher and pushing it closer to the beach.

He wanted something. There must be something to gain by keeping his promise. There were those who wished to become a blood witch, those who were failing at life and would do naught but evil as a *baobhan sith*. But that description did not fit Drake, so it must be something else.

He stepped out of the boat and pulled it to the beach.

"You're back," she said, unnecessarily. Her gaze traveled over him, from boots to black, wavy hair. He was a striking man; tall and lean and muscular. Blue eyes pierced her with purpose and intensity. His black hair was longish and in need of a cut. His beard, however, was trimmed and hugged the square set of his jaw.

"Aye. I've come to warn you."

She took an internal step backward, she was so surprised. "Warn me of what?"

He breathed hard from his labor, hands on his hips. "The villagers, they're plotting to lynch you."

Again this man, always full of surprises. No wonder she had once thought him suitable. She smiled slightly, amused that he thought she would be afraid of a few villagers. There was also a foreign twist in her chest. He had rowed all the way back to her, in the fog, like the devil was on his tail, just to tell her she was in danger.

"It won't be the first time. Why do you think I live on an island? I have been run out of more villages than you've had birthdays." She tilted her head, her smile coy. "You were worried about me."

His lip curled. His gaze remained steady. "I owe you a life."

She let out an incredulous breath, ignoring the mild sinking in her chest. "Then consider your debt now fulfilled. I am warned."

His brows lowered. "What are you going to do?"

She shrugged, crossed her ankles, and lowered herself gracefully onto the beach. "What is there to do?"

"You can't just sit here and wait for them to come for you. You have to leave. Hide."

She placed a palm on her chest. "You amuse me."

She looked fondly toward the hidden line of coast. "They are harmless. Tam probably stirred up a bit of trouble, but that man couldn't find his own arse with a dung beetle."

Drake's lips compressed. He blew exasperation through his nose. "You don't understand. They know how to kill a *baobhan sith*. Someone told him."

"I ken. I told him."

His surprise couldn't have been greater had she kicked him in the groin. He frowned at her and finally managed, "You?"

"Aye." She nodded, watching his eyes. What would he do now? He was not the type of man to give up, even when deeply unhappy. Witness his continued life after the death of his wife, whom, Hannah knew, he had loved deeply. He'd lived on though he obviously found it abhorrent. He no doubt would find Hannah's "giving up" distasteful.

"You *want* to die?"

Well, that wasn't why she had stirred Tam up, but Drake seemed so scandalized that she decided to continue that fiction. She leaned back, wrapping her arms around her knees. She wore a thin gown—all she ever wore most days, since few people came to the island—and it puddled in the sand around her. "I have lived a long time. Longer than any human has a right to. I'm ready to move on."

"Then move on!" He waved his arm elaborately, encompassing unseen distant lands. "Leave the island, move to Italy—but don't just give up and let them win."

"I didn't realize it was a competition with winners and losers."

"*Life* is a competition," he hissed through bared teeth. "The one who stays on top till the end is the winner."

Her heart skipped. She rolled forward with a sigh, feet tucked up underneath her and chin on knees. His passion excited her, sparked something inside like fine wine, making her want to sustain the feeling. So she pricked at him some more. "Then *you* win, Drake. Go enjoy your victory."

He made a sound—the beginning of a protest— that he cut off sharply. His boots crunched in the sand as he paced away, stopped, then paced back. Hannah never looked at him, though the beat of her heart sped up the tiniest bit. This man was an enigma. She knew he loathed her. And yet he could not abandon her to fate.

The woman in her wanted to tease him. The devil in her calculated how she could make use of his sense of duty to her. "What else did you overhear? Are they coming soon?"

"I know not . . . but I think they wilna wait long."

She nodded. She was ready. They would come during the day, thinking her helpless. But she had lived a long time and had found there were no new schemes under the sun. Men just replayed the old ones over and over again. She was in no real danger.

Beside her, Drake's hand curved around her upper arm, hauling her to her feet. As it was day, she had no more strength than a mortal woman, and she was at his mercy. It infuriated her and was the very reason she had retreated to the island: so she could remain in control. It was the very reason Tam and his gaggle would never set eyes on her during the day. People interacted with her on *her* terms.

"Let's go."

He dragged her to his skiff and tried to force her into it. She stiffened her stance and put her hands on his arms. They were granite, immovable.

"What are you doing?"

"This is suicide, and that is pathetic and sinful. I won't let you do it. You're coming with me."

"No. I'm. Not." But her words had as much impact as her hands did on his solid arms. When her stiff stance impeded his task, he simply slid an arm beneath her knees and swung her into the air. She still hadn't caught her breath when he plopped her down on a cross plank.

She immediately tried to stand, but he placed a large, warm hand on her shoulder and held her in place. She looked up at him, making herself relax the tight set of her lips. She was not accustomed to being dominated by anyone. It was unnerving and strangely . . . exhilarating.

"Why are you doing this? I released you from your promise. You are free to go away and forget about me. In fact, I really wish you would."

A lie; a bald-faced lie. She didn't want this to end. Not yet. Normally by this time she was fast asleep, and indeed, her limbs grew heavy with weariness, but her mind was alert to his every move.

He shook his head, climbing into the skiff while keeping his hand firmly on her shoulder. "It's not that simple. I canna let you do this to yourself. For all I know it is *my* fault. Mayhap you're unhappy because I did not come sooner—"

She choked on laughter. It amused her that he would think that a man held such power over her life. Hardly. She was not a weak human anymore who let men mold her and destroy her.

"You think this has aught to do with you? I am not so lonely that I would end my life over a man such as yourself."

He stared down at her, his eyes skeptical. "Whatever your reasons, I cannot let you do it. At least not until you give me a chance to try to fix whatever is wrong."

"It is not something that can be fixed. And if it were, you would not be the person to make it right."

"Well, let us determine that elsewhere. This place is no longer safe." He stepped out of the boat, hand still planted on her shoulder. "Aye?"

Hannah sighed. She was settled on this island. She had been here longer than she had lived anywhere else. But in truth, ennui had set in. She was bored and Drake represented a tantalizing diversion. She supposed the island was going nowhere. And maybe it was time to move on anyway, make a home somewhere new. It always frightened humans when blood witches didn't age.

"Very well."

He nodded and, cautiously, as if he didn't truly believe her, removed his hand from her shoulder. He gripped the boat's stern and pushed it into the water. She noted the ripple of muscle in his forearms. He was a fine man and well worth the diversion.

"We're leaving now?" she said, one brow raised in surprise.

He hopped into the skiff with her and took up the oars.

"You give me no time to change into appropriate travel clothes and tend my sheep?"

"No," he said firmly. "No time."

"Surely you can give me a few hours? I have no money, nothing to barter with."

"I have money."

"I am aware of that. But I do not want your money. Besides, I doubt you have enough to compensate me for what I am leaving behind."

His brows drew together in consternation. "Damn stubborn woman."

She smiled. He couldn't see it yet, but this dance they engaged in would inevitably end in pleasure and then death.

She looked forward to it.

Drake paced while Hannah went about her house contemplating her belongings, trying to decide whether to pack them. It felt to him as if she purposely drew this out, lingering over each item as long as possible for no other reason than to raise his ire. She was the type of woman to do that—to find the raw spots and start scraping. Of course, she wasn't really a woman at all, so mayhap that explained it.

He fixed her with a severe look designed to motivate her to move faster. Instead of being cowed, she pulled her thin shift over her head, exposing firm, supple, alabaster flesh, round in all the right places. His blood quickened at the sight; his tongue went dry. He turned on his heel and left the dwelling, mumbling that he would see to the beasts.

He stalked to the barn, which was set into the side of a hill, and unlatched the fence. When he threw it wide, the sheep trotted out excitedly. He watched them, an almost painful frown between his brows. It wasn't right. She was not a real woman, not human. She wasn't supposed to look like *that*.

He was not a fool. He came from a family of witches, and now his niece and her husband were blood witches. He knew they were not monsters. But Hannah was different. She was an ancient creature who had denied life to his late wife. Her choices were arbitrary and cruel. He could not forgive her for that or see her as anything but a monster.

He owed her a life. That was the only reason he'd come back.

Still . . . she *looked* like a human woman. An impossibly desirable woman. And he was a man with strong desires that he'd denied for a very long time. He grabbed the pitchfork and tossed fresh hay over the floor with angry, vigorous movements.

He felt a presence and turned. Hannah stood in the doorway behind him. She wore a gown fit for travel, but in a finer weave of cloth than that worn by the women he was accustomed to. A plaid arisaid was slung around her shoulders, and her blaze of cinnabar hair fell over her shoulder in a twisted plait. A satchel hung from her hand. The sun was behind her, hiding her face in shadows.

"What about your sheep?" Drake asked, stabbing the pitchfork into the hay at his feet and leaning on it. "They'll die."

She stepped into the barn and her face was visible again, softened by the dust-filled air.

"A boy comes to the island once a sennight to care for them, bring food and supplies." She waved a hand at the high shelves stocked with grain. "Where do you think this comes from?"

"I thought you used magic or some such."

She smiled. "Or flew it over on my toad?"

He shrugged and tossed the pitchfork aside. So she had not been concerned about her animals after all. She had just wanted to fetch her things.

"Are you ready?"

She tossed her plait over her shoulder. "I suppose."

He brushed past her, not offering to take her satchel, and led her back to the beach. It set wrong in his gut to let a lady carry her things while he went empty-handed. He had to keep reminding himself that she was not a lady; she was something else and was far stronger than he was.

"We cannot return by way of the village," he said over his shoulder. "I will row to the west, until we are clear of it before we go ashore."

She didn't reply. At the skiff he finally took her satchel and tossed it into the stern. It was not as heavy as he had expected. She climbed in and sat on a cross-plank, folded her hands in her lap, and waited. She appeared deceptively prim and obedient. An illusion designed to deceive stupid men.

Speaking of stupid men ...

What the hell was he doing? What the hell was he supposed to *do* with her? And why the hell couldn't he just be happy that she had released him from his promise? Why did he have to keep complicating matters?

He'd had the opportunity to put all of this behind him, and yet here he was. He pushed the skiff into the water and almost gave in to the urge to give it a final push—away from him. He would stand on the shore and watch her drift away. And be stranded on her island.

Instead he sat opposite her and took up the oars.

He felt her gaze on him as he rowed. He ignored her, keeping his own gaze fixed on a spot in the distance. She said nothing for a time, until he began relax, falling into the rhythm of rowing.

"What did you do with the witch-hunter?"

She meant Luthias Forsyth. He fixed her with a hard stare. "He is dead."

A fine auburn brow arched. "How did you manage that? *Baobhan siths* are very hard to kill."

"Mayhap; easier when they want to die. The challenge was keeping him alive."

Her chin rose slightly. "So you made him suffer?"

He wondered at her questions. Of course, she had been the one to turn Luthias, at Drake's own request—yet another thing he owed her for—so in a sense she was Luthias's mother, his creator. She didn't look unduly troubled by what Drake had said. Nothing ever appeared to trouble her, but surely something had to. Just because she was a blood witch didn't make her emotionless. Stephen and Deidra were blood witches and much the same as they had been before, outside of drinking blood and sleeping all day.

"Does it hurt you, his death?"

"Hurt me?" Both auburn brows rose in surprise, and she leaned back slightly. "No, but I didn't *feel* that he died. Usually I get some sense that they died or I dream of it. You are sure he is dead?"

Drake shrugged. "No, I didn't see him die. If he's not dead now he will be soon. He'd turned into a pathetic creature. He was waiting to be burned when I left him."

"You act as if you care so little, and yet you've spent many months making this man miserable."

"It was justice. Someone had to do it. No one in this godforsaken country gives a damn what happens to witches. They slaughter them like kine and care less. Someone had to do something."

"Is that what you've appointed yourself? Warden of witches? Here to make certain justice is served and witches are free to perform magic?"

His rowing paused only a moment. "You mock me? You, a creature yourself?"

Her lips curved. "Just because I am one doesn't mean I think we're doing good works. I am no nun."

He gave a triumphant laugh. "So you admit you are evil."

The full curve of her lips widened as her gaze traveled over him and he felt it, as if she'd touched him.

"Well, I'm not a good woman."

And in that one phrase there was an abundance of meaning. A vision of her skin as she pulled the gown over her head shimmered in his mind, and he forced it away angrily. "You're not a woman at all."

His venomous words elicited no reaction from her. Her expression didn't change—it remained seductive, teasing. "So I am a pathetic creature? Like Luthias?"

"I don't know what you are." He had to look away from her when he said that. He didn't know why, either. He knew how to read people, and the shift of his own eyes indicated he was equivocating. And yet he wasn't even aware of what or why he equivocated.

"Why are you doing this then, if you disdain me so?"

"I owe you."

A surprised laugh erupted from her, pulling his gaze back to her. "I do not see how that could be so. Apparently you don't owe me common courtesy, which is the least a person deserves, think you not? I find it difficult to believe you owe me so much and yet cannot speak with a civil tongue."

Drake's jaw clenched as he stared back at her serene face. Her words—a firm rebuke, as if from a mother to her miscreant child—burned through his heart. She hadn't the common courtesy to do that which came so easy and natural to her: create life where life faded. She had no heart, no emotions. She had let his wife die, destroyed his life and his future, and yet she sat here talking about *courtesy*.

Boiling rage and buried sorrow stiffened his lips, charred the words as they passed through them. "I am enduring you because it is what God expects of me. But I will not be your friend."

"Courtesy does not require friendship." The mother again, a slight, amused smile shadowing her lips. No fear. No feeling.

"Courtesy," he spat. "Do you say 'prithee' and 'thankee' afore you drain a man of blood? Or when you watch an innocent die, do you have the courtesy to apologize for being too evil to help?"

She regarded him for a while, long dark red lashes blinking slowly over green eyes. "You are surely a man of your word, Drake MacKay, to subject yourself to such a loathsome creature. Your wife, I'm sure, would be proud—"

Drake threw down the oars and pointed a finger in Hannah's face. "*Do not* speak of my wife. You desecrate her memory by even speaking of her."

She did not even flinch. Her eyes never blinked or left his to flit at the finger threatening her. There was no anger or insult visible in her expression. He could not wound her. Could not make her feel the misery he felt. Instead she contemplated him and said, "No, Drake, I think it is you who desecrates her memory."

If they hadn't been stuck in a skiff he would have thrown back his head and yelled his frustration. He needed to stalk away because he wanted to hit her. Except she looked like a woman and he would never hit a woman. He wanted to yell at her to shut up. But she would not care and would not shut up. Rage smoldered in his chest. He took up the oars again and rowed with new vigor. The muscles across his back and his arms flexed and contracted with each stroke.

He waited for her to *scrape scrape scrape* at the raw wound she had opened, but apparently she had the decency to shut her mouth.

His vigorous exercise eventually burnt away the anger until all that was left were the ashes of shame and he could not even look in her direction. Had Ceara seen how he had spoken to Hannah, she would have been aghast. He had forced her to leave her home, and now he treated her with contempt.

His heart sagged in his chest. Hannah was right; his behavior was not worthy of his late wife. If any desecrating had been done this day, he must shoulder the blame.

Chapter 3

$\mathcal{L}$uthias hid in the abandoned shell of a cottage that sat on a wasteland. Moors stretched in every direction around him. Death surrounded him. It filled him.

They would not find him here.

The sun sank in the sky, and he knew the weakness would disappear with the light. It was still so difficult to wrap his mind around all that had come to pass. He had gone from hunter to hunted. From right to evil. From human to monster. He huddled in a corner, trying to pull his ragged coat around his thin body. He was so hungry. It was unlike anything he'd ever felt before. His will shrank before this need. It clawed at his chest, and lower; his belly rumbled, and it felt as if someone had carved it out with a sword.

He'd given in to the hunger more times than he cared to remember. The first time had been a dog . . . that had been early on, and he didn't remember much about it. Just the warm rush of blood in his mouth and the surcease of pain. The second time . . . the second time he remembered better. It had been a human. A child.

He had been in pain, much like he was tonight.

He had escaped from the ubiquitous villagers that hunted him. Somehow they'd known he'd been skulking around the town. It was Drake MacKay who had informed them. He was always near, always informing on him. So Luthias had run and hid. It was easy to hide now. If he thought hard enough that he didn't want to be seen, somehow they didn't see him even when he didn't hide very well. A boy had wandered away from the others. Luthias had smelled him as he'd drawn near. He knew when others were near now because he could smell their blood. This lad's blood had smelled so young and fresh. Clean and untainted. The closer the boy had come, the worse the dry aching in his belly had grown.

And then the boy had been there before him, looking at him curiously, without fear. So Luthias had snatched him without thought. The rush of blood in his mouth had been warm and delicious—deliriously so. In fact, he hadn't even realized what he had done until it was too late and the lifeless, bloodless body had lain limp in his arms. He didn't remember the boy crying out or fighting him. It was as if someone else had done it, some monster that had taken over his body but then left him with the dead boy and the taste of blood in his mouth.

He had truly wanted to die then. He deserved to die. And yet he kept escaping. It was inadvertent. He never tried to escape. Usually he didn't want to. He looked forward to the burning, to an end to the pain. He had been tortured so often that he *should* have been dead, and yet he did not die. Prisons would be left open, and though he did not want to leave, it was too fortuitous, too convenient to simply be a coincidence that followed him around.

It was God. God wasn't finished with him yet.

Luthias could not imagine what the Lord would want with a wretch such as himself. He was no longer holy or good. He was a blood witch—vile and unworthy. He had thought God was punishing him. That he had offended God. And so he was humbled—given their weaknesses, made as depraved as they.

But then escape kept presenting itself. What was God trying to tell him? Pain tore him in half. He curled in on himself, moaning. He was empty. As if the blood had dried to dust in his veins. He was nothing. He had no tears, no spit. He could not urinate. He was a foul, empty thing. He hated himself and what he was.

And he smelled blood nearby. He didn't want it. The idea of the blood in his mouth excited and repulsed him. He gritted his sharp teeth and cried out with the effort to ignore the aroma and the pain that drove away sanity.

"Brother, what ails you?"

The voice brought Luthias's head up. A man knelt before him. He wore the tattered robes of a cleric—a parish pastor, probably. He regarded Luthias, his head tilted, a frown of concern between his brows. His balding head shone in the moonlight.

"What has brought you so low?"

Luthias opened his mouth to answer, but only a growl erupted from his chest. It was a growl of hunger, of warning. This man was in danger if he didn't leave. Luthias turned away from him, hands over his head.

The pastor was silent for a long while. He placed a hand on Luthias's shoulder. "Misfortune has fallen upon you. It is only by chance that I came upon you today. There is a lass to the north possessed by devils. A witch did this to her. I went to exorcise her of these devils, but I was not successful. I wondered why God sent me on this mission if I cannot help . . . and then I come across you, a poor soul in need of aid that I can supply. So come, sit up and partake of bread and ale with me."

The smell of blood was overpowering, pushing thought and logic from Luthias's head. Nevertheless, an idea wormed its way through the pain that filled his head, penetrating the blood-crazed thought.

The man was correct. God had his reasons for everything. He had brought this man here to find Luthias and share his story, to elucidate what Luthias had been too small and wretched to see.

Like the pastor, he had lacked the strength to combat the blood witches. He had been but a man. Now he was more than a man. He was equal to the witches he sought to punish.

But he was useless in his current state. He needed strength. He needed to feed.

The sun had gone and with it the weakness that gripped his body when light filled the sky. He turned. The pastor still crouched, but now dug through his sack, producing a round loaf of bread and a leather flask.

"I can help you," Luthias said, his voice a dry rasp.

The pastor turned toward him, bread in one hand and flask in the other. "Well, brother, let me help you first."

"The girl . . . do you want to help her?"

The pastor's head tilted, confused. "Of course."

Luthias lifted one hand, surprised to see how pale and thin it had become. The veins stood out, blue bulges along his wrist and the back of his hand. "Come closer."

The pastor leaned closer, his face still a mask of curiosity and confusion. "What is it?"

Luthias's hand snaked around the back of the pastor's neck. The man tried to pull back. His eyes widened in shock at Luthias's strength.

"Brother—," the pastor gasped, bread and flask flying as his hands scrabbled at Luthias's shoulders.

Luthias brought his mouth to the pastor's ear and whispered, "You are right. The Lord brought us together for a reason."

The pastor hit at Luthias and collapsed to his knees. "Don't do this!"

"Forgive me." Luthias sunk his teeth into the pastor's neck. The blood flowed and the pastor's body relaxed, a groan of surrender escaping him. Luthias sucked greedily, the pain fading as his body grew full and vibrant.

When Luthias finished, he sat up and wiped the blood from his mouth. The pastor lay on his back, arms splayed, mouth ajar. He was dead, and remorse clawed at the edges of Luthias's heart.

It was what God wanted of him. It had to be. Why else would he do this to one of his warriors on earth? But as Luthias looked at the body and tasted the blood, his certainty began to elude him. Whose will did he do? God's or the devil's? He fell to his knees and prayed for God to show him the way.

They traveled by moonlight and slept during the day. Hannah had not requested this arrangement, but she was grateful that it was Drake's preference. It was her natural rhythm. The last time she had made such a trek had been six months ago with the same man, when he had wagered his life for her help. She had traveled with him and his men, and they had exchanged few words beyond what had been necessary.

This time it was just the two of them, but little had changed. They traversed glens filled with wild rose and blackberry bramble, desolate moor, rock-studded mountains, all in near silence. After the first day he had acquired ponies for them; instead of walking in silence, they now rode in silence.

Hannah knew that what she had said to Drake about his wife had affected him. She just wasn't entirely certain *how* it had affected him. In many ways he was an uncomplicated man. Brash, reckless, and somewhat predictable. But in other ways . . . such as his adherence to some code of honor idealized in stories told by bards, but which, she thought, did not exist in reality . . . at least she'd thought that until she'd met Drake. His sudden, complete silence and withdrawal after she had chastised him had been unexpected.

She'd assumed that her words would have little effect past irritating him and that he would continue his rudeness. Instead, he now spoke to her with complete civility, but only when absolutely necessary.

She should have expected it. She remembered when he had brought his wife to her more than five years ago. Ceara had been her name. He had treated his late wife almost with a . . . reverence. It was a rare thing to find a man so devoted to a woman. Ceara had been frail. In the sharp bones of her skeletal features Hannah had seen what had once been beauty, but the beauty had been ravaged by sickness and pain. Her eyelids had been too heavy, her skin too pale. It had looked as though movement had been a massive effort for her.

The memory of his late-wife had shamed him into courtesy.

The darkness dissipated, and Drake found a dry place to sleep in an abandoned cottage that still contained many of the comforts of living: a heather-stuffed mattress, a table and bench, and an assortment of carved wooden cups and bowls. He chivalrously gave her the bed and unrolled his blanket on the floor near the door.

As Hannah lay on the mattress, listening to him move around the abandoned cottage, her curiosity overcame her usual stoicism.

"Why have you not remarried?"

He didn't answer immediately. "Who said I haven't?"

The strong odor of oil tingled her nose. She rolled onto her side to look at him. Across the room he cleaned his dag, swabbing the barrel with a rod topped with an oiled cloth.

"I do."

He didn't pause in his cleaning. "You're correct. I have not married again."

"There has been no one else, has there? You've lived like a monk."

"You wouldn't understand."

"Maybe I understand more than you think I do."

He shot her a dubious look, one brow cocked. "Losing Ceara was like . . ." He looked around the cottage as if the word he searched for hid in the walls or floor. He lifted his arms, dag in one hand, rod in the other, and looked down at them. "It was as if someone cut off my arms and I have to go through life never feeling silk pass through my fingers, the weight of a baby in my arms, the soft fur of my dog as he rests beside me, the trembling belly of a woman in want. It is never holding a body that fits perfectly with yours so tightly you will never let it go. It is losing that tactile ability. Going through life without any arms."

She had never heard him string together so many words, and certainly none so eloquent. His words brought sadness to her heart, an emotion uncommon to her. She rarely felt sad. In fact, she rarely felt anything.

"I understand more than you think," she said softly.

His gaze met hers and she saw the sneer he tried to hide. She supposed she should give him credit for that, for trying to hide his derision, though he did a poor job of it.

"You don't know me, nor have you any idea of what I've lost," she added.

He snorted softly and returned his attention to his dag. "Perhaps," he said, "if you didna hoard your magic, if you used it to help others, you wouldna find yourself so alone."

"It is easy for you to judge. You are a child. I have lived long enough to know that not everyone should be a blood witch. With power over life and death comes responsibility. I have found that those who wish to become a *baobhan sith* are the ones most likely to abuse that power. They are not people I wish to spend an evening with, let alone eternity. And the ones who would respect the power, they are the ones who understand that eternal life is not truly a gift but a curse."

He did not reply, but his movements became forceful. He jammed the rod into his dag much harder than necessary. He withdrew into himself again.

She rolled over and closed her eyes. She was not physically weary from the ride, but she was mentally weary. Somehow just being with Drake raised her awareness in a way that made her more intent, more watchful, and each morning when the sun rose she was even more drained than normal.

"If you hate me so much," she asked, surprising even herself by giving voice to the question, "why are you taking me to your home? Why not just leave me in some village?"

She heard scraping and footsteps, then a thump as he dropped a sack on the table. "What makes you think that I wilna leave you somewhere still?"

"If you meant to leave me, you would have done so already."

A rustling as he dug in his sack. Then a crisp, satisfying crunch. Hannah rose up on the bed to see. He was eating an apple, glossy red skin and stark white meat. It sounded delicious. Hannah sighed and lay back down.

"I have another," he said.

"No," she said wistfully. "I used to adore apples."

He bit into the apple again. "*Used* to? It sounds as if you still do."

Hannah shook her head. "No. I tried to eat them for a while, but they no longer had any taste."

At his silence she tilted her head up to see him. He held the apple up and turned it, studying it. He took another bite of the apple. It crunched as white teeth sunk into it. It sounded like heaven. He chewed it thoughtfully, then sighed. "That is unfortunate."

He teased her. Once it would have bothered her, though she never would have shown it. Now his attempt amused her.

"It is," she agreed. "But after more than eighty years, it no longer vexes me."

His teeth sunk into the apple again and held there as he stared at her, brows arched in amazement.

She nodded, brows raised to match his.

He quickly chewed up his bite of apple and swallowed. "Did you say eighty? You're eighty?"

"No, I am one hundred and seven. I have been a *baobhan sith* for eighty years."

He looked at his apple. "I would give this up to be forever young."

"You say that now."

He lowered the apple and gave her a dubious, dark blue squint. "You would trade eternal youth for an apple?"

Her mouth curved, but there was no joy in her heart. "Oh aye, I would."

He turned back to his apple. "I suppose I should thank you then, for sparing me a fate worse than death."

She rolled onto her back, staring at the peat-blackened ceiling with growing irritation. She didn't know why she was irritated, but it was there, twisting her belly tight. Why had she gone on this foolish excursion, and why did she continue to stay with him? She did not need him or any man. She was entirely capable of caring for and defending herself. In fact, when the moon rose, she was far stronger than him.

But during the day she was weak. A mere woman, subject to the whims of men. And though she might make them pay when the sun went down, until it did, she was still at their mercy.

She was with him because she knew he would not harm her. Whatever his reasons, he would protect her. As much as she hated needing anyone, away from the protection of her island she needed him by day. It wasn't for much longer. She would tire of him quickly. In the meantime, she would find a way to wipe that self-righteous smirk off his face.

Chapter 4

 $\mathcal{N}$early a sennight later they finally arrived at Strathwick. Drake's brother, William, and his wife, Rose, were happy to see him, but as he had anticipated, they were shocked at his traveling companion. They had met her briefly six months ago when she had helped save Stephen and Deidra, but they knew little else about her.

Though Rose faltered at first, her innate hospitality won out, and she whisked Hannah away to wash and rest. William led Drake to his chambers and offered him whisky.

"You look as if you need it, brother."

Drake took the cup gratefully and dumped it down his throat. The liquid burned as it slid down, warming his gullet and belly. He proffered his cup for more.

William raised a brow but readily poured more of the amber liquid.

"So . . . ," William started.

"Dinna ask," Drake said before William could finish his thought.

Drake turned away from his brother and crossed the room. Tension strung him tight. He should be exhausted. They had traveled all night and then on into the morning, past when they normally would have stopped. But he had known Strathwick was near and had not wanted to stop until they arrived.

Hannah had not complained. She appeared tireless, but he could tell by her delayed reactions that she had been fatigued. She was just too stubborn to show any sign of weakness.

William crossed to his chair and lowered himself into it. "How do you know I was going to ask anything?" His hair had long ago gone gray. Though not an old man, William was not young either. He was just past his prime, in his forties, still strong as a horse. And yet that silver hair . . .

It had always troubled Drake. They were as alike as they were different. Their features were similar; both had the same dark blue eyes. William was taller, but they were both broad. Drake, however, retained the black hair that William had possessed only as a lad. William had been in his teens when he'd first begun to gray, so the black was but a memory. But it was a memory of Drake's.

Every time he looked at William's hair now, with not a single strand of black left in it, he thought of death. Of how William would die one day and Drake would truly be alone. The last person who knew him, gone.

He tossed back the rest of the whisky and slammed his cup on the table.

"She really has you vexed," William mused, pouring more whisky into the cup and studying Drake. "I haven't seen you in such a chuff in some time."

Drake shook his head. "It's not what you're thinking."

"What am I thinking?" William asked innocently.

They both knew damn well what he implied, so Drake wouldn't dignify it with an answer. Instead he said, "She was in danger. I saw a lynching coming."

"So." William shrugged elaborately. "It's not your affair. You cannot help every poor soul out there . . . is that not what you always told me?"

"Aye, well . . . it is my affair. I owe her."

William's cup stopped halfway to his mouth, then lowered. "For what? For Stephen's life? I thought you settled that a long time ago."

Drake stroked down the wild hairs in his beard. "No, I had to take care of Luthias first."

Williams' entire presence went alert, head tilting, body leaning forward. "And that is taken care of?" His gaze turned hard and narrow as he waited for Drake's answer. It was William's daughter, Deidra, whom Luthias had hunted with single-minded intensity.

"Aye." Drake smiled in anticipation of his brother's reaction. It pleased Drake immeasurably to be the cause of releasing his family from this menace. "She'll no longer have to worry about him."

The lines beside William's mouth relaxed and the tension left his body as he sank deeper into his chair. "For that alone I owe you my life. What need you? Name it and it is yours."

William was no fool. He knew Drake had come to Strathwick for a reason. Drake rubbed his hand over his mouth. "Keep Hannah until she is ready to move.

She has portable wealth—some baubles she can sell or trade. See her to Edinburgh and onto a ship."

William's brows rose. "That is all?"

"Aye. She's really no trouble."

"Then why don't you take her yourself?"

Irritation boiled up. "I thought you said you'd help me?"

William set his cup on the arm of his chair and raised his arms palms out, in a calming gesture. "I never said I wouldn't do it. I simply asked why you cannot."

Drake paced away. "Because I can't." He honestly didn't know why. But he couldn't—or, more accurately, he didn't want to. A strange aversion filled him at the thought of being near her for days at a time. It felt wrong to voice it. She had done nothing to him. She had helped him when he had asked for it. She had released him from his promise. And yet . . . she had let his wife die, and then she had used his wife's memory to put him in his place. And it had worked.

It infuriated him. How was it that this woman knew his late wife so well? And even more vexing, in some ways she reminded him of Ceara. Her soft-spoken strength, her calm confidence. But in other ways she was nothing at all like his late wife. Ceara had been a fine woman, a woman of high moral character. A *good* woman. He had been a better man because of her.

Hannah was not a good woman. She was the kind of woman that drove a man to the edge with lust, and then pushed him over just to amuse herself. He couldn't remember the last time he had been so preoccupied with thoughts of sex. Something about her . . . reeked of it. She made a man think of sleepless nights and late mornings in bed, of filling himself with her and still going hungry.

No, he did not want to spend another sleepless day with this woman. For her to raise Ceara's memory in his mind, when he was possessed with visions of lying between her thighs . . . it was blasphemy and made him uncomfortable in his own skin.

Rose entered the room. She crossed straight to Drake, arms folded under her breasts, and said, "What are you doing?"

Drake glanced at his brother uneasily then back at his sister-in-law. "You are angry?"

Rose's brow wrinkled incredulously. "Angry? Why would I be angry?"

"Because I brought her here."

Rose waved that away with a slim hand. "She helped Stephen. He is a new man because of her. She is always welcome in my home. What I ask is what the two of you are doing together? A more unlikely pair I cannot imagine."

Her brows raised suggestively. Drake felt transparent, as if he exuded the lust he secretly accused Hannah of emanating. He turned away. "It is a long tale."

William, surprisingly, was able to impart the story succinctly, sparing Drake of having to speak on it anymore.

"Well," Rose said when William leaned back in his chair and resumed drinking his whisky. "We will certainly do all we can to help Hannah. But you"—she shook her head, her mouth pursed in disappointment—"you should be ashamed of your-self, abandoning her in such a manner."

Drake paced away. "You know who she is and what she did. She let Ceara die."

William and Rose exchanged a look. Rose crossed to Drake and placed a gentle hand on his arm. Her hair had gone nearly completely white like his brother's—and for the same reason—but her face was still young, her eyes bright with understanding.

"I doubt anyone could have helped Ceara."

"*She* could have. A *baobhan sith* is different. They can bring back the dead. I owe her because of Stephen—but that is all."

Rose studied his expression intently. "It's been a verra long time since Ceara passed, Drake. Maybe it's time to move on."

Drake's jaw clenched stubbornly. "A long time? Mere minutes to a creature that lives centuries."

Her hand dropped. "Verra well. We'll see to her then. You be on your way."

Drake felt his sister-in-law's disappointment keenly. He stood, hands on hips, and tried to think of some defense. But there was none. He felt guilty, as if he was wronging Hannah. But it was *she* who had wronged him, *she* who had brought him so low, *she* who now put his life in turmoil and his honor in question.

"I'll be leaving in the morning," he said abruptly, and left their judging eyes.

Hannah woke as the moon rose. Though the room she was in had no windows, she knew the moon hung high in the sky. She felt it flowing into her and filling her with strength. It tugged at her, calling her to feed.

It was time.

A *baobhan sith* did not require frequent feedings. She could go an entire moon cycle without blood, though she preferred to feed more often. The longer she went, the more reckless she became. It had been more than a fortnight. It was time to slake her hunger.

She rose from the comfortable bed Drake's family had kindly given her and walked silently through the slumbering castle, making herself unseen by all. Blood was all around her—servants, Drake's family, animals. Most of it was fresh and fine. But she would never repay hospitality with such a turn. They had welcomed her, accepted her. She would satisfy her hunger elsewhere.

She left the keep and crossed the bailey. Men manned the walls, guarding against intruders, but they did not see her, because she did not want to be seen. She found the postern door and let herself out.

The castle had a moat. The only way across it was to follow the berm to a wooden bridge. The village was on the other side, a good-sized cluster of cottages. Almost a hundred men, women, and children, and more than twice that in livestock. She should not have a problem finding a meal.

She wandered through the village, choosing a mark. There was much blood in this village, but it did not smell as sweet as it did in the castle. She was accustomed to dining on the less than desirable. It was necessary in order to live in harmony with humans. But on occasion . . .

" 'Tis late for a lassie to be out alone."

She had known he was there, but she feigned surprise when he appeared beside her: a lad, his dark, shaggy hair hanging in his green-flecked eyes. Young and strong and healthy. He would do.

She wadded the front of her shift in her hands. "My cat ran away."

He looked down at her with an indulgent, predatory expression. "Ye were in such a hurry ye didna bother to put yer kirtle on." His eyes roamed over her, hungry. The man had rape on his mind. She knew his kind all too well.

She looked down at herself and ducked her head in a bashful manner. It was beyond her to blush, but she could fake demur.

He put a large, warm hand on her arm and propelled her toward a stand of trees. "Let's have a look over here. I thought I saw a cat go this way."

She smiled up at him gratefully. "My thanks, sir."

"My name is Eric." His hand slid from her arm to her back. "You must be cold."

She leaned into him, nodding. "Kitty, kitty," she called, craning her neck forward as they entered the trees. "Where are you, kitty?"

He didn't question the fact that her cat apparently had no name. He didn't question this because he had already forgotten the cat. He didn't care about her cat and he didn't care about her. He wanted only to slake his lust, just as she wanted to slake her hunger.

Only one of them would find satisfaction tonight.

She let out a little gasp and bent, as if peering into

the trees. "I think I saw her!" She darted away, slipping from his grasping fingers like an eel. She heard his low growl of frustration, though a mortal woman would not have perceived it, and it excited her. She wended her way between trees that grew tight together and heard his lumbering, graceless footfalls behind her. She continued calling to her nameless cat, her tone hopeful, for no other reason than to keep him on her tail.

And then, when she was ready, she let him catch her.

He grasped her elbow and spun her around. She gazed up at him, wide-eyed, as he took both her elbows and propelled her backward against a tree trunk. He was smiling.

His head dipped toward her ear. "Shhh . . . quiet. We dinna want to scare it."

The anticipation of blood, the nearness of it, the sweet, metallic scent, the heat of his skin, drew her incisors longer. His greedy hands moved over her buttocks and thighs to press between her legs. He didn't even know her name, and he mauled her. She despised men like him.

He drew back, probably to smash his mouth against her and suck at her as men were wont to do. She smiled . . . and saw the moment he noticed her teeth, the widening of his eyes, the bobbing of his Adam's apple.

She enjoyed that moment—the second his face registered understanding that he would not burn through her like a lard candle. When he realized that he had picked the wrong woman and would never make that mistake again.

He tried to back away, but his tight embrace had

become his prison. Her fingers dug into his biceps and he couldn't break free. She sunk her teeth into his neck. Blood flowed, pulsing with the beat of his heart. His body relaxed. The frantic fluttering in her belly calmed as the blood warmed and filled her.

She hadn't been feeding very long when she heard someone approach. She lifted her head. The young man she'd been feeding on blinked blearily, gazing through her.

She looked beyond him and saw Drake. He stood about fifteen feet away, his hand resting on a tree trunk. His eyesight was not nearly as keen as hers at night, so she didn't know if he saw her as well.

"What are you doing?" His voice held a strange edge of disbelief and anger.

Hannah sighed. She released the young man and whispered to him, "Go home. You drank too much. This is just troubled dreams."

"Drunk dreams . . . ," he mumbled as he stumbled away, picking a path through the trees until he was no longer visible.

Drake didn't move from where he stood, didn't take his gaze off her. "How dare you feed on my brother's people?"

Hannah sighed deeper this time. *How tiresome.* He couldn't possibly understand, and she knew he wouldn't listen to any explanation she gave. "He is fine. He will not even remember this tomorrow."

"He wouldn't even wake tomorrow if I hadn't followed you." His voice was ominous, derisive. She felt a lynch mob in that statement.

So he had followed her. She frowned, wiping the blood from her mouth as she leaned back against the tree. Strange that she hadn't known he'd followed her.

"I did not intend to kill him. I would not have taken enough to even make him ill. He would have been fatigued tomorrow and perhaps the next day, but after that he would be perfectly normal. In fact, he would be able to get a good drunk for far less ale than usual, so it's a service I do, saving him some coin."

The last was meant to amuse, but he seemed anything but. He approached her. She wiped at her mouth again, then became irritated with herself. There was no blood on her lips. It was a nervous gesture. Even when she was nervous she never showed any sign of it. She was always in control of herself. It annoyed her that suddenly she was less aware of herself.

When he was an arm's length away he inspected her narrowly. Her body was still flush from fresh blood. The warmth filled her cheeks, made the skin along her arms and neck prickle.

The taste was in her mouth. She wanted more.

"If you're hungry," he said, "feed on me."

Her heart trembled in anticipation. She wanted nothing more at the moment: to wrap her body around him, to smell the warm skin of his neck. He would not try to rape her; he would not try to hurt her.

"No," she said.

He took a step closer, as if he sensed how tenuous her control was. "Why is my blood unacceptable?"

"It is not unacceptable. That man would have raped me had I been a mortal woman. I feel no remorse for taking a little from him when he has probably taken so much from others."

Drake's head turned slightly, as if to look after the man, but his gaze remained fixed on Hannah.

"There are animals I can feed on." She pushed away from the tree. "I'll not touch any more of your brother's people—even the rapists and murderers."

"What murderers?"

She smiled. "There are always murderers."

He studied her dubiously. He didn't seem angry, which surprised her. She started to move around him, but he put a hand out, stopping her.

"Is that what you did on your island? Fed on animals? Your sheep?"

She nodded. The hand that touched her arm rose to her face. Her heart paused. The false warmth that slowly seeped from her body rushed back when his fingertips grazed her cheek. His thumb touched her lips. His eyes followed his fingers. Her heart started again, racing in a way that made her fear something must be wrong with it. She couldn't remember the last time she had been touched by a man in such a manner. It was tender, gentle. It made her skin warm, a sensation she hadn't felt in a long while without the aid of blood.

His thumb nuzzled between her lips, pushing her top lip upward and exposing her incisor. His gaze rose from her mouth to meet her eyes. Why did she let him touch her? She could have tossed him into a tree, but instead she allowed him touch her with intimate familiarity.

His hand fell away. "You have teeth like an animal. I do not remember them being that way."

She ran her tongue over her teeth, grazing the razor-sharp tips of her incisors. "They are not always like this."

"I do not understand this feeding you do. If the feeding causes your victim no harm, then by what means do you choose them? Because you believe him to be a rapist? Why not kill him, or at least wound him? If he doesn't suffer for it, why bother?"

The way he phrased it made her flounder for an answer. "It is a matter of respect," she finally said, and she supposed it was. She respected humanity. After all, she had been human once.

He took a step back, as if she'd pushed him. "You respect me?"

"You are not a bad man."

"Then why do you choose not to change me? Apparently I am not a good enough man." He scowled at her, arms crossed over his chest. He reminded her of a boy denied a pleasure he wants very much. He was pouting. After a moment he shook his head slightly. "I don't believe you. I think you meant to lay with that man."

Now *that* was amusing. She had not lain with a man in more years than Drake had been alive. She raised a shoulder. "Think what you will."

She tried to brush past him, but he caught her elbow. "He had his hands all over you. You don't want that from me, do you?"

Her eyes narrowed at him. "How long did you stand there watching?"

"Long enough to see he was about to have you backed up against a tree." He moved her backward until her spine touched the tree again. He had long black lashes, and they had fallen heavily as his dark blue gaze moved over her face.

Normally, such behavior would have been met with contempt by Hannah. Men were ruled by their loins, and it disgusted her.

Or at least it used to.

When Drake did it, she was not disgusted. She could easily have broken his hold on her and gotten away. *Easily.* And yet she did not. She hadn't kissed a man in a dozen years, and even then it had been unwanted. Suddenly, she wanted to feel his mouth against hers. She slid her hand up his chest and curled her fingers into the front of his shirt.

He looked down at her hand, then raised his head. The look in his eyes surprised her. The dark blue blazed, as if lit from a fire within. His nostrils flared as he inhaled. His response was so intense she couldn't tell if it was anger or passion. She pulled him down to her, using the front of his shirt, and got her answer.

His hand covered the base of her skull and he closed the remaining distance between their lips. His kiss was not what she had expected. She had not expected gentleness, and she did not get it, but she had expected an easing into, as was common when two people were new to each other. There was no easing.

His lust flowed into her as fresh and intoxicating as blood. He kissed her hungrily, as if he wanted to consume her. His beard was not rough, as she had expected, but soft and smooth against her skin.

His other arm wrapped around her waist, gathering her close and pressing her all along his solid body. Heat emanated through his clothing, enveloping her in warmth. Her heart beat as it hadn't in forever, it seemed, full and straining, as if she were human again and not a dead thing.

She wanted this feeling, wanted to hold onto it. Her lips parted and his tongue slipped inside. He groaned and mumbled something, a curse, she wasn't sure. His tongue wrapped around hers and his hands began to roam. At first, her body welcomed it. His hand was large and warm, and it felt good as he stroked all over her. To her breast.

A shock jolted through her, from her breast to her groin. She pulled back, startled by the sensation. He grunted and turned away, releasing her abruptly. His hand covered his mouth, and she tasted blood on her tongue. Her mind was still fuzzy from the kiss. She wasn't certain exactly what had happened.

He straightened and lowered his hand, looking at the blood smeared on it. "Ouch," he said, but there was no anger in his tone. He breathed hard, his chest visibly expanding with each breath.

"That was not intentional." Her mind still spun and twisted from what had just happened. She had never kissed a man and felt that way. Had never felt such a jolt go through her from a mere touch. Even now, as she tried to analyze it, she didn't know if it was pleasure or pain, or some strange combination of the two.

"It was worth it," he said, his tone low and rough, sending a mild aftershock through her body. *Pleasure, definitely.*

His gaze narrowed on her suddenly. "Was that some sort of *baobhan sith* magic?"

"What?"

"What I felt—that's how you lure men, isn't it? You cloud their minds with lust until they cannot think."

She blinked. She could, at times, suggest things to other blood witches or humans and control their behavior. Most of the time they did not realize that their thoughts were not their own. However, that was not the case here. She had done nothing of the sort.

"Is that what you think? That I used magic to make you kiss me?"

He squinted thoughtfully, as if studying her even closer would give him the answer he sought. Finally he nodded. "Aye. Some of the thoughts I've had since I took you off the island . . . they cannot be my thoughts. I would never kiss you—my wife's killer." He nodded slowly. "You did this to me, didn't you?"

She raised a brow, unsure whether to be insulted or flattered. Insulted that he thought she would use magic to force him to kiss her? Or flattered that what he felt was so strong and different that he sought magic as an explanation for it?

Her mouth curved into a smile as she brushed past him. "You flatter yourself to think I would waste such useful magic on you." She continued walking away from him, her steps slow and measured. She did not look back.

This time he let her go.

Chapter 5

After a night of fitful sleep, Drake rolled out of bed just before dawn. Though his mind had refused to quiet down all night, come daylight he didn't feel particularly alert. His muscles ached from the journey and his head felt stuffed with straw. He splashed cold water over his face in an attempt to clear his head. Aftereffects from Hannah's magic? She had done something to him last night. He'd been overcome with the need to feel and taste her. That was not like him at all. In fact, it had been years since he'd been with a woman. He'd been something of a womanizer in the days before Ceara, but he had never been as desperate as he'd felt last night, as if he might perish if he didn't take her hard and fast against the tree. . . .

He left the castle in an attempt to walk off these troubling thoughts. The sky hung low, a slab of slate across the sky. It tasted like rain.

He crossed the moat, entering the trees that grew to the water's edge to the south. A few hundred feet into the trees a burn flowed. It ran shallow here, so he walked beside it until it emptied into a pool so clear he could see silverfish darting beneath the surface, above the black and pink pebbles that covered the bottom. He shed his clothes and waded in until the water lapped at his waist. His skin shivered and puckered from the chill. He dove beneath the surface. The cold water braced him, sharpened his mind. He broke the surface with a gasp. His arms and shoulders rippled, protesting the shocking temperature, but he dove under again, invigorated by the water and exercise.

When he broke the surface again, he froze, sinking down until the water lapped at his bottom lip. Someone or something crashed through the forest. He scanned the trees surrounding him. Whoever it was made no effort to be quiet, and they were still some distance away. He started toward the shoreline, watchful of the trees surrounding him. He could hear the rasp of harsh breath and the rustle and crash of someone struggling through the trees.

Drake grabbed his clothes and melted in between the trees, dressing quietly as he homed in on the spot where the intruder would emerge. A man burst through the trees carrying a limp figure in his arms. Something jerked in Drake's chest. The man was familiar. His long blond hair was dirty and unkempt, his clothes torn and filthy. The man's head swiveled around, as if he was disoriented and trying to fix his location. It was then that Drake recognized him— Stephen Ross, and the limp figure he carried was Drake's niece, Deidra.

Drake emerged from his hiding place, one boot on and the other clutched in his fist. "Stephen!"

Stephen staggered, nearly dropping his load. He

clutched her against his chest as his legs collapsed and he stumbled to his knees. Drake raced to him, relieving him of Deidra. Her head lolled against Drake. Her skin was shockingly white, and even through her clothing her body felt unnaturally cool to Drake.

"Deidra?" Drake shook her gently, lowering her to the ground. "Deidra, do you hear me?" He touched her face, taking her chin between his fingers. Again, her skin was too cool. "What is wrong with her? Is she . . . ?"

Stephen shook his head, struggling to his feet. "There's no time for this. We must get her to her father."

Drake couldn't argue that logic. He lifted Deidra into his arms and, without a word, led Stephen back to the castle. The minute they were inside the castle walls Stephen seemed reenergized. He pushed ahead of Drake and shouted, "William! Rose!" over and over until they were inside the keep.

William and Rose tumbled down the stairs, bleary-eyed and half-dressed. William's confused expression broke when he saw his daughter's dangling limbs. He didn't ask a single question. Right now, nothing anyone said mattered.

William took Deidra from Drake and cradled her against his chest, eyes closing. Rose stood at his arm, red hair, liberally streaked with white, falling down her back and over her shoulders. Her mouth pulled into a tight line, her eyes studied the inert figure. Somehow Drake's brother and his wife *saw* ailments. Drake didn't understand it; he never would. It was their witchcraft.

They could see sickness and heal it. It was amazing and wondrous, but it also killed them both slowly.

But they did it anyway. And now, Drake knew, William would give his own life to save his daughter's. Instead of the collapse that usually accompanied a healing, however, William opened his eyes and gazed down at his daughter's blank face, his forehead creased with misery.

"I cannot heal a *baobhan sith*."

Stephen's hopeful face went slack, his eyes stricken. "You have to! Why can't you?"

"Because she's already dead," Rose said softly.

Stephen turned his grief-filled eyes on her. "*How?* She's not supposed to die! She's a blood witch—why did we do this at all if she can just die?"

Rose hastened to clarify. "To become a blood witch one has to die—and when they are . . . reanimated, there is no color . . . nothing for us to heal." She shrugged. "You've gone beyond mere human magic."

Stephen's hands came together as if in prayer, fingers touching his lips. "Will she die?"

William shook his head, his brow furrowed. "I dinna ken . . . I didna think a *baobhan sith* could be killed . . . what happened to bring her to this?"

"Were you lynched?" Drake asked, remembering how the villagers had planned to go after Hannah.

Stephen shook his head and ran a shaking hand over his face. "No . . . no . . . or, not exactly. It was Luthias." He turned on Drake, his brows lowered thunderously. "You said you took care of him. You said he would trouble her no more."

His words sliced through Drake like a sword. He took a step back, one hand rising to palm his forehead then push through his hair.

"Damn it," he muttered. Then louder, "Damn it all."

"Luthias is a blood witch now," Rose said gently. "They are not so easy to kill."

Stephen sneered. "Aye, and whose brilliant idea was it to make him one? To make our greatest enemy powerful and impossible to kill?"

Stephen was right. It had been a stupid thing to do. At the time, it had seemed the only *right* thing to do. Make the man who'd spent his life hunting and killing witches become the hunted. It had been pure justice. And it had worked . . . for a time. But apparently Luthias had found a way not only to save himself but also to thrive and continue his hunt.

Drake's jaw hardened. He hadn't done it alone. In fact, it was not even possible for him to turn Luthias into anything.

"I'll be right back," Drake muttered, and headed for the stairs. He took them two at a time until he reached the landing, where he barged into Hannah's room.

The shutters were tightly closed and the room was dark. "Hannah, wake." He strode into the room. It was cold and smelled like roses. No answer or sign of life, so he found the table and lit a candle. The light from the flame did not extend far. He crossed to the bed, candle held out before him.

She was there, a slim lump under the covers, curled on her side. Her copper hair spilled over most of her face, obscuring it from view.

"Hannah," he said loudly. "Wake!"

She didn't stir. Was she ignoring him? Or did she really sleep so soundly? He remembered on their journey that she seemed to sleep through most anything. He set the candle on the floor beside the bed and placed a hand on her shoulder.

"Hannah." He shook her shoulder gently. Still nothing. He shook it harder and said her name louder. He knew better than to think she was dead, and so he grew annoyed at her unresponsiveness.

He pushed her to her back and took both slim shoulders in his hands. He shook her hard. "Hannah, wake." Her hair slithered off her face, exposing pale features and delicate pink eyelids. He shook her again, and this time she came awake with a start, eyes wide, inhaling a loud, painful, "Hah!" as her mouth opened into a shriek of horror. She twisted and hit him. The blow would have landed him flat at night, but during the day, she possessed no more power than an ordinary woman did.

"Hannah, peace. It's Drake."

She stopped struggling and turned her bewildered gaze on him. She swallowed hard, and then he saw it: her mask of indifference had slipped. He was suddenly certain that was all it was, a mask. It fell back over her face.

"I was dreaming." She rolled to the other side of the bed, away from him, and stood. She turned to him with a frown. "Why are you here?"

"Deidra and Stephen are here and something is wrong . . . Luthias nearly killed her."

She stared at him blankly. "Luthias?"

"Aye, Luthias."

"I thought you said he was dead."

Drake scowled and waved this away. "Well, he's not."

"He attacked another *baobhan sith*, you say?"

Her questions only increased his impatience. "Aye! And nearly killed her—sucked her dry. She might die yet."

Hannah blinked and shook her head, as if confused and disoriented. She took her gown off the back of a chair and slid her arms into it.

"Impossible." She tied the gown under her breasts. "A blood witch doesn't feed on other blood witches." But she didn't say it as if she disbelieved him, more like she was trying to wrap her mind around the idea.

"I guess he didn't know the rules."

She swept past him, giving him a sarcastic sideways smile.

He followed her down the stairs. William had started a fire and laid Deidra on the floor beside it. Rose had found a fur blanket to wrap Deidra in. Stephen hovered over his wife, looking completely destitute. Drake knew that feeling. His stomach hollowed out. He had been there with Ceara. He had watched her decline and waste away while he'd hovered uselessly, wanting desperately to *do* something, anything. And being useless.

Hannah knelt beside Deidra. She touched her face, turning her head to the side and viewing the ragged punctures on her throat. She stared at the wound for several long seconds, her lips pursed with evident displeasure.

She stood and looked at Stephen. "Tell me exactly what happened."

He came toward her, the hope returning to his eyes. "We had gone to Edinburgh and were returning . . . we sleep by day, so we rented a room at an inn. We were roused . . . but we do not wake easily, so we were stuffed in a bag in the back of a wagon afore we actually woke. When we were cut out of the bags we were in a house . . . and there was Luthias. He was well . . . better than well, he looks ten years younger. He spewed his gibberish about how God chose him for this mission, except now he believes he was turned into a *baobhan sith* for the purpose of killing other blood witches." His mouth flattened and he looked down at his wife. "There were three of them and two of us. They held us down and Luthias . . . bit her, drinking her blood. The wolves came then—they sensed something, or she called them, I know not." He ran a trembling hand over his face, looking lost and confused. "I used the distraction to free us."

Deidra could communicate with animals. Although Luthias had made his loathing of all witches clear, something about Deidra's brand of magic offended Luthias more than other witches did. Maybe it was because as a mere child she had nearly killed him. No one really knew, but since that day twelve years earlier, his vision had narrowed to one goal. To punish Deidra.

Tension bunched Drake's shoulders. He couldn't bear just standing here doing nothing. This was his fault, and he had to do *something* to rectify it.

"We have to go." He stared at Hannah until she raised her calm, expressionless gaze to his.

"I should have made certain he was dead. But I didn't. I will fix this."

Stephen turned on him, pale blue eyes blazing. "He mentioned you. He said, 'Where's Drake now, eh? Mayhap this will bring him home.' What did he mean?"

Drake's blood crystallized in his veins. He did not want to tell them how he had spent the better part of the last year. It was no wonder Luthias's focus had shifted.

"What?" William breathed the single word, an incredulous hiss.

"It appears our friend has found a new target," Hannah said, her considering gaze on Drake. She waved a hand at Deidra. "He sent you a message."

William surged forward, eyes fixed accusingly on Drake. "Why?"

Stephen's hand shot out, stopping William. "Not now." He turned his pleading gaze to Hannah. "Will she live?"

Hannah stared down at the unconscious woman. Dark curls jumbled in disarray around Deidra's small, pale face. She looked like a child. Drake's heart squeezed as he remembered her as a child, little heels digging into his ribs as she climbed on his back and demanded that he be her steed. He would crawl around the castle on all fours until his knees ached from it. Then he'd made leather pads for his knees so he could carry her longer. It had been so simple when she'd been a child. If his failure caused Deidra to die . . . he couldn't live with himself.

Not another one.

Finally the corner of Hannah's mouth turned up the slightest bit. "She's not actually alive."

Stephen's lips pursed, and he exhaled. "You ken what I mean."

She nodded wearily. "Aye, I do. In truth I've never seen this happen before. But she *is* a blood witch. Feed her blood—good blood, fresh blood—and she should regain her strength. In time."

"So that's it?" Stephen asked, looking from his wife to Hannah. "There's naught you can do?"

Hannah put a surprised palm on her chest. "Do? What could I do?"

Stephen's lips flattened, apparently not having the answer to that question.

"I know what you can do," Drake said. "You can help me destroy Luthias."

Her eyes narrowed the slightest bit as her gaze turned on him. He might not have thought anything about that slight narrowing before this morning. But seeing her earlier, all raw fear, he knew she wasn't as cool and unflappable as she wished him to think.

"How do you suppose I might do that?"

He advanced on her, meaning to loom, to intimidate. "By making me strong like you. By helping me find him and kill him for good."

"None of this would be necessary if you had just left him dead." She put her fingertips to her lips in mock surprise and shock. "In fact, we wouldn't be having this conversation at all if you hadn't insisted I turn him into a blood witch."

Drake's brow furrowed. The thought had occurred to him, and it infuriated him every time it did. "You could have said no."

"But you insisted."

He smiled suddenly, recalling her harsh words to him. "Have you no free will? You should have said no. 'With such power comes responsibility.' How very irresponsible of you to do something just because a mere mortal man wished it. Have you no will of your own? No judgment? What good are all the years you've lived if they bring no wisdom?"

Though her expression didn't change, her eyes hardened to glass.

He snorted. "One would think you were desperate for the attention of a man the way you agreed to my every wish."

He heard Rose's surprised intake of breath. No doubt he'd fallen to a new low in her estimation, but Drake didn't look at her; he kept his gaze fixed on Hannah to see if she had any reaction to his words.

Her smile tightened. "It appears you actually have a valid argument—at least a portion of it. My judgment has been faulty."

Drake wanted to laugh his triumph, but he settled for a smug smile. "Good. Now change me so I can be of use."

Her hands went to her hips. "And make another mistake? I think not. I have made enough unwise decisions of late." Her gaze swept the entire room, encompassing everyone. Her gaze lingered on Stephen as he lifted his wife into his arms and left the room.

Hannah turned to Drake resolutely. "I will rectify this shipwreck."

That was acceptable. He gave a curt nod. "We'll leave at dusk."

She left the room, her bare feet silent as she padded away.

Drake finally looked at his brother and Rose. "I'll make sure this is over."

Rose stared at him, her mouth hard, arms crossed under her breasts. "I'll see to Deidra."

William watched her until she was gone. "She is right, you know."

"Who?" But his brother didn't fall for his stall for time.

"It was wrong of you both to create a monster out of an abomination. Rose and I, we play with life and death every day . . . but we do not create demons. You've grown reckless. He is after you now."

Drake's jaw went rigid and his neck burned. He didn't need a lecture from his older brother. He knew his shortcomings.

"I vow I will make this right."

William sighed deeply, with the resignation of one who knows his cause is hopeless. He inclined his head. "Then I put my trust in you."

The weight of trust weighed heavily on Drake's heart as his brother left him alone. Drake was finished letting people down. He would find Luthias and end him.

Chapter 6

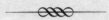

$\mathcal{H}$annah and Drake set out late that night. His brother supplied them with horses, and Rose gave Drake a bag full of supplies, raising her shoulders apologetically at Hannah as she said, "I didna know what to pack for ye to eat."

Hannah just smiled. "I do not eat."

Rose smiled and brushed her hands together as if brushing away the problem of attempting to extend hospitality to her. "Good, then."

The moon was high and shed a soft light over everything. Hannah loved the night. She always had, even before she'd become a blood witch. As a blood witch, the world was clearest to her at night—every rock and tree and blade of grass was sharp and perfect and beautiful to her. Her eyes were different at night, keener. Drake did not see as she did. She had been a blood witch longer than she had been a human, and she couldn't remember what a world shrouded in darkness looked like. Her eyes saw everything.

Her eyes saw Drake far better than she'd ever seen him during the day.

Because of the dark he was not aware of her scrutiny. She could look at him all she wanted and he did not know. That was important—that he not know.

Since last night in the wood, when he had kissed her with such intensity, she had wanted to look at him. Nay, *stare* at him. As if she would understand his kiss if she looked hard enough, as if his face were a book that held the answers.

He had done something unexpected during the time she had slept. He had shaved off his beard.

She wondered what had motivated him to do that. She liked the way he looked without it. For some men, shaving off a beard revealed a weak chin, or an oddly shaped face, or pockmarks. Drake's unveiling revealed nothing of the sort. He was a very handsome man. He had a strong jaw and chin. His sensual mouth had been visible in his beard, but unframed by whiskers it looked different. Softer.

He was not completely scarless, though. Across the pale, smooth skin a scar striped him. It spanned from his ear over the jutting part of his jawbone and ended in the soft skin just below his chin. It was white, indicating it was not a fresh scar.

"What happened to your face?" she asked, reining her horse in closer to his.

He smoothed a hand over his jaw and chin. "Nothing. I shaved."

"That is a shaving cut?" she asked dubiously.

"Oh, that." His fingers sought the scar and traced it absently before his hand dropped to the saddle horn. "It was given to me by a Swedish giant when I tried to steal his magic cup."

She stared at him for a moment, waiting for him to say he jested. When he did not, she repeated, "A Swedish giant?"

"Aye." He nodded slowly, sagely.

"Magic cup?"

"Well, it did not turn out to be very magical. So it was for naught."

"You do not jest."

"No, I do not."

Then she recalled the reason why he would seek a magic cup—the same reason he had brought his wife to her all those years ago.

"So it did not cure Ceara." It was a statement of the obvious, but he shook his head absently.

"No, it did not."

And though she asked no more questions, he kept talking as if she had. "The cup, you see, was supposed to impart eternal youth to all who drank from it. Except it didn't."

Hannah's lips tightened. Something about the failure of his desperate hunt to save his late wife troubled her. Ceara's death weighed heavily on Hannah, and she resented that. It had not been her responsibility, and she didn't like fingers pointed at her. Refusing to help a stranger was not the same as killing. And yet . . . he had such a great love for Ceara. She didn't understand it, but she admired it. And she did not want to. She didn't want to feel anything in regard to Drake.

"Her death was verra painful, you know."

Hannah nodded, even though Drake could not see it. "Aye, I know." And she did, better than he could imagine.

"Do you?" He looked outward, at the night sky, not at her. "It started with the babies . . . our first child was born . . . wrong. Deformed. He didn't live long. After that she had miscarriage after miscarriage until I was afraid to touch her. She was always hungry and thirsty and yet never gained weight. She stopped feeling things in her feet. In the end even my brother couldn't save her feet. She went blind. She would convulse and my brother or Rose would bring her out of it . . . but they couldn't fix what truly ailed her. One day she told me no more, she was done. William and Rose respected her wishes though I cursed them for it. She made it through several more fits, but each time she woke, something new ailed her. She couldn't remember me. Then she didn't know who she was. Finally she just didn't wake."

Hannah's heart contracted. He recounted the events with little emotion. In fact, he seemed surprised, as if he had forgotten some of it and found the memory foreign and unreal.

Hannah had not meant to speak of her refusal to help Ceara. She didn't think he truly cared. She was a convenient scapegoat. But something about the way he held himself responsible for not discovering the cure or forcing Hannah to help moved her, made her want to ease his burden.

"My decision not to help your wife was not made out of spite. It was not an arbitrary decision."

Drake turned, his dark blue gaze clearing to fix on her. "It wasn't?"

"No. I smelled her blood before I even left my

home. It was bad, diseased. It would have made me gravely ill to drink it."

He stared through her for a long time, his mind working something out. "*Could* you have saved her?"

Hannah sighed and nodded. "Aye. But I didn't know you. Why would I cause myself months of agony for complete strangers?"

"How do you know? Mayhap it would not have been as agonizing as you think. William only suffers a few days when he heals truly desperate ailments."

"It is not healing, Drake. It is dying. It is transformation into something new. These are quite different things." His brow still creased obstinately, so she said, "You think you are the first supplicant to come to me for aid? You think I've never drank tainted blood to help someone unworthy of my efforts?" She stopped. Emotion rose up inside her, black bitterness she could barely contain. Its name was Simon. She would not go there again, not after all these years.

"What is a bit of illness to someone who cannot die?"

Her lips twisted and she fought against it, keeping the line of her mouth neutral. "What have humans ever done for me but take and take and then try to kill me when they're finished taking? After you got what you wanted, what then? Who would stay with me afterward when I was too ill to walk? Who would care for me through the illness, bring me fresh blood? A plague such as your wife suffered from could take a very long time to recover from."

His gaze returned from the distant place it had been to focus on her briefly before turning away.

This time she let the bitterness show. He couldn't see it anyway in the darkness. "Aye, that's what I thought," she continued. "Because no one stays. Why should I help when people will leave me to suffer alone?"

He turned to her. In the darkness he could not have seen her expression, yet his eyes focused on her, their intensity piercing. "I see," he said after a long moment, his voice weighted with meaning. It was not just a polite response—she could hear it in his voice, see it in his eyes.

What did he see? He didn't say and she didn't ask.

They rode on the rest of the night in silence. She stole glances at him. He seemed contemplative, staring into the darkness, looking outward, then down, a small frown occasionally pulling at his brows, only to disappear moments later. She wondered what he thought about. Their conversation?

The horizon began to lighten. The sharpness of Hannah's vision faded, and, with it, her strength. They came upon a cottage. The walls still stood, but half of the roof had caved in.

"This will do," Drake said. "Get some sleep."

She slid off her horse and wandered into the cottage with her bedroll. There was nothing inside but a dirt floor and the missing half of the roof. She moved some of the thatching to the shadowed part of the cottage and laid her blanket atop it.

She rested on her blanket and listened to him talk softly to the horses as he rubbed them down. His voice soothed her, but she did not sleep. She was still awake when he entered the cottage with his own blanket. He dragged more thatching near her. Her heart did an irritating little leap, and she scowled. He only lay near her because she was under the covered roof section.

He apparently sensed her displeasure, because he said, "What? I cannot lay here?" He looked mildly irritated, brows drawn into a scowl.

"I care not."

The strength continued to drain from Hannah's body. She needed to sleep, but her mind was too aware of him, lying so close. The atmosphere felt heavy, as if he, too, lay consumed with thoughts.

"I understand." He said the words so suddenly that they startled and confused her.

"What do you understand?"

"Why you sent Ceara and me away."

Something clutched tightly in Hannah's chest—the heart she had thought was all but dead. It had been slowly showing signs of life recently, but now it ached sweetly, in a way that was familiar. Yet the memory was so distant that she couldn't grasp it.

"I do not ken if it troubles you still," he said slowly, as if choosing each word carefully, "but if it does, fash on it no more. You did what most people would have done."

Her voice was locked deep in her chest, blocked by something warm and liquid. It stunned her to realize that she could not speak, for if she tried, her voice might break. She could not recall the last time she had cried. Her tears had dried up scores of years ago, and she liked it that way.

At her continued silence he lifted to his elbows and turned to look at her. "I thought you might have fallen asleep and I would have to say it all again later."

She shook her head. "Thank you," she managed. It wasn't as cool and precise as she would have liked, but she did manage the two words without a single wobble.

He did not lie back down, though. He continued to lean on his elbows, his gaze now turned to his hands. "My whole life I felt alone . . . until I met Ceara. My parents, my brother, his daughter . . . everyone close to me was a witch. But not me. Then William married into a family of witches and I was surrounded by them. I was the only normal one of the lot. I wanted to be different, to be part of the secret society, but I was always on the outside. Then I found Ceara, and she was like me—her family had a shine that she didn't inherit, and for a little while, I wasn't alone. We *knew* each other afore we ever met." He turned his head to look at her. "So you see, I do understand what it is to be alone—and more, to be afraid of dying alone."

Dying alone. Hannah knew she would die alone. She had resigned herself to it long ago. It seemed strange. After all, she was a blood witch. She could live forever.

But she didn't want to. Living was a lonely business, and she had been doing it a long time. She wished to go where everyone else did when their time was finished. She was tired of being on the outside, watching everyone live and love and die while she remained, watching. There was nothing left for her to do or see anymore—and no one to love.

"Is that what you believe?" she asked. "That you will die alone?"

He rubbed his fingers over the black stubble around his mouth and nodded.

"That is why you fought so hard for Ceara's life."

His brow furrowed and he shook his head slightly. "More that I was afraid of life without her."

"Is it as awful as you imagined?"

"It's worse."

The tightness in her chest released, and a rush of warmth flooded her. She had not lost what he had, but his devotion to Ceara moved her inexplicably. She touched him, fingering the curling black hair near his temple, then pushing it behind his ear. He turned his head toward her, and one brow curved upward in question.

In response, her fingertips traced over his brow and his eyes shut.

"I have seen miracles in my life," he said in a hushed voice. "I have been surrounded by them, blessed by them, and yet, when it came to my wife, I was powerless."

"You are not powerless," she said. Her hand slid down, her palm stroking over his cheek, over the slight bump of the scar. He pushed onto his hands and moved over to her, his dark eyes smoky with desire.

She rolled onto her back, gazing up at him, palms resting on his shoulders. Her limbs were heavy, but her mind was alert. They watched each other in silence, communicating with their eyes but committing nothing to words.

She had felt alone her whole life. Before she'd become a blood witch, she had been alone. She had slept in the same bed as her husband and she still had been completely alone. She had lain under him while he had grunted and thrust into her and still, she had been utterly alone. In eighty years, that had not changed.

Until this moment.

Gazing up at Drake, her hand touching his solid body, she felt whole and filled and connected. He lowered his body until his lips touched hers. It was a soft kiss, not at all like his last kiss; that one had been hungry, desperately taking. This one took comfort and companionship, then gave it back. Her fingers slid into his hair and she pulled him down so his body pressed into her. At this cue his kiss deepened, grew demanding. She met his tongue willingly, her leg sliding up to wrap around his. She wanted this. It had been so long since a man had held her this way, kissed her this way. It had been a long time since she'd wanted one to.

His fingers pulled at her bodice, unhooking it and sliding in to cup her breast through her shift. She arched up, pressing her breast into his hand. There was a frenzied fluttering beneath her breastbone, making thought irrelevant and demanding only more sensation, deeper, harder.

He rolled away suddenly. She gasped when his lips broke contact with hers, so disoriented and agitated was she at the loss of his mouth, but his hands gripped her waist, pulling her on top of him so that she straddled him. He wanted her too; she felt it pressed into her and she moved against him, sparking an ache of desire throughout her lower body. He groaned and pulled her down, kissing her as his hands pulled at the ties of her shift until her breasts were bared, then he buried his face in them. He kissed them until he found her nipple. He sucked hard, teeth scraping over them, sending shards of pleasure through her so intense she cried out, grinding her hips into him until the deep throbbing broke over her.

He gave her no time to recover. Her body still shuddered and pulsed when his fingers sought her down there, stroking moans from her, then his cock replaced his fingers and he pressed up into her, so deep he touched her barren womb.

"God, you feel good," he gasped as she moved, palms on his hard abdomen, sliding up and pushing down, moving her hips so he hit her right *there*, and gasping each time. He moaned, his eyes locked on her, hands sliding up her belly to rub her breasts, then sliding down to guide her hips.

It felt strange and wonderful. She had never done it like this—eyes open and speaking all that was in her heart even though she never spoke a word. She had never looked into a man's eyes as he'd rutted on her . . . but this was different; not a man relieving himself in her but two people taking comfort and pleasure in each other.

Pressure built deep inside and her breath grew short again, her fingers curling into the crisp hair on his stomach. His hands gripped her waist and he rolled over, lying between her thighs and thrusting even deeper inside. His deep thrusts sent her over the edge and she cried out, her body convulsing around him.

"Bite me," he breathed into her ear. His hand slid beneath her neck, bringing her head up so her lips pressed against the smooth skin of his neck. She couldn't think, pleasure enveloped her body, wiping away coherent thought. She licked his neck and sucked at it.

"Bite me," he demanded.

Though it was day, she could still smell his blood faintly. Blood witches rarely fed during the day, but it wasn't unheard of. At his urging and her body's upheaval she did as he bid, her teeth sinking into his neck. He grunted, his body tensing. He was in pain. She was hurting him. Of course—her teeth were retracted. She had not been prepared to feed. Fury washed over her in a wave. She pushed at him, palms scrabbling across the wall of his chest, anger and betrayal replacing her passion.

"Get off of me!"

He obliged, rolling off her. His hand was pressed against his neck, and blood seeped through his fingers. She tasted it, felt its wetness on her lips. She wiped it away violently.

"You said it didn't hurt," he said, taking his hand from his neck to look at the blood. Two crescents of bloody marks marred his neck, not the usual puncture wounds left when she fed.

"That hurt," he repeated.

"Why did you do that?" Her voice shook. Her entire body trembled violently. The taste of his blood made her stomach cramp with hunger.

"Because you need me to be a blood witch too if we mean to end Luthias."

"I don't *need* you at all, you fool." She got to her feet, pulling her shift closed. Her loins still clenched and were moist from his intrusion; the pleasure he'd given her still lingered through her body. It made her angrier. "I can finish him without any help at all."

He stood, too, lacing his breeches. "I made a promise." His moves were angry, but she could see that he was angry at himself. He had failed. It had all been a ruse, a game, to draw her in and make her do his will. When would she learn? One hundred and seven years, and she could still be duped by a pretty face.

"And I released you from it." She shook her head, hands on her hips. "It takes more than a bite for the transformation."

"I ken, but I thought if you drained me dry, you would do it."

"You think I have no control over my hungers?"

He grabbed his water flask and poured some into a rag, then slapped it against his neck. "I know not. And never would know until I tried."

She was humiliated, but she would never let it show on her face. Instead she snorted softly. "And I thought you might actually be useful."

His head jerked around. "Useful?"

"Aye, but it appears you are not even good for pleasure." She turned back to her blanket and lay down.

"You seemed to like it."

"Until you ruined it." She put her back to him and closed her eyes.

His movements were violent as he also lay back down. "You said it wouldn't hurt."

It wouldn't have if it had been night and she had been prepared for feeding. His lie pierced her again. She felt dirty and used, and it had been a very long time since she had felt that way. She was such a fool to think they'd had some connection, that there had been something between them. Men were all such lying bastards.

Chapter 7

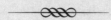

$\mathcal{D}$rake barely slept. His neck stung, and the weight of their sex lay between them. He didn't think she was sleeping either, but he didn't check to verify. He thought perhaps she faked sleep, her pride too bruised to face him. But there had been anger there, after; her eyes had fired and her face, animated. He kept seeing her passion, then her anger, and they both pleased and troubled him. Finally his aching belly drove him to search for food. When his clattering about did not rouse her, he gave in and leaned over her. Auburn lashes lay soft against her pale skin. Her face was slack.

It appeared she actually was asleep, and it irritated him. He was irritated that his plan to make her change him had failed. He was irritated that she was such a cold woman that even the throes of passion could not cloud her mind. Or perhaps it was him—he did not please her enough. He angrily threw his food and utensils back into his sack. *He* had found it pleasing. So pleasing, in fact, that just watching her sleep, looking at the way her hip sloped down to her narrow waist as she lay with her back to him, the way her red hair flowed over her shoulders, made him hard and wanting to lay with her again.

Which infuriated him. He left the cottage with his small crossbow and went in search of game. It was a mild day, and the insects buzzed around him. He stepped quietly among the brush and trees, but he was too distracted by his churning thoughts and either missed opportunities or frightened them away. He set several traps, then returned to the cottage. Hannah looked as if she hadn't moved. She slept like a dead thing—hard and heavy. He lay near her and watched her until he finally fell asleep himself.

When he woke, it was dark and Hannah was gone. A little frisson of panic ran through him. He wandered out into the cottage's yard, where the horses were still hobbled. As he relieved himself at the side of the cottage, he became aware of the distinct sensation of being watched. The moment he recognized the sensation rippling all along the back of his neck, he turned.

"Hannah?" he said cautiously.

"You're awake." She stepped out of the darkness. He knew she could see far better than he could in the dark. The darkness made her appear ethereal, otherworldly. Her hair stirred in the breeze, and her features were soft and partially shadowed.

He turned away and said in a gruff tone, "Aye, why didn't you wake me? We need to keep moving."

"We're not far. No reason to rush."

Irritation surged through Drake. "Why didn't you mention that before?"

"Because I didn't know until I woke."

"Well then, where is he and why are we sitting around here?"

"You were sleeping."

It should have been awkward after what had happened, and he did feel a bit awkward, but she didn't seem any different. Just as cool and enigmatic as always. She had emotions. He'd seen them. Why did she lock them down so tightly?

"Well, I'm not now." His words came out grumpy. He went to the horses, then stopped, hands on hips. They were saddled and ready to go. She brushed past him and swung up into her saddle in a single smooth move. She looked down at him, her lips curved into a secret little smile.

"Then why are you still down there?"

Though she pointed them in the right direction, Drake led the way. He wanted to go by his snares. She didn't question his route, but when he dismounted and dug around in the bushes, coming up with a large hare, he thought he heard a gasp of surprise from her. By the time he was beside her stirrup, though, she was completely composed. He conceded he might have imagined the sound. He studied her face from below, but it was too dark, and he doubted he'd be able to discern anything even if he could see her.

The hare was still alive. He held it by the ears as it struggled. "I thought you might be hungry."

She looked from the hare to his eyes but did not move to take it.

"Since I interrupted your last meal, I wanted to make sure you are getting enough to eat."

When she still just stared at him, he rushed on, "I know it's not a human or even a hart—I dinna ken what you prefer—but it is fresh."

The hare kicked out violently, and Drake moved back so it didn't spook the horse. Hannah leaned forward and ran her hand over the trembling hare. It immediately went limp and heavy. She took it from him. "Thank you." Her voice was soft and composed.

He peered at her face in the dark, wishing he could see her expression. He nodded and left her to feed in private.

They traveled for several more hours before arriving at a large village. "Here," she said. "He's been here."

"But he's not here now?"

Hannah shrugged. "I know not."

"I thought you felt him?"

Hannah's clear brow creased, as if she tried hard to find the words to make him understand. "I do, but it comes and goes. And . . . he is most unusual, in that I think"—her finely shaped brows drew together in disbelief—"I think he knows when my mind touches his, and he retreats." She shrugged, as if the idea was foolish, but it made Drake uneasy.

"What mean you? Do you speak to each other? In your minds?"

Deidra and Stephen had never mentioned such magic. He found the prospect both unsettling and intriguing. He would like the power to see other's thoughts but didn't relish others having access to his.

"If I think about one of my blood witches, sometimes I see what they are seeing or I see their memories and thoughts."

"One of *yours*? Do you have a lot?"

"Nay, but more than I'd like."

Drake wondered how many that equaled, but she wasn't revealing anything. The night seemed close and very dark. Drake's gaze tried to penetrate the dark alleys between the stone and thatch buildings. He saw movement in the shadows one minute, then wondered if he imagined it the next.

There was little activity in the streets. It was night, and the inhabitants were behind closed doors. When they passed, however, the sound of latches falling across doors could be heard. The villagers knew something dark had invaded their peace. Luthias? Or Hannah?

"Where are we going?" Hannah asked, looking over her shoulder as the houses began to thin.

"The first place I can imagine him going." He nodded his head to the building in front of them. A kirk. It was the largest building in the village. Several stone crosses stood out front; the knot work covering them was worn almost smooth, but still visible.

He turned to look at her and found himself alone. His muscles hardened. He reined his horse in and turned around. He could barely make her out in the darkness; he saw only the blaze of white on her horse's nose. She had stopped and was frowning at the kirk.

"Come on," he said.

"I cannot go in there."

Drake looked back at the kirk, then to her. "Why not?"

She did not answer his question and instead said, "Luthias is not in there."

"How do you know?"

"Oh, I know. Do not doubt me."

She did sound confident. Drake turned back to the kirk and considered it with a heavy sigh. Luthias was a church man, and in his own warped way, served God above all else.

"There's a house behind it where the pastor probably lives. Can you go in there?"

"Aye." She rode around the kirk, giving it wide berth. Her behavior made Drake uneasy. If she could not even enter a kirk, she must truly be an abomination. This was something else Stephen and Deidra had not mentioned.

They dismounted and entered the house cautiously. The kitchen was a detached building to the back, with a garden between it and the house. The breeze lifted the scent of mint and thyme into the air. Hannah lifted her head, like an animal catching a scent. The more he watched her behavior, the more uneasy he grew. He did not like putting his life in her hands. The kitchen was dark, so they entered the house from the back. It stank of the lard candles that illuminated the interior. A long table with benches sat before a fireplace, and several chairs and cabinets were situated around the room. Along one wall was a heavy curtain that probably hid a door leading to other parts of the house. A wooden desk with paper and an ink pot sat against the wall. Other than furniture, the room appeared deserted.

"Hello?" he called. "Anyone here?"

"Someone's here," Hannah whispered. She moved silently around the room, her steps liquid. "He's hiding."

How she knew this, Drake had no clue, but she stopped at the curtain and looked back at Drake, a slender brow arched with the amusement of a cat stalking its helpless prey. She pulled the curtain back.

The curtain hid a wall—and a man pressed up against the wall with his eyes squeezed shut. His eyes popped open and his gaze snapped from Hannah to Drake. The tense set of his shoulders relaxed, and he let out a breath.

"Thank the Lord. I thought he'd returned."

"Who?" Drake asked, approaching the man cautiously.

"The reverend's friend."

Hannah and Drake exchanged glances.

"Why would the reverend's friend frighten you?" Hannah asked.

The man looked at her, really looked at her for the first time, and his fleshy face flushed a mottled red. He quickly averted his eyes. "He . . . uh . . . he . . ." He seemed to have lost his thoughts, and he rubbed at his forehead. Hannah did tend to have that effect on men. Drake's thoughts often scattered around her. A vertical line of impatience formed between her brows, and he realized that this was not magic, not some spell she had cast. It was just Hannah.

"The reverend's friend," Drake prompted.

"Ah, aye." He craned his neck to peer around Drake. "He wasn't right in the head it seemed . . . but the rev-

erend thought he was special—that he would help him
with the witches that plague the village. And he did
seem knowledgeable." His gaze darted about the room.
"We shouldn't be here when he returns." His gaze
took in Drake, looking him over from head to toe, his
brows lowering in a suspicious frown. "Who are you?"
He glanced at Hannah but quickly looked away.

"I am Drake MacKay, and this is Hannah O'Shea.
We are looking for Luthias Forsyth. He is an older
man. Tall with a balding pate; thin face, small gray
eyes."

"That's him!" the man said excitedly.

"And you are?" Drake asked.

"Robert." He pushed away from the wall and started
toward the door. "I really dinna want to be here when
your friend returns."

"Why?" Drake asked.

"He did something to the reverend. Look." He
waved a hand, urging them to follow.

He pushed the curtain further aside to reveal a door.
It led to a small, spartan room resembling a monk's
quarters. It contained only a cot, a shelf with a candle,
and a Bible. On the cot lay a white-faced old man.

Hannah stood over him.

"The man ye search for said he wasna dead, that he
would wake later. But I dinna ken. He looks dead to me."

"Is it too late?" Drake asked Hannah.

"Aye, he'll be waking soon." She turned to Robert.
"How do you know Luthias is coming back?"

"Because he told me to stay here, that I should
be here when the reverend wakes . . . that I should be

available, was what he said. He said he would be back for him later." Robert looked at the reverend, and his expression was one of pain and indecision. "But I dinna think the reverend is waking. I think he's dead."

"Aye, Robert. You should go." Hannah didn't look away from the reverend as she said this. "Posthaste. To the kirk and stay there till morning."

"We should all go," Robert urged, eyes darting wildly. "This is wrong—it feels wrong. Something bad is going to happen. I dinna think your friend's mind is right. He's been in the moonlight too long."

Hannah laughed softly. "Aye, that's one way to look at it." She looked at Robert over her shoulder, her expression grim. "Something bad will happen if you do not leave now."

Robert swallowed hard. He looked at the reverend for a long moment, then nodded and hurried from the room.

"What should we do?" Drake asked, joining Hannah to stare down at the white-haired old man.

She held out a hand. "Give me your sword."

Drake unsheathed his sword from where it lay slung across his back, then handed it to her. She held it in front of her, gripping the hilt in both hands. She inspected the blade, then looked down at the sleeping reverend. He stared back at her.

Drake's heart leapt in his chest, and he barely kept himself from jumping backward. The reverend's lips drew back, revealing gleaming yellow incisors.

Hannah raised the sword over her head and

brought it down across the reverend's neck. The eyes went blank.

Drake stared in shock at the decapitated man. There was minimal blood. Hannah handed Drake the sword. He fumbled to take the hilt, suddenly averse to touching the blade. She grabbed the reverend's head by the thatch of white hair and turned to Drake.

"I need a sack."

Drake blinked. She looked like she asked for a bit of jam for her bannock, not a sack to stow the head she'd just severed from its neck. He didn't know what he had expected. He had been fully prepared to help kill Luthias, but a man of God, lying on his cot sleeping? How did one prepare for that?

"We're taking it with us?" he managed to sputter out.

She looked at him as if he was an imbecile. "We cannot leave it here."

He almost asked why, then decided not to bother. He rummaged through the reverend's trunk until he found a homespun sack. She dropped the head in, then handed it to him.

"Why do I have to hold it?"

She scanned the room, her mouth serious and flat. "Because he is coming."

He wiped the blade of his sword across the reverend's headless torso and held it ready. "He's here? Now?"

She shook her head and left the room, exiting back into the main room. "Not yet. But he knows. He felt the reverend die, and he will come."

This blood witch business was so odd that Drake counted himself lucky she had refused to turn him into one. He followed her as she crossed to the door. She stood in the doorway gazing out into the night. Her hair hung loose, rising in the wind to flutter around her arms. She listened to something beyond his senses.

She is beautiful. The thought struck him hard and fast. She was like some warrior woman of ancient times. He'd never known anyone like her. His pulse thrummed, anticipating confrontation. He tried to focus, but his gaze strayed to her cool, composed face. This part he hated, the waiting, the anticipation of the fight. He liked the fight and the heady rush of winning, but the waiting killed him.

He felt a change. He wasn't sure how or why, but the air changed, sparked almost . . . or maybe it was Hannah.

"Fash not," she said without turning around to look at him. "This will not take long."

She stepped back away from the door, and Luthias stepped in. "No, it will not."

He was different. Drake noted that immediately. Stephen and Deidra had looked no different when they became blood witches—but then they had already been in their prime. Luthias, who had been old, had shed years. He looked strong and vibrant. After the change, when Luthias had refused to partake of blood, and lynch mobs had hounded his every step and tortured him, he had been haggard and thin and sickly.

The blood had changed him.

He grinned at Drake, all teeth and thin lips. "I've been waiting for you, Drake. I knew she'd bring you to me. How is Deidra, by the by?"

So smug, so knowing. Drake's temper boiled over. He rushed forward, his sword arcing toward Luthias. Drake feinted at the last moment, coming at him from the opposite direction. Such a move should have given him the upper hand, but Luthias darted at the last minute and hit him.

It happened so fast that Drake did not know what happened. One minute his sword arced through the air, the next his face slammed against the cold stone floor while pain exploded through his skull.

Before he could open his eyes he heard fighting—grunting and crashing. Panic gripped him anew. This wasn't the easy feat that Hannah had anticipated. She was in trouble, and he lay on the ground doing nothing. His sword scraped along the stone as he forced himself to stand. He turned unsteadily and saw Hannah crumpled on the floor. Luthias stood over her. He dropped to one knee.

If Luthias killed her, Drake didn't know what he would do. To see her, such a strong woman, broken, sent strength flooding his limbs. He raised his sword and charged at Luthias.

Luthias turned, unafraid, uncaring, waiting for Drake's attack. It was hopeless, but he couldn't stop; he *had* to do something. Luthias grabbed Drake's sword by the blade—a move that surely cut his palm—and raised his other hand to strike. Hannah rose silently behind him. Her eyes were wild.

She gripped Luthias's neck in both hands and twisted it. She threw him against a wall.

Drake wiped a shaking hand over his face. His head still throbbed, but the rush of the fight was draining from him.

Hannah turned. "No time to gawk. Get the head and go."

Drake blinked at the urgency in her voice. "You broke his neck."

But Luthias was getting to his feet, and he had Drake's sword. Drake asked no more questions. He grabbed the sack, following Hannah as they raced into the night.

Chapter 8

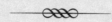

$\mathscr{H}$annah was actually unnerved. Drake had never seen her so flustered. They had fled blindly at first, unthinkingly, with no other goal than to put as much distance between themselves and Luthias as possible. But when Drake was reasonably certain that they were safe and he began to think coherently, he suggested they lay low for a while in a large town. The larger the town, presumably, the harder they would be to locate. Hannah agreed without argument.

He rented a room at an inn and stood vigil while Hannah curled up on the bed and slept like a corpse. Drake did not know how she could sleep after what had happened. Apparently blood witches slept no matter what. His body was rigid, the details of the night frozen in his mind. The vision of Luthias rising, his head sagging at an angle haunted him. Drake usually had some type of plan regardless of the situation, but tonight he had naught. They had not even disposed of the reverend's head yet. Drake's gaze strayed to the corner, where the sack rested, mocking them.

The conclusion his circling mind kept coming back

to was that they could not defeat Luthias. At least, not as the situation currently stood.

When the sun dipped below the horizon, Hannah stirred. Drake sensed when she was awake, though she did not move from where she lay curled on the bed. He watched her for a time, waiting for her to sit up or speak; but she did not move. He wondered why she lay there, unmoving. He crossed to the foot of the bed so that he could see her face.

She stared at the stone wall. He said nothing for a time, watching her. Things were far worse than he'd imagined for her to lay there, mute. He'd come to rely on her strength, her steadiness. He might be impulsive, but she tempered it. His throat tightened and his lips rolled in. Frustration built in his chest like a wall, stone by stone.

When she finally spoke, her voice was soft. "I want to go to Italy."

Drake's frustration instantly transmuted to anger. "You want to run away from your problems."

Her gaze shifted to him though she did not move her head. "I want to run away from *your* problems. None of this is mine. I did not ask for it."

"It was *you* who showed the poor judgment in turning Luthias." It was cheap of him to throw that in her face. He had wanted her to do it; it had not been her idea. Nevertheless, she was the one with the power, so she shared responsibility.

Her eyes shut and she did not respond. She looked small and fragile lying on the bed, knees curled up almost to her chest. But she was not fragile and they were not helpless.

"You said you could handle Luthias, that it would be no problem," he continued. "You were wrong. If you had just turned me it would have been two of us and he would be dead now. Still, you alone managed to incapacitate him long enough for us to escape. He is not invincible. Imagine what two of us could have done."

Her mouth tightened, pushed out into a stubborn moue. She said, "I surprised him. It was a trick. He will not fall for it again."

He leaned forward and braced his hands on the bed, one on either side of her legs, and said urgently, "Which is why you need me to be a blood witch."

She shook her head, her eyes opening blankly again. "No, he was too strong. He is creating more like him, an army."

His hands curled into fists in the bedcovers. "That is why we need to stop him now!"

She didn't move or speak. He pushed forcefully off the bed and spun away, pacing across the room. "Fine. If you don't do it, I will return to Strathwick. Stephen will turn me. I know he wants Luthias dead as much as I do. He will not be so stubborn."

"Good. Now you have a plan. Leave me."

Drake almost did, but her stubbornness provoked him. His fists opened and closed as he walked toward the door. He stopped and turned back. How could she give up after only one attempt? Together they needed to analyze what had happened, study Luthias's weakness, and formulate a new plan. He needed her to do that, however.

She could run, but she wouldn't be rid of him so easily.

The bed was large enough for a family. He lay on the other side of it and yanked the blanket over his shoulder. "I paid for the room and I'm tired. *You* go. Night is your time anyway."

He felt better having said it. But Hannah made no move to leave. She continued to lie in the same spot and didn't say a word.

He was surprised to find that after he lay there a while his body grew heavy and tired. It had been some time since he'd last slept.

He woke a little while later. Moonlight poured into the dark room from the open window, illuminating a portion of the room in silver-gray. He turned his head to look at the other end of the bed, feeling in his bones before his vision verified it: she was gone.

What now? His earlier words about going to Stephen had been a threat, but it was an option and one he had not considered before. And now he wondered why. He supposed it was the promise he had made to Hannah, but that mattered little now. Stephen would change him. Drake didn't need Hannah.

He sat up in bed and rubbed his hands over his face. No more traveling all night at least. He should have gone back to sleep, but his body had become accustomed to the new rhythm, and he was now wide awake.

He gathered his things up in the dark, crammed them into his sack, and left the inn. His footsteps were leaden as he crossed to the stable. No lantern lit the stable's interior, so he propped the door wide. He had only taken a few steps inside when he saw her. She leaned against the stalls, waiting.

Though he would never admit it to her, relief flowed through him. She hadn't left.

He brushed past her. "I thought you were off to Italy."

"I am." She turned to watch him enter the stall. "But before I go, I had an idea."

He saddled his horse, waiting for her answer, not wanting to seem eager. When she didn't give it, he asked, "What is your idea?"

"It takes an army to beat an army, aye?" There was a note of self-satisfaction in her voice that he liked. Her idea would be a good one.

He turned to face her in the dark. "You have an army?"

He couldn't make out her expression, only the pale oval of her face, but he imagined he heard a smile in her voice when she replied, "More of a nest."

"So there are more of you?" The idea staggered him. Prior to Stephen and Deidra's transformation, she had been the only blood witch he'd known of, and her existence had been questionable—a thing of legends.

"More than you'd expect. One or two sometimes choose to live in a large town; the large cities often have a nest or two . . . London, Paris, Rome—"

"And in Scotland?"

"Edinburgh."

Drake exhaled. "Of course. Will they help us?"

"When I tell them what Luthias has done, I believe they might."

She acted as if she didn't care, but here she was,

with another idea. He resisted the smile tugging at him.

Drake took a step toward her, wishing he could discern her expression in the darkness. "Why do you not live in a nest?"

She shrugged. "I dislike the city."

He stood inches from her now and could still barely make out her features. Her head tipped back. Her skin was pale and luminescent in the moonlight, her brows dark arcs over dark hollows.

"Why is that? I don't think you enjoy living alone."

"A person can be crushed by humanity and still be alone. Besides, humanity is all death and loneliness."

He inhaled deeply. He could smell her when they stood this close. She had washed with rose water. It drifted up to tickle his senses. He loved the way she smelled.

"The life of a blood witch, as you choose to live, seems hardly any better. Why not live with your kind?"

"The ones I have known do not share my respect for life."

"Ah," he breathed, understanding her. "They live among humans because they are a ready food source. Like your flock of sheep."

The dark line of her mouth curved slightly. "Aye."

Morals. Ethics. A monster who did not feel could not possess these things. His hand rose, the back of it brushing against her skin. Satiny, soft, inhumanly sensual to his fingers. Touching her made him want more, to open his hand against her skin, to knead and taste. . . .

Her lashes fluttered from his touch.

"You were frightened today," he said softly.

One delicate brow arched. "Weren't you?"

"Aye, but I have a healthy respect for things other-worldly. You, my dear, *are* otherworldly, and seem afraid of naught."

His hand stroked, unwilling to give up the luxurious feel of her skin. She didn't protest or move away, and he thought of the last time he had touched her, their bodies melded in intimacy.

"Until recently, I have never had reason to fear."

"You've never been accused of witchcraft? Or lynched?"

"I didn't say that. Death does not frighten me."

His hand paused against her cheek then slid under, his thumb stroking the underside of her chin. "If you were not afraid for your life, what then frightened you?"

"You did."

That caused him to laugh. "Me?" She could throw him against a wall and crack his skull with one hand. He was nothing to her.

She nodded slowly. "Aye, you."

He frowned dubiously. "You were afraid of me?"

"No, stupid man. Afraid *for* you."

And he understood. He had never been as she was—caring for no one and nothing. He had a family he loved, who loved him, but he had been alone and uncaring of his own fate.

His other hand rose to cup her face. He still could not see her eyes, but she gazed back at him. He felt it.

He kissed her. Her lips were soft, inviting. Her hands curled into the front of his plaid, pulling him closer. He loved how she did that, how she was so eager and enthusiastic. It was the only time she showed any emotion. He thought of what she had said before, that she had been using him for pleasure. At the moment, he didn't care. He wanted her to use him again.

He pushed her backward, his hands bunching up her skirts. When her back hit the stall, her leg slid up to wrap around his. Her kiss was deep and passionate, and he was lost in it. She fumbled with his belt, and he pulled back to help her.

He felt strangely urgent, as if he must take her now, against this wall. He had to possess her, exert some kind of power over her. He thrust into her, nearly lifting her off the ground. She cried out. He groaned with the incredible relief of being inside her, with her all around him, warm and pulsing.

She tore her mouth away to gasp, her fingers digging into his arms. He still couldn't discern pupils at this distance, but he could tell she gazed at him. Her lips parted, her breath fanning against his face. He thrust again, deeper this time, and she tightened all around him as a little cry escaped her throat.

"You feel beautiful," he said as his hands slid up to cup her bottom. He thrust harder and deeper as her thighs wrapped around him. His heart swelled and pumped against his ribs. When his climax gripped him, he nearly fell to his knees. He braced a forearm against the wall above her head and sagged forward, his breath sawing in and out of his chest as he willed his heart not to explode. His forehead rested against his forearm.

He became aware of the sounds and smells in the

stable: horses shifting and blowing, the odor of dust and hay and manure mingled with their sweat. He slid his head down to bury his nose in the curve of her neck. He inhaled the sweet scent of her and realized that the sweat he smelled was his own. He rubbed his nose against cool skin.

He drew back to look at her. He could feel the dampness of his own skin, but it was too dark to see her skin. So he placed his palm against her cheek. Cool and dry.

Something curdled in his chest and he pulled away from her, retying his trews and buckling his belt. He felt strange, unbalanced. Uneasy confusion curled in his belly like a dying worm. She had enjoyed that, he was sure of it. He was not a complete novice in the ways of women, and she had been in heat. And yet her temperature had not risen at all.

He deluded himself. She was different, not human. And old. She wasn't moved by such things as making love anymore. He thought he was taking possession of her, but in truth, she wended her spell all around him until he was too ensnared to even know himself. He couldn't let that happen.

He turned to her. "Are you ready to go?"

She had pushed her skirt down. She leaned against the wall, staring at him. Finally, she straightened. "Of course." Her voice was cool, emotionless. Just like the empty cavity of her chest.

Fresh anger swept through him. She held all the power and he was sick of it. He would find a way to shift it before this was over.

Chapter 9

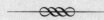

$\mathcal{T}$hough tales of bloodthirsty creatures abounded in Scotland, a nest of blood witches in Edinburgh was not a tale told to frighten children. Luthias had heard of them once long ago and had dismissed them as local lore. He had not dismissed much, but the idea of a nest of blood witches living freely amongst humans and never being caught or stopped had not seemed likely.

But now . . . now everything had changed. Things that had once sounded absurd were now perfectly within the realm of possibility. He felt incredibly powerful as he waded through a sea of humans. They were insects. All of them with someplace to go, some pressing matter to accomplish. This moment could be their last, and they spent it on such petty concerns. Even now, when Luthias had become a vile creature, he had found a way to lift himself up above all of that, to still honor and worship God. Even the lowliest creatures could be saved. He had to believe that.

But it was difficult when he smelled them, their blood. Rich and thick and full of life. *They were not for him.* God had shown him a better way, and Luthias was so grateful for it.

It had been a struggle, as everything in Luthias's life had been until now. He had killed a pastor in a frenzy of hunger and blood lust. Then, in a wave of regret, he had tried to return the man's blood to him. He had cut his own wrist and poured the blood down the man's throat. But the pastor had not woken.

Night faded, and Luthias's exhaustion overcame him. He slept. He woke stronger than he had been in a long while and decided the least he could do was give the pastor a proper burial. He was digging the grave when a rustling sound frightened him. He thought that perhaps someone had chanced upon him and the hunt would begin again. He wanted it to be over. He was so very weary of the world. Part of him hoped that was exactly what it was; the lynch mob had come for him with fire and sword and would burn him until he finally didn't wake craving blood.

He crept closer to the sound. His heart jacked painfully against his ribs. The place where he'd left the pastor's body was nothing more than crushed moor grass. He stood frozen, listening to the odd sounds that he now recognized as *feeding*, that sickening-sweet sound of a blood witch sucking the life from its victim.

Horror immobilized him. Was this another of God's punishments? Or was it a test? He had turned Luthias's victim into a blood witch to taunt him? Or was he to dispose of it? He didn't know what to do.

He hid in the moonlight, rooted from indecision, listening, disgusted and intoxicated. He loathed himself for desiring blood, but the loathing did nothing to quell the desire.

The pastor crept out of the tumbledown building where he had been feeding, and he stared at Luthias. Blood smeared his face, coated his hands like gloves. He held his hands out in front of himself and looked down at them, his eyes wide as he cried, "Father! Oh God!"

Luthias didn't know whom the pastor spoke to, him or God. All he knew was that he saw himself in that monster, and what he saw filled him with compassion. So he did what he could not do for himself. He killed it.

And then fed on it.

That was when Luthias's luck finally changed.

But that knowledge did not come to him immediately.

Guilty and sickened, he buried the corpse. He did not know whether he had done the right thing, but really, what was right anymore? He went through the rest of the night certain that if he had finally done God's bidding, he had gone about it all wrong. He wasn't supposed to have eaten it. Why had he eaten it? Some part of Luthias, some foreign part that lived in his head and gave him memories and knowledge that were not his own, told him that feeding on another blood witch was wrong, forbidden. But Luthias knew that it wasn't God who spoke to him. It was the evil thing that took over his body and craved blood. So he ignored it.

Daylight came and he found a place to hide while waiting for the sun to steal his strength.

Except, for the first time, it didn't. He remained strong and alive in the full glory of daylight. He walked among the humans, a god in their midst and they did not know, could not fathom. He praised God for making him *more.*

He would have liked to have said that he understood then what happened, but it took him more time still. His day strength faded and the hunger returned. But this time, he contemplated what he should do about it, how he should handle this blood-weakness so that he did not continue to offend God with his wicked cravings.

And whenever he considered God in his plans, He put another blood witch in Luthias's path. A male and his mate. They had a wee farm and seemed oddly peaceful. They lived away from humans and fed on animals. They welcomed him and pitied him. They said it was wrong for a blood witch to turn a man of God and that whoever had done it was cursed. It surprised Luthias that he liked them. So he decided to save them. When they slept during the day, Luthias ignored the voices in his head telling him that it was wrong, wrong, *wrong*, and he killed them. And supped on them.

He grew stronger. That was when he finally understood that he was once again doing God's work. When he obliterated the dead things, he became stronger, capable of doing more such work in the Lord's name.

He also understood that alone he could not take on Hannah and the MacKay witches. He did not care about mere witches for now—it was Hannah and Drake he wanted. The ones who had done this to him, turned him into a demon, then tortured him. He would need more like himself. And only men of God could be trusted. Men like him. So he sought them out, pressed them into service—for not one of them came willingly—then sought out the storied nest. He would find Drake and Hannah and show them the real meaning of justice.

They entered Edinburgh during the day. Hannah had wanted to go straight to the house of the blood witches, where they could sleep in relative safety, but Drake had refused. He had been acting odd since she had agreed to continue this folly. She had thought he would be pleased. And indeed, he had seemed so at first. He had taken her hard and fast against the wall in the stable. He was the only man in a very long time who had made her feel *alive*.

He had been tender afterward, touching her face and neck. And then he had walled her out. She wanted to believe Drake was different from the men in her past. She had almost convinced herself of it. But she had been wrong. He was no different.

His reluctance to sleep in a nest of blood witches, however, was understandable. He might wish to become a blood witch, but he didn't wish to be their dinner. And that was the way it probably would have gone, for a blood witch did not sire other blood witches indiscriminately. But most blood witches weren't complete animals: They respected another's human pets, and though Drake would no doubt balk at being considered a pet, that was the way they would see it.

They found an inn and slept until nightfall. Hannah

had grown accustomed to sleeping beside Drake. And though they started out the evening on opposite sides of the bed, he ended up with his arm around her and his body pressed along her backside. She slept deeply, so deeply very little could rouse her, so she wasn't conscious of their sleeping positions—until she woke. And then, for a few moments at least, she pretended that he held her because he wanted to.

But then he stirred and she threw his arm off, as if finding it there had been repugnant. She needed him to know he had no power over her.

He grumbled something as he rolled out of bed.

"What was that?" she snapped.

"If your hearing was as sharp as you claim it is, then you should know."

"Even sharp hearing cannot discern words run together as if you have a mouth full of food."

"I said, are you ready?"

That wasn't what he had said. She crossed to the basin and splashed water over her face. She was tiring of his quicksilver moods. He treated her like a whore, to be used and then ignored. She dried her face and turned to look at him. He leaned insouciantly against the door, waiting with studied boredom.

"I am ready," she said. "The question is, are you?"

He frowned slightly, as if he thought he had misunderstood. "Am I ready?" He pushed away from the door and advanced on her slowly, almost angrily. "I have been ready since the beginning. It is I who pushed you every step of the way." He stopped before her, hands on his hips. "Of course I am ready."

"Good, because they will want to eat you. And you will find after you are there only a short time that you will want them to."

He tilted his head slightly. "I cannot see that happening."

She bit her bottom lip in a small smile, wanting to tease him, but she decided that their relationship was too strained to attempt teasing.

His eyes narrowed. He saw that she suppressed some urge and caught her arm. "What?"

"You are so . . ." *Ignorant* was on the tip of her tongue, but that was not quite right. She waved a hand in front of her, palm up. "Innocent."

His eyebrows shot up. Clearly *innocent* was not a term he would have applied to himself. "Innocent, aye?"

"Aye, you think you know so much about me, about what I am, but you know nothing."

"What you really mean is that I'm ignorant."

She wondered how far she would take this. There had been a time when she had controlled others for no other reason other than that she could. It had been an empowering experience, to be strong and in control after so many years of being subordinate to everyone. But that had worn thin when she'd seen herself becoming that which she had once fought to escape. Now she only did it to protect herself. But he tempted her. He thought that because he lived among witches, he understood *her*. He understood nothing.

What harm would it do? It wasn't as if she planned to feed on him.

She tipped her chin up toward him, letting calm flow out of her and into him. Her mind reached for his, urging him to relax and release his troubles. He studied her expression with a frown. The lines of strain relaxed from his face, and his eyes went hazy and distant.

She walked toward the bed. "Come with me."

He followed.

She gestured to the rumpled covers. "Lay on the bed."

He hesitated for a brief second, then lay down.

"On your face."

Obligingly, he turned over.

With great satisfaction, Hannah smiled down at him lying there obediently. She stopped projecting her thoughts and feelings on him. His head turned from side to side. He rolled off the bed abruptly.

"What the hell?" He rubbed at his eyes and glared at her. "What did you do to me?"

"What the others will do if you are not careful and stay close to me." *You need me.* She didn't say it, but the thought filled her with pleasure.

He scowled at her, hands on hips. "I will not look them in the eyes."

As if it would be that easy. She shook her head knowingly and pulled her arisaid around her shoulders, pinning it with a brooch. She started to brush past him when his hand on her shoulder stopped her. She glanced down at his hand, large and warm, cupping her shoulder, then up at him. His eyes, blue as the night, gazed back at her. Her pulse picked up pace. He confused her, the way his temper changed.

"Mayhap I am ignorant of some things, but we're in Edinburgh. Take off the arisaid."

His words hit her like a shock. She glanced down at herself, feeling suddenly foolish. She looked every bit the Highlander, and he was dressed as a lowlander, in leather breeches and a worn leather jack. Living as she did on her island, she was insulated from the political climate. But if one thing hadn't changed in a century, it was the lowland hatred for Highlanders.

She shrugged his hand off and removed the arisaid, tossing it back over the end of the bed. "Let's go."

They went out into the city on foot. The streets were still choked with people. Men, mostly, but some women, too. Men in their city clothes strode though the crowd, off on some enterprise. Men in their home-spun trudged home with their tools and dinner pails. Men and women with no homes begged for alms, eyes rheumy and cracked and filthy hands outstretched. Children that had nowhere else to go chased a dog, shouting and laughing and throwing dirt clods at it.

They were prey. All of them were, but especially the children. No one would miss them. They had no place to call home.

Hannah glanced at Drake. His gaze scanned the streets around them, watchful. He missed nothing. He had asked her where they were going, but she hadn't told him because she hadn't known. And yet she did, or at least she would know when they arrived.

His gaze locked onto the child at the same time Hannah noticed it, but she doubted the child caught their attention for the same reason.

She started to put her hand out to warn him, but she decided to let the skeptic learn a hard lesson. She drew back, lagging behind him.

The little girl wore a blue dress that had once been fine but was now dirty, the hem tattered. She was too young to be on the streets. But of course death came to everyone, regardless of their age or whether they had young children or anything else. It took and left those behind to fend for themselves.

The girl's face was small and elfin, her green eyes large and long-lashed. She sat on the ground just inside an alleyway, skinny knees pulled to her chin, gazing out at them wistfully, two fingers in her mouth.

Drake went to her as if drawn by a string. "Little one." He squatted in front of her. "You all alone?"

Green eyes gazed at him, unblinking. She scrambled to her feet and raced away into a dark alley.

Drake straightened and followed the child, never turning to see if Hannah followed. He glided like a dream walker. Hannah trailed along after him.

"Little one," Drake called, his steps quick. "Come back—I dinna bite. You must be hungry. I'll get you a bite to eat."

Hannah found herself mildly alarmed at the irony, and her step quickened. She didn't want to chance catching up too late.

They emerged on the other side of the ally. The child huddled in the dirt near a midden pile. Drake leaned over her.

"Come now, you cannot eat that. Let me . . ."

Hannah rushed to them and found the child feeding on a dazed Drake.

"Get off him, you little beast." Hannah kicked it. The child tucked and rolled, coming up on the balls of her bare feet, fangs bared and bloodied.

The child, no longer very sweet looking, hissed at Hannah, but didn't run.

Hannah knelt beside Drake. The child had barely had a chance to taste him. The daze was already fading.

He shook his head, blinking. "What the hell?"

When his gaze settled on the child she looked peaceful again, with large, soulful eyes in her small face. Blood smeared her lips.

"That's enough," Hannah said firmly. "He's with me."

"We can share." The childlike voice was laced with unnatural maturity. "I'm so little, I don't need much."

"He *is not* food."

The child looked Drake up and down with obvious disdain. She turned to leave, shoulders squared now.

"Wait," Hannah called.

The child turned, her expression no longer one of childish innocence but of long-suffering boredom.

"Where are the rest of you?"

A pale blond brow rose. "The rest of us? There is no *rest of us.*"

"You are not with them? The other blood witches? Craig? Anna? Where are they?"

The child's lip curled. "Craig and Anna are dead."

Hannah put a hand out, touching the wooden wall beside her. Her stomach hollowed out sickeningly. "What? Dead? How can that be?"

The child smiled bitterly. "I know not. And yet it is so."

"All of them are dead?"

The child shrugged. "I think so. But I didn't go back to find out for certain."

"What happened?" Drake asked. He seemed to have collected himself from the shock of a child nearly supping on him. "How is it a whole nest of your kind were killed? I thought you were long-lived, nearly indestructible?"

"A man came. He was one of us, so we welcomed him. Then he turned on us. He had others, waiting to overpower us. What he did is forbidden." Her small mouth thinned. "And it happened during the day."

Hannah gasped. Drake jerked around to look at her, brows raised in surprise.

What the child spoke of was unheard of—it simply wasn't done. Hannah was so stunned that she couldn't think of what to do next. She turned and took two steps in the opposite direction, palm pressed to her chest. Luthias was feeding on other blood witches— and during the day. This was much worse than anything she had dared to imagine. Her hand curled into a fist. She turned back to the child and Drake, both of whom watched her anxiously.

"Take us there."

The child looked at her as if she were mad. "I will never go back there."

"Why?" Drake asked. "Do you think he is still there?" The look he gave Hannah after he asked this was enigmatic—both excited and fearful. He longed for the confrontation and dreaded it. Hannah simply dreaded it.

"I dinna care," the child said. "It is a place of death and I will not return."

"Then tell us where they are," Hannah said.

The child considered her for a full minute before shrugging. "I'll take you partway."

She turned and ran out of the alley. Drake ran after her. Hannah sighed and lifted her skirts, bringing up the rear.

The child led them through a maze of streets and alleys until they were in a finer area of the city. Walls and gates surrounded these houses. Well-trimmed shrubs rose above them.

"It's the brick house on the end." One pale blond brow arched in an expression far beyond her physical years. "I wouldn't recommend knocking."

She turned on her dirty heel and sprinted away.

Drake stared after her. "A child," he breathed. "Why would someone turn a child? It's . . . it's . . ."

"Grotesque?" Hannah finished for him. "Unnatural?" She nodded slowly. "Aye, it is, but consider this. You are a parent and your child is dying. If you could spare them pain, let them live out a full life, keep them with you—would you?"

"But as a child? It's . . . obscene. The mind matures, but the body . . ."

Hannah smiled grimly. "There is really nothing pretty about being a blood witch, Drake. Is that what you thought?"

Drake shrugged. He looked unsettled and a bit gray,

but he seemed to shake it off as he turned toward the house. He slid her a sidelong look. "Does he know we're here?"

"If he were in there, he probably would. But I am almost certain he is not."

Drake studied the house dubiously. "Well, you've been certain of a host of other things that you were completely wrong about, so I think I will err on the side of caution."

Hannah scowled, which surprised a laugh from him. Her belly dipped, and warmth spread through her. Her frown lifted momentarily, charmed by his fleeting pleasure. "What amuses you?"

His gaze moved over her face as if he'd never really looked at her before. "You. It is rare to see so much expression on your face."

Hannah didn't know how to respond to that. It was true that she showed little emotion. She meant to appear so. But seeing the pleasant surprise on his face made her want to coax the expression forth again just to make him look at her so.

But of course she would never say that, so she said, "Come, let us enter with caution."

He grinned at her and waved his hand for her to lead the way.

Hannah walked the rest of the way to the house at a brisk pace, stopping at the tall wrought-iron gate that surrounded it. The gate was locked. Hannah glanced around; finding the street deserted, she put pressure on the gate until the lock broke.

Drake watched the curtained windows quietly.

They slipped inside the gate. Hannah led him around the side of the house to the back, where they found a porch littered with various cleaning items—a broom, a bucket, a mop. Hannah climbed the steps to the back door. It had not been pulled all the way closed. She pushed on the door and it swung inward on oiled hinges, making not a single sound.

The interior was dark. Her pulse throbbed faster. She sensed nothing, but the emptiness was disconcerting.

"This should be the kitchen," Drake whispered.

Hannah knew he could see nothing, but he was correct. It was an empty kitchen. Empty of people and empty of the food most houses kept. Her nose picked up the faint odor of cheese and ale. But that was for their human guests. The scent of blood and death permeated the house.

Hannah slipped inside. Drake followed her in and closed the door softly behind them.

She reached back and took Drake's hand. He clasped hers without hesitation. His palm was warm and firm, and she felt safer even though here, at night, he could not help her if she was in danger.

She moved through the kitchen. Beside a large wooden table in the center a man sprawled on the floor. It was nearly impossible to tell the difference between a human and a blood witch, once dead. Hannah released Drake's hand but held his arm to indicate he should stay back. Then she knelt and lifted the body's lip.

Razor-sharp incisors. She felt heat against her back. Drake had knelt beside her.

"What is it?" His warm breath tickled the hair on the back of her neck and she nearly shivered.

She pivoted slightly and pressed a finger to his lips. If anyone was here, they would hear them. Their hearing was far more sensitive than a human's.

His lips were full and firm against her finger. She remembered how they had felt against hers. . . .

And wondered why she thought of all this now. Was she really so depraved that she could imagine such things in a house of death? She shook it off and stood, taking his hand and leading him further into the house.

They discovered several more bodies, the throats of some ripped almost completely open. She wondered if those were the ones who had resisted. Hannah knew many of them, had lived among them once.

Now they were all dead.

She went to the large window and drew the curtains wide, letting in moonlight. Drake blinked and scanned the room. It was still dark, the worst of the carnage hidden, but he should see the dark lumps of the bodies scattered near the back of the room.

It was a fine house—a large manor—with furnishings that were all imported and obscenely expensive, some of them very old. Many of the blood witches were far older than she was and had accumulated wealth beyond her imagination—and she had a vivid imagination. And this was not their only house.

They had houses scattered across the continent. They traveled between them. When an area became hostile, they left it for a time.

They were city dwellers, where the food was abundant, the pickings easy, and the chances of discovery slim. It was a good system and it worked well for them. Everyone was cared for and protected. They rarely lost one of their own.

But now an entire house of them had been wiped out and the authorities had not yet discovered it. And when they did, what would they make of the massacre? What would they make of the victims' teeth? Perhaps they wouldn't even notice. There were so many bodies; they might not even inspect each one individually.

"Damn," Drake breathed, wandering around the room and squatting down to study each body in turn. He shook his head and again whispered, "Damn."

Damn was right. They were up against something she couldn't comprehend. What Luthias had done was forbidden. A blood witch simply did not feed upon its own kind. It was cannibalism and no less grotesque than humans dining upon each other.

And yet Luthias had done it, blatantly. Defiantly.

Hannah leaned against the round lacquered table beside her while she attempted to steady her whirling thoughts. She did not know what to do now that they were all dead. If a house full of blood witches could not fend off Luthias, how could she expect to, with nothing more than the help of a human?

Her uneasy gaze turned to Drake, who was squatting beside a female blood witch. Hannah had known her. Her name had been Clarabelle, and for a short time they had shared a room in a house similar to this one. Clarabelle had discovered her living much the same as she had when she'd been human, minus the husband; Clarabelle had introduced Hannah to the elegant lifestyle of a *baobhan sith*. Hannah had stayed among them for a time, accumulating knowledge and funds, but the life had not appealed to her. At the time, Clarabelle had been angry at her defection and had told Hannah she was no better than a child who refused to eat meat—foolish and ignorant. That had been more than half a century ago.

Drake squatted beside Clarabelle's lifeless body now. His elbows braced on his thighs and his hands formed a steeple that covered his nose and mouth, obviously as horrified as she was.

He turned his head, dropping one hand and rubbing the other over the black stubble on his upper lip and chin. His eyes sought her in the dim room. He opened his mouth to say something, but Clarabelle sat up suddenly and clawed at him. Hannah's heart jerked.

Drake fell back as Hannah rushed forward. Clarabelle's long fingers circled Drake's forearm, and her fangs were bared.

Drake didn't fight her, and Hannah first thought he had been entranced. Then she saw that Clarabelle was simply too weak to do much more and Drake was well aware of it.

As if just sitting was too much effort, Clarabelle fell back to the floor with a pained sigh and released his arm.

Hannah knelt on the other side of her. "Clarabelle, it's Hannah—what happened?"

Clarabelle's lashes drifted open. She gazed at Hannah for several minutes, her brown eyes registering no recognition.

"You know me?" she rasped, her voice dry as sand.

"Aye, it's Hannah O'Shea. We were friends . . . once."

Clarabelle stared at her for a long time, then her gaze turned to Drake. "I see your inclinations haven't changed at all. You still keep them as pets."

Drake slid Hannah a curious gaze but didn't comment.

"They're all dead?" Clarabelle asked, her eyes closed again.

"Aye, I think so." Hannah glanced around. "But then, we thought you were."

Clarabelle waved a limp hand toward Drake. "If the smell of this one's blood hasn't roused them, then they are dead."

"How is it that you are alive?" Drake asked.

Clarabelle shook her head. Ragged punctures speckled her neck. Her skin was pasty and white, shocking against her dark hair. "I know not. I dinna yet know that I will live"—her eyes opened—"unless your pet here is willing to give up some of his delicious blood." She smiled lasciviously, yellowed fangs gleaming in the moonlight, pale limp hand raising toward him.

"No," Hannah said, "but I will bring you something."

Clarabelle let out an amused snort, as if she had expected no other answer. Her hand dropped to her side. "Make it a child . . . a young, fat one."

"I will bring you an animal."

Clarabelle's sigh was deep and resigned. "I pray you, no rats."

Hannah glanced up at Drake. "Will you go out and get something? A pig, mayhap?"

He blanched but nodded after a moment.

When he was gone, Hannah said, "Tell me what happened."

Clarabelle's head rolled to the side. Her black hair, normally pulled back into a tight chignon, had come loose and spilled in thick locks all around her. "It happened so quickly. Craig discovered the man in town . . . he brought him to us. I thought him a bit strange, but then many new blood witches are who haven't yet found their way. I thought it odd that anyone would sire a churchman—more of a joke, I suppose." Her voice was soft, her eyes closed. "He asked a lot of questions. The same questions most new ones ask . . . and then he asked one that made us all uncomfortable." Her head rolled to the side and her eyes opened so that she could look at Hannah. "He asked why blood witches did not feed on each other."

Her eyes closed again and she lay very still.

Hannah touched her. "What happened next?"

Clarabelle's lashes fluttered, then opened. "What?"

"What happened next?"

She frowned, as if she didn't remember their conversation. "We slept. It was day, after all. Craig and some others had been discussing whether to expel him or not. No one liked him. But we never had the chance. He attacked us in our sleep. He wasn't alone." Her voice trailed off. "We didn't have a chance . . ."

Hannah sat beside Clarabelle for the next hour, waiting for Drake to return. She wasn't sure when it happened, but with barely a whispered sigh, Clarabelle died. Hannah spoke her name loudly several times and shook her, but she was gone. An empty shell that had lived far longer than a body was ever meant to exist, but still, she could not have been prepared. One who doesn't die is rarely prepared for death.

Strangely bereft, Hannah wandered to the front of the house. It seemed foolish. She hadn't seen Clarabelle in so long, hadn't even thought of her. Why should she feel sadness at her passing? But she did. Perhaps it was sadness at her own mortality. She could die, too. Perhaps as alone as Clarabelle was at the end.

Hannah wondered what was taking Drake so long. She hoped nothing had happened to him. She stopped at the window, and saw him sitting on a stone bench in front of the house. A fat, squat goat stood beside him, its head on his leg. He stroked his hand over its neck.

Hannah sighed, the tension draining from her. She leaned her forehead against the window, watching him for a long while. He had apparently fetched a goat but then hadn't have the heart to hand it over to die. Something in Hannah's chest shifted, opening up more room, and her heart expanded.

She left the house. Night was giving way to dawn and with its retreat went Hannah's strength. Drake looked up at her but said nothing. She crossed the garden and sat beside him on the bench.

The plump goat bleated up at Drake. It would have been a decent meal for any blood witch.

"I couldn't do it," he said, not looking at her. "He came with me so willingly."

"It doesn't matter. She's dead."

His head swiveled toward her, his lips drawn tight. "I am sorry."

"For what? She would have killed you without a single regret. Why do you feel remorse for her death?"

He shrugged. "I know not."

"If you are a blood witch, you will out of necessity have less respect for life."

"You don't."

She smiled sadly. "You are wrong there. I let your wife die, did I not? And it would be a lie to say that I wasted time fashing on it."

He scratched at the goat's ear. It shook its head but moved closer.

Hannah did not know why she had confessed that, and worse, why she had reminded him of the very thing he loathed her for. Their relationship was troubled enough without her making it worse.

"My brother, William, as you know, is a healer. Every time he heals, it sucks life out of him. It doesn't kill him, mind you, but it makes him unwell. It used to make me angry when strangers would show up, demanding he heal them or their friends and family." He shook his head. "They didn't care what he suffered, or how it slowly killed him. It's the way of the world— people are born, they live and hopefully love, and then they die. Some get to stay in the dance longer than others."

Hannah didn't quite know what to say to this; it

was unlike anything else he'd ever said to her. Perhaps it was another trick? She studied his expression as he rubbed at the goat's ears. He was pensive, deep in thought. She wondered how long it had taken him to come to this philosophy.

"When William healed," Drake continued, "he only suffered for a few days. You would have suffered for much longer and, as you pointed out once before, you didn't know me or Ceara. We were nothing to you, strangers." He shook his head. "There is nothing wrong with respecting your own life."

"No. I am a coward."

The confession was wrenched out of her, along with a memory from long ago. Of a human she had loved and helped, who had left her to suffer. She had refused Ceara because of this, but she had not let herself dwell on it.

Drake straightened, the cobwebs of deep thought clearing from his eyes. His dark blue gaze was direct and probing. "Why would you say such a thing?"

"I do not respect my own life. I was merely afraid of the pain and of suffering alone. There was someone once . . . he left me alone and very ill. . . . It is a very unpleasant memory." She shrugged. "Otherwise I would have done it. I had nothing better to do." She spoke lightly, or she tried to, habitually making light of her own feelings. But she had to look away, unable to maintain eye contact when she spoke so honestly.

And with that admission a blanket of melancholy settled over her. It was all true, and she would eventually settle into another such life of rote and boredom when this brief period of excitement ended. She had been long past loneliness, but now she suspected the pain would be more acute than ever. And it was all thanks to Drake.

"Whatever your reason," he said, "there is no benefit in doing it for people you do not even know."

Hannah tilted her head and narrowed her eyes at him. "Are you forgiving me, Drake?"

He slanted her an enigmatic look. "I suppose I am."

"That's a good thing, since I have decided to change you into a blood witch if you are still willing."

His mouth curved into a flat smile. "I thought as much."

"I cannot do it until tonight." She rubbed an illustrative finger over her top teeth. "They don't work during the day, so let us return to the inn."

He gave the goat a final scratch and stood. "Go on, boy." The goat bleated at him, its stubby tail wiggling, but after a second it wandered over to a patch of grass and began munching.

Drake stood over her, palm out. She looked from his open hand to his face. His eyes were clear and direct and strong. *He* was strong. And she was a coward. She was afraid to change him. Afraid because then he would truly be in her world and when he left her the utter emptiness would be unbearable.

Chapter 10

$\mathcal{D}$rake lay on his side in the small bed beside Hannah, unable to sleep. How could he? When she woke, he would die and wake as something different and new, a creature that subsisted on blood. He had never really wanted this; he had only known and accepted the necessity of it. But he had never thought she would do it.

There was a time not very long ago when he would have welcomed death, but that day had passed. He did not wish to die anymore. He thought that might have something to do with the woman beside him.

He watched her deep, undisturbed sleep. He would sleep that deeply when he was like her. He couldn't recall the last time he had slept well. Perhaps that in itself was worth the sacrifice. He thought of the goat today. Could he feed on that? He didn't know. He didn't want to, but it was preferable to a human. Hannah had learned to.

Her hair was vibrant; it appeared so slick it would slip through his fingers like gold dust. He slid his hand into it, cool and silky; he liked the feel of it sliding over his fingers and hand.

She was beautiful. He had known that from the first moment he had seen her, when he had carried his dying wife to her island. He had known it the day he had returned to take his revenge and found her wounded and bloody and unafraid. He had chopped down her door with an ax and she had shot at him. But he hadn't killed her that day because he had seen the smallest glimpse of the woman who now slept beside him. It had only been a glimmer, and he had questioned what he thought he'd seen many times since.

But he no longer had any doubts. There was a woman inside the blood witch. And she was amazing.

Her lashes fluttered. Drake's hand stilled. He had not meant to wake her. Her lashes rose, and brilliant green eyes gazed back at him.

"I woke you. I apologize." He didn't withdraw his hand from where it tangled in the fall of her hair. The eyes that looked at him intently were as expressionless as they always were, as lacking in emotion. And that bothered him. He knew it was schooled, that she had somehow worked at this utter lack of feeling. He wanted to know why.

"I was not asleep," she said.

Was she troubled by the same thoughts that kept him awake?

"Who were you," he asked, "before you were a blood witch?"

One brow arched slightly, causing a faint furrow in her smooth white brow. "What an odd question."

He propped his head on his fist. "Has no one asked

you about yourself? I want to know what your life was, before."

Her lashes dipped and rose. "It was nothing like this."

Drake's lips thinned and his eyes narrowed. "You ken what I mean."

She seemed genuinely surprised and somewhat wary of his interest. "My name was Aedammair, and I'm Irish."

"I gathered the latter from the O'Shea."

"No, that was my husband's surname. I decided to take it after we wed."

Husband. Of course there had been a husband once. He felt a little stab of jealousy and more intense curiosity.

"How did an Irish woman find herself in Scotland?"

"I came as a child with my mother. Some Scotsmen came to Eire for wives. They brought back my mother . . . and Gareth's mother."

"Gareth?"

"My late husband."

"So you were a wife once."

She laughed softly, but it was false, bitter. "Not a very good wife." Her lips thinned and she exhaled with harsh annoyance, rolling onto her back to stare at the ceiling. "I tried very hard, but I could not please him. In my own defense, I'm not sure any woman could have."

"Some men are very hard to please. My father was such a man. I think only his dogs pleased him." When her head turned to look at him, his hand slid to the back of her head to gently knead the base of her skull. "How did your husband express his displeasure?"

"With the back of his hand."

His kneading paused. So her husband had beaten her. "Did you become a blood witch while he was still alive?"

"I did. I became one because of him. So I would never have to fear another man." She held his gaze, unwavering.

"And did it work?"

"Aye." But her voice was filled with reservations.

He wondered what her choice had brought her. Loneliness? Her cool exterior kept her in a position of power and everyone else at arm's length. She never seemed to let down her guard. He supposed a hundred years of building a wall made it pretty thick. Drake knew he had done his part to lay some of those stones, but now he wanted to chip away at the mortar.

"Have you any children?"

She shook her head against the pillow. "I miscarried many times. I am not sorry that being a blood witch means I cannot have children. Losing babies is . . . is . . ."

Drake's hand opened over her neck, cradling her.

Hannah smiled at him suddenly, lopsided and insouciant. "You seem concerned. You think that any of this troubles me now? It occurred more than a lifetime ago. It is as if it happened to someone else. I am long-lived. That part of me is dead."

He thought that perhaps this was true. But it was also true that she had separated herself from others for so long that she didn't know how to break through the wall. She really was dead to the world of the living.

"Who are you now?"

His question caused one slim copper brow to arch. "A monster." She said it with pride almost, and yet he knew she was not fond of others of her kind.

"A monster that refuses to kill humans. Who keeps them as 'pets.' Isn't that what your friend called it?"

"I'm sure Stephen would disagree with that assessment."

Drake smiled. "You never meant to kill him. That was your clumsy attempt to create a companion."

Her face froze, the delicate jaw locking. Her gaze moved past him, rose to look at the window behind him.

It was still day. She couldn't escape him yet.

She tried anyway. She rolled away. His fingers snagged in her hair, and she cried out. She grabbed her hair and yanked it out of his fingers. She rose to her knees on the mattress.

"*This* is why I became a blood witch."

He grabbed at her hair but she jerked her head back, long copper locks flying over her shoulder.

"Because of men pulling your hair?"

"Because of men using their strength to push women around."

Drake rose to his knees in front of her. His hands rose to take her by the shoulders, but he let them drop to his sides. "When have I used my strength to push you around?"

The muscles in her jaw spasmed and pulled tight. It

wasn't his strength that overpowered her but his honesty. He cut too close to the truth, and she didn't like it. She didn't like it because it meant he was starting to understand her. He fought to hide his satisfaction, knowing she would not appreciate it right now.

"That's not what I meant," she said.

"What did you mean?" He couldn't resist touching her. His hands rose to delicately trace the smooth silk of her arm. Her lashes fluttered and her lips parted the slightest bit.

"Or is it something else that overpowers you?"

She turned her face away. He caught her chin in his fingers. He held her gently, so that she could easily break away if she wished. She let him turn her face so that she looked into his eyes.

They stared at each other in silence, and he realized that she would give him nothing. She would not answer his questions or show him in any way that she cared about him. But he thought she did. He *thought*. He didn't know. So he didn't push it.

She moved backward slowly, as if he were dangerous. When she came to the edge of the bed, she slid off quickly.

"Come," she said, sliding her shoes on. "It's nearly dark and we must have your first kill ready for you so that you do not do anything you will come to regret."

It was finally night, and Hannah was strong once again. Their room at the inn was awash in candlelight. Drake sat at the sturdy wooden table downing small cups of whisky in silence. She had told him repeatedly that it wouldn't hurt, but she supposed it was the idea of his impending death and transformation that had him unnerved. She didn't relish the fact that his blood would likely make her ill, but she couldn't fault him either.

It gave him something to focus on other than her, which was a relief. His earlier questions had irritated her. She didn't know why. Perhaps she did. She just didn't enjoy thinking about it.

He had made her think about Stephen Ross and how she had attempted to change him into a blood witch to trap him into being her companion. It had not been one of her finer moments.

And it annoyed her that not only did Drake know about that but he was also so quick to recall it. It was apparently at the fore of his mind. There was nothing she could say or do to change what had happened. She found the whole incident repugnant now and wished everyone, herself included, could just forget it.

She had hoped Drake would remain with her when this was all over. She had become fond of him. Nay, *fond* was too tame a word. She wasn't yet ready to pin a word to it, but what she felt consumed her, like the hunger for blood. Just to look at him now as he poured whisky in his cup with unsteady hands made her weak and aching inside. How was it that merely looking at a man could make her so foolish?

A soft grunting in the corner drew their attention. It was a pig. Drake had chosen it. They had walked through the streets for hours, and he had not been able to make a choice. When he had narrowed it down to a goat or a pig, it had taken him overlong to choose between the two. Hannah had chosen for him. He had seemed tight-lipped and unhappy afterward and insisted on buying a bottle of whisky from the ostler. The worst part—for Drake, at least—was the fact that the pig had come along with them, as docile and obedient as a dog, and it now lay in the corner sleeping with soft, grunting snores.

Drake turned back to his bottle and drank directly from it, giving up the civility of pouring it, since more spilled on the tabletop than went down his gullet. Hannah's lips turned down in disgust. She wasn't even hungry. She didn't want Drake's blood, especially heavily diluted with alcohol. The smell of it now made her eyes water.

But once she got started she feared she would lose herself anyway. Before Stephen it had been thirty years since she had tasted human blood. And his had been like nectar—a forbidden fruit. She didn't want to be like the others—the blood witches Luthias had killed.

He stood unsteadily and turned to her. "I'm ready," he slurred.

Hannah sat on the bed, waiting. She patted the mattress beside her. He swayed, then crossed the room and sank down beside her, his shoulder leaning heavily against her.

"This won't hurt." She had already told him this several times, but it had no effect.

"Like sleeping, aye. Gude. I'm tired."

She took his face in her hands. Whiskers scraped her palms. Her thumb moved over the slightly knobby bump of his scar. He blinked slowly. She wondered if he would be different as a blood witch. Eventually they all were, but some of them . . . some of them were different immediately. As if the blood contaminated them somehow.

"You're bonny," he said. "I trust you to kill me."

He trusted her. Her lips twisted up into a smile she didn't feel. She kissed him. He tasted of whisky, and his lips were unresponsive at first. But when her tongue grazed his bottom lip, he seized her, drawing her in closer as his tongue tangled with hers.

She pulled her mouth away and kissed his jaw. She could feel his heart beating all through her, the pump of his blood. Her teeth sank into his neck and she heard his sharp inhalation. *Easy, easy.* This was where some fought and struggled. A blood witch could easily overpower any opposition, but when it happened it could get a little messy.

But Drake did not struggle. Other than that single exhalation, he relaxed into it. His blood should have been sweet, but it was heavily laced with whisky, a beverage she had never appreciated. Especially when it had made her late husband violent.

But she drank. She had to drain him dry, end his life for this to work, so she drank until her head swam. She closed her eyes but that didn't help; the darkness only swirled in frantic colors.

His body had long grown slack, and she lowered him to the bed. When he was dead she laid her head on the pillow beside him. His blood should have made her stronger—and it would eventually—but for now she was merely inebriated and ill. He needed to drink some of her blood to complete the transformation, but that would have to wait. For now, she couldn't move without her belly lurching. *It will fade. Just sleep it off.* So she remained beside his cold, dead body and fell into the spinning whisky void. Her last thought before oblivion took her was that she hoped she didn't sleep too long to rouse him. If she did, he would never wake.

Chapter 11

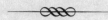

*H*annah didn't know how long she had slept. It was unusual for her to sleep at all at night, but every time she tried to open her eyes, her sour belly turned and she had to close her eyes and focus on controlling the queasiness. Distant voices pushed their way through the thick mud of her mind. Something was wrong about that, but her mind couldn't grasp what.

"Aye, he is dead," a male voice said.

"Has she given him her blood?"

"I know not."

Brief silence, then, "It would be better if she had, but it matters not."

Hannah recognized the voice and it sent shocks of panic through her. It was day; she could tell by the lethargic weakness that gripped her limbs. She forced her eyelids open.

Three men surrounded the bed, watching them. Looming directly over her was Luthias Forsyth, his bald pate gleaming in the daylight.

His thin mouth stretched into a smile. "Good morning, Miss O'Shea."

Hannah's voice stuck in her throat, choking her.

How was he here? How had he found them? And how was he so . . . *vibrant* in the morning?

"Aye." He nodded, studying her. "I found you, didn't I? Surprised?"

Hannah's mind still scrambled. Never at her best in the daylight, she had the added problem of a thick fuzz that blanketed her brain and a dull throbbing at the base of her skull. Her hand reached out, patting the bed beside her. Drake was still there, stiff and cool and motionless.

"At first, if you recall, you kept after me. In my head from time to time."

She remembered. She hadn't actually kept after him, but as a blood witch she'd sired, he had been there, in her head. But that had eventually faded to no more than a feeling. She had not created many blood witches, but each one was there, somewhere, in her head. She could home in on any one of them anytime she wished. They shared blood, so they were connected. But with Luthias . . . that ability had become unreliable.

He smiled. "You have noticed that I've been absent for a time." He sat on the bed beside her, large, skeletal hands gripping his knees. "Well, I haven't really been gone. I've been there all along. You just do not ken I am there anymore."

Hannah's heart, already galloping in her chest, jerked. He was in her head? In her thoughts? And she didn't even know it? How was this possible?

"A twist of fate, actually," he said as if answering the question in her head, and she wondered if he was.

"When you turned me, I thought that God punished me for failing him. But I see now that wasn't his intent at all. He gave me the strength to finally vanquish my foes."

"And when we are vanquished?" Hannah asked, finding her voice, though it was thin and breathy. "What of you?"

He laughed softly, a mellow sound, full of good humor. "I doubt the world will ever be completely free of evil. But if such a thing were to pass, I would submit myself to God's will. I always submit myself to God's will."

Hannah stared up at him and realized she was about to die. She could not fight three men in the day-time. It was unlikely she could best them at night. And without Drake's help it was impossible.

The sudden rending in her heart made her close her eyes and exhale. *Drake.* He wasn't supposed to have died. This wasn't supposed to have happened. She was supposed to have made him strong so together they could destroy this abomination they had created. Luthias was a bully—just like most men—and she would finally die at the hands of a bully. Perhaps it was inevitable. She should have died long ago at her husband's brutal hands. Instead she had killed him. Fate had caught up with her at last. A sob rose from the pit of her belly, expanding in her chest. She fought it down, teeth clenched, throat tight. She would not shed tears in front of him.

She waited for it, but Luthias and his men didn't do anything. It was unlikely they were hungry after their recent massacre, but one didn't have to be hungry to feed.

"So what now?" she asked when she could speak again.

"I had initially planned to feed on you while your lover watched . . . but your blood stinks. It's polluted. So I will pass. For him . . ." Luthias's gaze shifted to Drake. "Something special. I have been planning it for some time." He rubbed his long-fingered hands together, eyes shining. "After he spent months torturing me for his own pleasure, I couldn't just kill him. No, that is too easy, death is too good for him . . . just as he obviously found it unsatisfactory for me." He smiled at Hannah, his incisors long and sharp and white. Everything about him was frightening and unusual. That his fangs were exposed during the day . . . it was wrong, it shouldn't be.

"I do hope you gave him some of your blood." He sniffed, his brow lowering. "Though I do not think you have. Not yet." Luthias brought his wrist to his mouth and bit it. He leaned over her and put his wrist to Drake's mouth. Hannah's arm rose to bat it away, but his arm was solid, like stone, immovable. He didn't leave it at Drake's mouth very long, but then it didn't take much blood to create a blood witch.

He removed his red-smeared wrist and stood. "Bag them."

Before Hannah could catch her breath, a rough homespun sack was thrown over her head and her ankles and wrists were bound. She struggled, but it was fruitless. The closeness of the sack to her face made breathing a chore. As it was daytime, she could no longer maintain consciousness. Her last thought was that when it had really mattered, she had failed.

It was night.

Hannah woke with a scream. Her hands flew upward, palms pressed into the ceiling.

The ceiling was cold and hard and much too close. She sucked in musty air and coughed. She blinked. It was pitch dark. So dark that even her excellent vision couldn't penetrate it.

She lay still, trying to calm her panicked thoughts and spasming heart. She was no longer in the bag, but neither was she at the inn. Something pressed against her side. She turned her head.

Drake. She had not sired him, therefore she could not sense him. When he woke, her control over him would be minimal. And he would be hungry.

She cast her gaze down to her feet. Their enclosure ended just past Drake's boots. She struggled to get her arms up over her head. It ended a few inches past the top of her head. She lay on hard stone. The left side of her body pressed against stone, and when she reached across Drake, stone met her fingers.

They were in a box. A stone coffin. A sarcophagus.

Hannah's breath hitched with near hysteria before logic pushed its way through her thoughts. Tombs had lids. How else did they get dead people inside them? She braced her palms on the stone above her head and pushed. It didn't budge. She pushed harder, with all her strength.

Still, nothing.

Of course Luthias would not have made this easy. In fact, he'd surely tested this himself. It was probably impossible for them to escape. Drake would wake, feed on her until she died, and then he would lay in this coffin forever, going insane from hunger. The end would be fast and easy for her, but for Drake . . . endless torture.

Fear from the horrific images that danced in her head galvanized her. She couldn't get her feet up to push with them, so she pushed until the palms of her hands ached. Her mind glazed over with panic, and her body drew on reserves she didn't know she had. But it didn't matter. The lid didn't move an inch. The unthinkable truth that had been nudging at her thoughts burst through. Something heavier than a stone lid trapped them. Earth. Lots of it. Luthias had buried them.

Her breathing hitched and grew ragged. Her face felt wet. This bizarre behavior frightened her even more until she realized with a start that she was crying. Her fingers touched her cheeks and came away damp.

Tears.

When had she last cried? She honestly couldn't recall. She had forgotten what it felt like until the sobs ripped through her chest. Years of misery burst forth. She wailed her grief and frustration, clawed at the stone tomb until her fingers were damp with her own blood. There was no one to hear her, no one to care.

Her sobs had died to hiccups when she heard a

sound. She tried to silence herself, but she still sniffled. It didn't take long for her to understand what she had heard. A low moan of pain rose from beside her, vibrating through to her body.

Drake was awake.

Drake had always thought dying would be an extremely painful affair, that it would be another battle he had to fight, just like everything else in this life. But death had come quietly, like sleep. The piercing of Hannah's teeth in his neck had pricked and stung, but only for a moment. He had expected something much more violent—a rending or puncturing of flesh.

Her fangs were small and delicate, and they pierced him gently. Within seconds he had descended into a sort of dream world where he was only partially aware of his surroundings. They had lain on the bed, her hand cool against the side of his face; her breath had blown against his skin, neither warm nor cold. It had been pleasant, relaxing. And then, without quite realizing how or when it had happened, he drifted away.

The darkness was complete with no thought, just a warm, comfortable floating. Then the sensation that he was not alone pricked him. He turned, suddenly having a body again.

The room he stood in was foreign to him. A vast hall, lit only by candles, inhabited by a woman with several children.

They all sat before an enormous dollhouse of a size and extravagance that Drake had never before seen. The woman was beautiful, with long, curling dark hair spilling down to her waist and plump breasts over-flowing her bodice.

One of the children looked up from his task—a boy with dusky skin, large black eyes, and a mop of jet curls.

"Look," he said and pointed at Drake. "He is new."

The woman looked up. It was Gillian MacDonnell, the Countess of Kincreag—his sister-in-law's sister.

She stared at him, and he saw the sadness soften her eyes. "Drake?" she whispered, disbelief in her words. "Oh, no."

Her distress meant nothing to him, though some part of him thought that perhaps it should.

"How are you here?" she asked. "Can you speak? Or are you but a wraith?"

"I can speak." But it was difficult to force the words out; he had not expected that. All he really wanted to do was drift off to sleep.

"Why have you come to me?" she asked, standing and stepping around the dollhouse.

He didn't have that answer. He didn't know how he had traveled such a distance in such a short amount of time, or why he stood in Gillian's doll-house room.

"I am a blood witch," he said, though that didn't explain why he was here now.

"A blood witch?" Her fingers pressed against her lips. "How did this happen?"

"Luthias still hunts. He is so strong. Too strong."

She shook her head, confused. "I thought he was dead."

Shame washed over him. Even in death he couldn't escape his deadly mistake. "No."

She seemed genuinely distressed, twirling a ring round and round on her finger. She continued to fire off more questions, her voice strident, but Drake could no longer understand her. He was fading, weak and wavery. He held his hand in front of his face. He was smoke. He was nothing.

There was no sense of passing time. Just . . . nothing.

A sound penetrated his vacuum. A woman crying. Her broken sobs tore at his heart. What troubled her? His bodiless self turned toward the crying, wanting to hold and comfort. The voice was familiar somehow, though not the weeping. But the closer he got, the less he could focus on the cries. A pain rose up in him, gripping his belly like a toothed trap and holding it fast.

He was in his body. All the pain and violence he had expected of dying became manifest in this moment. His body was being ripped apart, crammed into consciousness like shot rammed into a gun muzzle.

When his eyes opened, darkness and confusion and pain suffocated him, crushing him. He gasped, inhaling stale, musty air. And in that breath of air he understood one thing only.

Hunger.

His belly cramped and twisted, as if being wrung out. He thought he might die if he didn't feed. Now.

Chapter 12

Panic infused Hannah with new strength. Frantic, she punched at the lid of their stone tomb, hoping to break it. Drake writhed beside her, not yet fully awake. The lid was too thick, and he kept knocking her arms away. Even with her strength at its fullest she was helpless, buried as they were. Then he seized her. She fought at him instinctively. She was the stronger. She could kill him.

But he was wild, mindless in his hunger. None of this was his fault. He didn't know what he was doing, and he would barely remember it later. She could not harm him.

She wedged her arms between them, pushing his face away with her forearms. His fangs grazed her wrist, drawing blood, and he latched on like a leech. She cried out as his teeth sunk and held.

She brought her other fist up, hitting him hard beneath the chin. He released her, tearing her skin and releasing the scent of even more blood.

She didn't know how much longer she could keep him off. The dark stone walls closed in on her. He was too close, too strong. She did not wish for him to suf-

fer when he remembered himself, but she knew he
was in pain now and could not bear it any longer. She
didn't want to fight him. She gave up, her arms sagging and her body going slack.

He slid on top of her. She was trapped. She couldn't
push him off if she wanted to, as his back was against
the coffin lid; but she didn't want to.

His face was in her neck, then his teeth sunk in. It
was nothing like the first time she had been bitten.
That time she had grown dazed and fallen asleep, as if
she'd been drugged. There had been little or no pain.
Now the pain shot through her, from neck to shoulder.
She could feel the blood draining from her body. She
tried to cry out, but all that emerged was a whimper.
She wasn't human anymore, the rules had changed.
You only got one painless death. It was only fair after
living so long that the final one hurt like hell.

And it was hell. She went limp, hoping her lack
of fight would make it go easier, hurt less, but nothing helped. Her neck burned, her body felt as if mer-
cury had replaced the blood in her veins. She prayed
for death to take her, but he stopped suddenly and she
was still alive.

No! her mind cried out. She could not lie in this
coffin in eternal pain. Her own hunger had renewed,
a clawing in her belly, but there was nothing she could
do about that. She was too weak.

He lay against her, unmoving, an obscene parody
of the aftermath of their lovemaking. The awakening
of a new blood witch was unpleasant to begin with—
overcome with confusion, with a mind that had been

erased like a slate, all that was left to the new blood witch was a jumble of confusing emotions. She imagined that his confusion would increase tenfold when he realized he was trapped in a stone box. Her belly dropped like a stone as she waited for him to comprehend his situation.

He jerked. He tried to push off of her, but he was wedged between her and the stone lid.

"Peace," she whispered, surprised at the effort it took to speak.

"Where am I?" His voice was hoarse, full of panic.

"It's complicated."

"Why can't I move?" His voice rose with urgency, his body rigid against hers.

"We are trapped. The man who changed you—you must remember him? He put us both in here, a stone tomb, and buried us."

He said nothing for a long while. Her vision had faded. Not because day approached but because she was dying. She was an empty vessel. Very little blood coursed through her.

"Who are you?" he asked cautiously.

"I am Hannah. I am . . ." The thing that cares for you, perhaps even loves you. But she couldn't say that. Who was she to him? She didn't know how to describe herself or their relationship. Finally she said, "I am your friend."

He inhaled suddenly, smelling her. His breath warmed her neck. "You are more than a friend."

Her weak heart kicked. She turned her face so that her cheek pressed against his. The stubble from his whiskers scratched against her skin. He struggled and grunted until his hand was on her neck, stroking over where he bit her.

"You're weak," he said. "I feel you fluttering inside. Fading."

"Aye. We're trapped in here. You needed blood."

His hand left her neck and he braced both palms on the bottom of the tomb on either side of her. His jaw clenched against hers. His arms stiffened as he pushed his back against the tomb lid. He strained and grunted, and Hannah's heart went out to him.

"It won't work," she said. "I've already tried. We're buried underground. You'd have to break the stone and dig us out . . . but it's too thick."

He slid off her, back to his side of the tomb. The absence of his weight pressing into her left her cold and empty. She heard a dull thud. She couldn't see, but she knew he'd punched at the stone lid just as she had. He punched again and again, grunting with each hit.

She wanted to put a hand on his arm, to calm him, or to help him. But that was impossible. Her body was lead. She waited for him to realize that they were trapped and would die here, when she heard a crunch and a fine shower of dust filled her eyes and mouth. She coughed and blinked.

"Hit it again," Hannah urged, though it made her head spin to speak with such force.

He punched again. This time chunks of stone tumbled down on them. A few more punches and dirt poured in, filling Hannah's mouth.

Oh God. She spit out dirt and turned her face away.

She had not thought of that, of being smothered by earth filling her mouth and eyes and ears. She clamped her mouth shut and squeezed her eyes closed.

Drake kept at it, digging mindlessly. Dirt continued to fill the coffin, restricting what little movement she'd had.

After some time she realized she was alone. He had dug his way out, and she was trapped in the broken coffin, covered with dirt. There was no reason for him to save her. He didn't know who she was. She was nothing to him now. She imagined him running into the night, confused. Tears seeped from her eyes, creating mud and infuriating her at her weakness.

Suddenly fingers dug at the dirt around her face. A burst of cool air blew over her.

"Take my hand," Drake said.

Hannah couldn't open her eyes; mud coated her lashes, gluing them together.

"Take my hand," he said, this time his voice fierce and demanding.

Hannah forced her arm to raise. It obeyed and hope shot through her, sweet and sharp. He grasped her wrist and pulled. It hurt, as if he pulled her arm from her torso. The hole he dragged her through was ragged and scraped her face and arms.

"You did it," she rasped, sucking in air—still stale, but fresher than that in the tomb. He set her on her feet and released her. A swarm of bees immediately obscured her vision and buzzed in her ears. Her knees crumpled beneath her, and she slumped to the ground.

He pulled her upright, hands under her arms. "You are weak. You need blood."

There had been no bees. She had fainted.

He wiped at her face until she could open her eyes and see him. Her vision cleared slowly. His hands were filthy, crusted with dirt. Dirt dusted his face and clung to his hair.

She had been unable to do anything. Perhaps with more time she might have dug them out, but she was not confident of that. He'd drunk her blood—not a pig's blood, not even a human's blood, but a *baobhan sith*'s blood. And he was far more powerful than she was.

They were in a mausoleum. Three stone tombs filled the inside of the stone building. Old and forgotten, each one with a thick coat of filth. They had been buried between two of the tombs. A mound of dirt was at their feet and, beside it, the hole Drake had dug to free them.

His head rose, eyes shifting. "He knows I am awake."

Hannah didn't have to ask who. As a freshly sired blood witch, Drake would have a strong connection with Luthias.

"We need to go. We don't want to meet the man who created you—not yet. I doubt we would live through it."

He swung her into his arms. "Where are we going?" he asked as he strode out of the stone building and into the sunlight.

He had no past. No memories. For the moment he

was completely dependent on her. He would do whatever she asked. She laid her head against his shoulder, feeling safe and protected. She needed blood. Human blood would revive her like nothing else, but when he remembered himself he would hate her if she made him bring her a human.

There was something about the blood of a *baobhan sith*. Just as it served to reanimate a dead human to produce something new and stronger, so the blood of a *baobhan sith* appeared to alter another blood witch. It made them strong during the day and stronger than an average *baobhan sith* at night. The more Hannah thought of it, the more she believed that she could not have freed them from the tomb.

"Wait," she said. His long strides took him rapidly through a graveyard marked with stones of various size and elegance. "Luthias had to suspect you might be able to free us. This might be his plan—to hound and torture you as you did to him. He will probably return. Try to block him from your thoughts."

He nodded.

"We will hide and—"

"And I will bring you one to feed on."

She nodded. "Aye . . . how did you know what I was going to say?"

He shook his head, the line between his brows deepening. "I know not."

"Hmm . . ." She stared up at him, bemused, as he turned back toward the mausoleum, which was meant to house a great personage or family.

But he passed the mausoleum, instead taking Han-

nah to a collection of tall tombstones behind it. He set
her between them so that she was hidden from sight.

"Rest here," he said. "I'll be back."

She could do nothing else, though what she wanted
to do was lean forward and watch him leave, to call
him back and die in his arms. But she couldn't do anything. She was so weak that she could do nothing more
than lean back against the cool stone and wait to die.

Drake didn't know how he knew things. He just did.
He knew his name—Drake—though he hadn't known
it when he'd awakened. It had come to him later. Other
things were coming to him, too. He had family, but
past that he knew nothing—not their names, what they
looked like, whether they were mother, brother, son.
That woman, Hannah, she was important to him. She
must be someone special to have given her blood to
him. They had been trapped together because they had
been found together. He also knew she was not his sire.

He returned to the mausoleum. There was no place
to hide save inside a tomb, and Drake was not getting
back inside one of those. The hole he'd dug was hidden
between two tombs and not visible from the doorway.

He knew Luthias would come. He didn't know if he
would come alone or send someone. He didn't know
if he could take them, but he did know that the only
thing that would help Hannah was *baobhan sith* blood.
She was dying and that was not right. Blood witches
didn't die from lack of blood. Something was different
about this. Different because he was different.

He squatted down beside the door of the mausoleum and waited until night gave way to day. He wanted to check on the woman. He imagined her dying in the sunlight while he waited here. His chest hollowed out. She would die anyway if he didn't bring her blood; this thought kept him there, waiting.

He heard footsteps outside the mausoleum door. Drake's body tensed, ready. The door opened and a dark figure entered.

Drake saw the back of his head—brown and gray wispy hair, shiny scalp visible. The man froze just inside the door, his head tilting in Drake's direction. The blood witch sensed him.

Drake leapt forward and swung at the blood witch. Prepared for the attack, he leapt aside so that Drake's fist only grazed his jaw. He seized Drake and dug his strong fingers into Drake's neck. Drake drove the heel of his hand into the man's face, breaking his hold.

The blood witch grabbed the front of Drake's leather jack and flung him to the ground. He drew an enormous blade from his boot and slashed at Drake.

Drake rolled, swinging his leg around and knocking the blood witch backward. Before he could scramble back to his feet, Drake fell on him. He hit the man, knocking the knife away and pounding the blood witch's face over and over again until he went limp.

Not dead, of course, but momentarily incapacitated. Drake sat back on his knees, marveling at how he wasn't even tired. And if *he* wasn't tired, then this blood witch would not be down for long.

Drake slipped the blade into his own boot and tossed the blood witch over his shoulder.

Hannah was just where he'd left her, except she'd slipped off the tombstone. She lay so still that Drake's heart squeezed in panic and he jogged the rest of the distance to her.

He dumped the blood witch beside her and pulled her into his arms. Though she was not dead yet, she was dying.

"Hannah, wake."

Her head hung backward, limp, copper hair streaming down to pool on the ground. She was too pale, her eyes hollowed out.

He shook her gently. When that didn't work, he shook her harder.

She stirred, mumbling something.

He slapped at her cheeks and shook her again. She blinked, then squinted up at him.

"I brought you something. You must feed," he said.

Her gaze shifted to the blood witch sprawled beside her. She shook her head. "I cannot . . . not during the day."

"You must." He pulled her beside the blood witch. "You're dying."

She shook her head again. "I cannot. My teeth won't . . . during the day."

Her voice had become soft and wispy. Panic rose in Drake's heart. He couldn't lose her. He didn't even know her, but then again, he didn't know anyone. He didn't even know himself. She was everything he knew right now.

He felt vaguely that he had done this before, held a woman he cared for in his arms as she died. Panic and fear gripped him so tightly that he thought he might crack. There must be a way. She was so weak she could not hold her head up. He didn't know how she would make it until evening.

He pulled the blade from his boot and took the blood witch's wrist, slicing the blade across the wrist, then pressed it to Hannah's mouth.

She lay immobile for a moment, then her eyes sprang open and she began to drink. The blood witch groaned and shook his head. He tried to yank his arm away, but Drake held him tight. The blood witch's face distorted in pain and panic. He had no doubt done this to other *baobhan siths* and was not enjoying the reciprocity.

Drake hit him again until he was unconscious. They couldn't chance Luthias sensing something and coming to finish the job himself.

Hannah's eyes were closed as she fed, her long lashes lying soft against her pale cheeks. Her lashes rose, and she met Drake's gaze. He didn't know how he knew her or what their history was, but in her clear green eyes he recognized her and his chest tightened in a painfully sweet way. He would kill for her—in fact, was that not what he had just done?

He tried to imagine what this would have been like had he been alone in the tomb when he'd woken. He didn't want to contemplate such confusion and loneliness. She was the only link he had, and he would not let her out of his sight.

Chapter 13

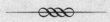

Sunlight blinded Hannah, so she closed her eyes, inhaling the blood like an elixir. She had never fed during the day. She had never fed on another blood witch. And she had never, never, never imagined she would be doing these things with a man who had just clawed their way out of a grave. The world she had known for eighty years had been flipped over on her, showing her an even uglier underbelly. At first her mind had recoiled from it. It was wrong, it was unnatural. But once she got a taste, her body craved more. She was bone dry, weak and insubstantial. The blood shot power all the way to her fingertips.

Drake gazed upon her throughout, intent. She wondered what was going through his mind. He wouldn't remember anything at this point. She was nothing and no one to him. She wasn't even his sire . . . and yet he had taken care of her.

She stopped when there was no more blood. The blood witch was dead. She knew that what she had done was forbidden. She felt in her marrow the very *wrongness* of it. But then so was everything that Luthias had done. He had changed the rules of survival.

Drake sat on his heels, studying her. "You look much better."

He looked no different than he had as a human. Strong and handsome, his forearms resting on his thighs, his large hands dangling between his legs. His black hair was charmingly mussed, and there was a shadow of dark stubble on his chin that grew everywhere but on the white scar that slashed across his face. His hair and whiskers would continue to grow, but how fast was directly dependent on how frequently he fed.

Hannah stood. "It's the *baobhan sith* blood. That is what makes them stronger." She touched her teeth to her bottom lip. Her fangs scraped the skin. They had never come out during the day before.

"We should kill him now," Drake said, standing too. "While we are both as strong as he is."

He lifted the body of the dead blood witch and tossed it over his shoulder. Hannah followed him as he carried it back to the mausoleum where they had been trapped. Everything felt different. The air even. Her hearing and sight had always been sharp at night, but during the day they'd been dull. Now she could see far-off birds nesting in trees. She could hear a peregrine call from so far away that it could not be seen. Her body—it felt strong, powerful, capable of anything.

She said, "If Luthias can monitor your thoughts, perhaps you can monitor his?"

Drake dumped the body on the floor and braced his feet, pushing a stone lid partway off one of the tombs. He didn't respond immediately, but a frown formed between his brows as he reclaimed the body and stuffed it into the tomb. He leaned against the tomb and scratched at his whiskered jaw.

"I cannot feel anything right now. I felt him earlier, watching me . . . but now there is nothing."

"You are better than a mere blood witch. There is very likely more that we are capable of than we can guess." Hannah pursed her lips. She had sired Luthias, so maybe the key was in her. But this power was too new, and she feared that if she reached out she would alert him to the fact that they were alive and free. She would wait. Besides, Drake didn't even know who he was.

"Before we do anything, you must begin to remember yourself," she added gently.

"Aye, that would be good. I dinna like the big empty space in my head."

He pushed the lid of the tomb back in place, and they left the mausoleum. Hannah decided the best and safest place for him to be during this process was his own home. Having his own familiar things around him would hopefully speed the process. Once Luthias knew they were alive—and it was inevitable that he would—he would come to them.

In silence, they returned to the inn to collect their horses and belongings. Hannah couldn't stop glancing over at Drake; every time she did, she found him frowning, as if looking deep within himself. It had been a very long time ago, but she remembered how it felt to have no past, no context with which to understand the present or future.

When they were away from the town, Drake finally asked, "Where are we going?"

"To your home. To Creaghaven."

They stopped only to rest the horses. They did not need rest or nourishment or even sleep anymore. They would get to Creaghaven in half the time that they would have otherwise.

Drake's memories about his life returned slowly, and it made Hannah uneasy. Each time he made reference to his past she watched, waiting for him to look at her with accusation and revulsion. Thus far his late wife hadn't been mentioned. And although he hadn't touched Hannah, she could tell he believed they were lovers. She did not dissuade him, since it was true. But his memory came in chunks, and she didn't know in what order they would return. . . . The memory of his wife's death and Hannah's refusal to help her could prove volatile to them. He was no longer a human that Hannah could control. He was as strong as she was now. Maybe stronger.

"My brother is a witch," he said the second day of their journey. It was a mild day, perfect for travel. Hannah couldn't remember the last time she had been able to enjoy the daylight—the sun on her face, the butterflies flitting about. Days had been for sleeping for so long that she had forgotten the pleasure of warm sunlight.

They had been riding in comfortable silence for some time when Drake made this statement with no preamble, indicating to Hannah that the memory had just descended on him.

"He . . . heals people . . . but not with herbs and

charms and such . . . with his hands." He held one of his hands in front of his face and looked at it wonderingly. He dropped his hand and frowned. "I admired him . . . but I also became vexed because healing hurt him, made him weak and sick."

Hannah nodded approvingly. "Aye, that's right. Is this the first you remember about your brother?"

"No . . ." But his voice was hesitant, and she assumed it was the first substantial memory he'd had. "I have remembered things from when we were children . . . but I couldn't remember my own brother's name or much else. He is William." His gaze cut to Hannah. "And I remember you now."

Hannah's heart jerked in her chest, but she kept her face bland. "Is that so?"

"Aye." And he said no more.

Her mind raced, wondering what he remembered. She wanted to ask, but she feared sounding too anxious. Instead she asked, "Do you remember anyone else from your family?"

His brows lowered as he strained to remember, but finally he shook his head. "I think my brother is married . . . but I'm not sure. And . . . I think I am married." He looked at her sharply. "But not to you."

Hannah's throat tightened. "No, we are not married."

"And my wife?"

"She is dead."

The tight set of his shoulders relaxed slightly and he said, "Oh. Good. I mean, not good, but at least I am not . . ." He said no more, looking sheepish.

She understood what he meant. It was one thing to

forget family and friends and your entire life, but to forget yourself, the kind of person you were, was quite another. To question your own morals or lack of—that was far worse. He was not the kind of man to be faithless to his wife or anyone else, and something inside had told him that. But he also knew Hannah was not the woman he had married, leading to all manner of conflicts if his wife had still been alive.

"Do you remember your wife?" Hannah asked, striving for a tone of nonchalance.

"No." He gave her a sideways glance. "Do you?"

Hannah started to say she didn't know her—and that was true, she hadn't really known Ceara. But Hannah did remember her. She had met her once and had let her die. After hesitating long enough to make Drake's eyes narrow suspiciously, she finally said, "I didn't really know her."

One brow raised dubiously, his eyes sharpened. "How did we meet?"

"I know not how you met your wife."

"No, not her—you and me."

She found herself at an unusual loss for words. She maintained her thoughtful expression, however.

His mouth curved into a smile that made her weak. "You don't remember," he said.

"I remember," she replied, the corners of her mouth deepening in response to the slight teasing in his voice.

"But you don't want to tell me."

"Not particularly," she said. "But perhaps I should."

His head tilted. "This is getting very interesting. Proceed."

"Very well. You tried to kill me once."

He blinked and drew back slightly. "This is how we met? With me trying to kill you?" His brows lowered with disbelief. Clearly he knew himself enough to know he wouldn't attack a woman without provocation, because he followed with, "What were you doing?"

She gazed back dispassionately. "I had tried to kill a friend of yours."

Black brows arched mysteriously. "I have much to remember, it seems."

"You will remember it all, in time."

"And you will not deign to help me?"

Her lips pursed together, pensive, and finally she said, "We should stop if we are to speak of this."

Immediately, he drew rein and dismounted, looking up at her expectantly. Though she hadn't expected any different, she sighed and dismounted too.

"The horses need a rest anyway," she said and let him hobble her horse.

While he gave the horses water and oats, Hannah played over in her mind what she would say. It would be very difficult. Hannah did not like difficult conversations. She generally avoided them.

When he finished with the horses, he touched her elbow and led her toward a fallen tree. She gazed up at him, liking the memory-less Drake a great deal. Once his memories returned, their relationship would return to the same mixture of anger and passion that had characterized it before. The passion she loved; it was the anger that left her drained and unhappy. And it was all because of his late wife. She needed to get this over with. She was tired of the waiting and the anxiety—the wondering when and if he would turn on her.

She sat on the log and he sat on the ground beside her so that she couldn't see his face. It was a little unsettling looking at the back of his head. She wondered if she should slide down beside him so she could see him better. She rarely felt nervous, and at the moment she felt excessively so; decided she didn't really want to see his expression as she told him these things.

So she sat quietly, hands clasped on her lap, waiting for him to say something that would prompt her leaden tongue to start. After several endless minutes he said, "Tell me about the first time I saw you."

Hannah moistened her lips. "Your wife was dying. You brought her to my island, believing I could heal her. I did not turn her into a *baobhan sith*, and she died."

There. She'd said it.

He twisted around to look at her, his brow troubled. "Why?"

"You have smelled human blood?"

He nodded.

"Then you know that some of it is good and some of it is very bad. So bad you would never dream of drinking it. So tainted that you know in your bones that it will poison you."

He nodded again, a grudging understanding in his averted eyes. He turned away, facing forward again.

A stone fell in the pool of Hannah's heart and sunk. Her lips tightened and she continued. "So she died. Many years later your niece's husband, Stephen Ross, came to me, wanting the same thing. Except he was not sick, he was lame." She was silent, suddenly unable to go on. He didn't turn and look at her this time; he waited quietly, and her chest tightened incrementally as the moments ticked by. In some ways this part was harder to tell. It wasn't about her refraining from helping. It was about her causing harm.

She smoothed her hands over her skirt several times before she could go on. When she spoke again, her voice was softer. "I had been alone for a very long time. I thought he would make a fine companion. It was what he'd come for, after all, and it was what I wanted. Equitable, aye? But sometime during our visit, he changed his mind. And I didn't."

She waited for some sort of reaction from Drake. A look, a head shake, something, but he didn't move. She could see part of his profile, and his expression was blank, staring . . . listening.

Waiting.

"So I bit him anyway. But he had a knife and a rosary and he managed to escape."

He turned now, quizzical. "A rosary, you say?"

"Aye."

"Why would papist idolatry harm you?"

Hannah smiled wistfully. "That is an excellent question. When I became a blood witch, I was Catholic, so it's not idolatry to me. And it can harm us because we are unnatural. We are not of God."

He turned his head a little more so she could see his face. His mouth had gone to a straight line. "That is not welcome news."

"No, it is not. Contrary to what others believe, I have never met the devil. But symbols of God strike terror in my heart. They burn me when I touch them. I am an evil thing and now you are too. When we die, I do not know what happens to us . . . but I have long since stopped fearing it."

Drake contemplated this in silence, and she hoped that the change in subject had closed the matter of Stephen Ross. She had said all there was to say. But then he asked, "What happened next?"

She sighed, resigned to revealing every unpleasant detail. He would remember it all anyway, and when he did, he would remember what she had left out. "Then you showed up. You chopped down my door and tried to kill me. But something stopped you. I . . . I don't know what. You hated me for not helping your wife and you hated me for not helping Stephen. But you didn't kill me. I often thought, afterward, it was because you saw in that moment that I didn't care whether I lived or died, and you knew that the worst punishment you could mete out was to make me go on living."

His head lowered so that his chin nearly rested on his chest. She wondered what he thought of her saying that. As unpleasant as it sounded, it was probably true. It was exactly what he had done to Luthias. Death had been too good for Luthias; only his suffering would have served justice. And that was no doubt what he had wanted for her.

"Stephen and his wife were in trouble, so you brought me to them and asked me to turn Stephen into a *baobhan sith*."

When she said no more, he asked, eyes fixed on the ground, "And that's it?"

"More or less."

"So we are not . . .?"

"Lovers?"

He nodded.

"Aye, we are that too."

His arms were crossed over his chest, his chin down as he apparently thought through all she had said.

Her belly churned as she waited for him to say something. "Do you remember any of it now?"

He shook his head. "No. I do not remember my wife, and I do not remember my niece or her husband. But I do remember you. I remember making love to you." His chin rose, and he turned, full-bodied, so that his elbow rested on the log beside her. His eyes met hers, deep blue and hot enough to burn her.

The churning in her belly turned to a quiver.

"I remember it endlessly. It plays over in my head, and I wonder why we do not even touch now. Why you stay away from me."

She had wondered the same thing, and the only answer she had was fear. She didn't like that answer. Fear rules when you had something to lose. But there was no fear now, just anticipation.

"I did not want to make this more difficult for you. I do not know what you will remember first, or how you will feel about those memories or me afterward."

"What do you mean?"

"What if your first memory of me is how I let your wife die? What might you do?"

The corner of his mouth turned up in a small smile. "That couldn't possibly be my first memory of you."

"You don't know that."

"I do. My first memory of you is when you gave me your blood. That memory precedes all else and is more significant than anything that happened in the past."

His words caused a softening in her chest that she did not want to feel. He only thought that now. But without the full collection of his memories, he was not truly Drake MacKay. Until he was himself, fully and completely, his declarations meant little.

She reminded herself of this fact, but her heart still squeezed painfully, tender feelings for him nearly overcoming her. She smiled down at him and placed a hand against his cheek. What would his memories bring?

His hand covered hers. He turned his face to her palm and pressed a kiss to it, turning the quiver in her belly to a flutter. His eyes met hers and his grip on her hand became stronger, pulling her off the log and to her knees in front of him.

He did not rise to his knees but continued to lounge against the log, relaxed, eyes moving over her appreciatively. She gazed back, her body shivering with anticipation, admiring his long, lean legs and flat belly. She wanted to see his skin, to touch it.

She wore travel clothes. They had once been fine, but travel had frayed the hem and torn the lace at the ends of her sleeves. His hand slid up the side of her waist to just under her arm, where the points to her bodice tied off. He pulled on them with agile fingers, unlacing until the stiffened material loosened.

"Looks as if you remember something," she said, watching him beneath her lashes.

His mouth curved. "Some things you never forget."

His hand slid beneath the bodice and cupped her breast through the material of her shift. She let out a little gasp and swallowed, but her gaze never wavered from his. His thumb rubbed slowly back and forth across her hardened nipple. Desire pooled low in her belly, a sharp aching. She refrained from biting her bottom lip and moaning, though that was exactly what she was moved to do.

He pushed the bodice up and out of the way so that it dangled from her other shoulder. He shifted forward, finally breaking eye contact when he was eye level with her breasts. He kissed her nipple through the material. She did bite her lip when his kiss grew deeper, drawing the nipple further into his mouth and sucking. It struck her low and sharp, deep in her belly, an almost painful arrow of need.

His hand came up, cupping and kneading her other breast. She took his head in her hands and pressed him closer, her fingers weaving through silken black hair. His hand left her breast to pull urgently at the front of her shift, exposing her breasts completely. He circled her waist with his hands and pulled her to him so that he could lick and suckle at her breasts at his leisure. She wrapped her arms around his neck as her body burned and throbbed low. She straddled him, pressing the core of her against his belt to get some relief.

His hands were free now to roam, and they slid

beneath her skirts, stroking her thighs. His fingers found the damp place between her legs and slid home. She cried out, moving against him, wanting more. She felt his hand fumbling with his belt and her mind cried, *Yes!*

He pressed up inside her, and she did cry out then.

"Aye," he said, low and rough. "Talk to me."

She looked down at him, startled that he had broken the silence with words. But he kept her moving, hands on hips, and she gave him what he wanted, moaning as she slid up and down him, her mind clouding with building passion.

One of his hands slid between them, and his thumb touched her briefly. It was like a shard of glass stabbed through her, piercing her deep and almost breaking through the dam.

"Drake, yes—do it again."

He smiled wickedly, a sheen of sweat on his upper lip. "You like that, aye?" And he gave her more until her body shuddered and jerked, and still he rubbed and thrust. Finally, he spent himself and she sagged against him, completely boneless, her mind thick and sluggish.

After a while he slid her off so that they lay side by side in the grass beside the log.

"With memories like these," he whispered, his breath tickling her ear, "I will not want to remember aught before you."

She smiled, her heart content for the first time in decades. And to their surprise, they slept for the first time in days.

Chapter 14

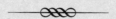

It was the first time Drake had slept since the change. It had been odd to fall asleep. He had felt no fatigue or weariness during the day, but now, lying in the soft grass with Hannah pressed against his side, a deep somnolence enveloped him. He drifted pleasantly, partially aware of his surroundings for a time. Birds sang, the wind blew across them; Hannah's body was a pleasant weight on his arm.

A long time seemed to pass before he realized someone sat on the log nearby. It did not startle him. In the dream it was completely natural that he should turn his head and find a woman sitting there. Her long blond hair flowed over shoulders thin as blades. Her face was all eyes, big and brown and unblinking.

"Ceara." The name sighed out of him like a prayer.

"What have you done, Drake?"

He could not move, could barely think. He could only stare at her as memories flooded him, each one slamming into him like a stone striking his chest. He remembered the day he had first seen his late wife: she had thrown a rock at his head and knocked him off his horse . . . it had actually been her father's horse and he had been stealing it. He had been angry until he'd caught a brief glimpse of her as he had made his escape, golden hair blowing in the wind. He remembered later hearing that she had been kidnapped and held for black rent by a rival clan. He had rescued her, then married her. Those were the good memories, the ones he welcomed back.

But there were others. He remembered watching her waste away and how brave and strong she'd been and how it had shamed him that he had been useless to her. He remembered the day his marriage had turned into a friendship and how that had not troubled him because he had loved her anyway, even if there had been no passion or excitement; there had been caring and loyalty, and that had been good. He remembered the bloody kirtles from the miscarriages, the tears, watching her hold other women's children in her twiglike arms as her eyes misted.

It was all pain, the memories now, piercing through him, fresh, as if they had just occurred, and he thought he was better off without them.

And he remembered Hannah.

Not the Hannah he had just made love to, but a cold woman, a hard woman, a woman with no mercy in her heart. A dead thing and now he was one too and Ceara wanted to know why.

"Because I was not strong enough. This was the only way." He heard himself say the words though he could not feel his lips move.

"What have you done?"

He didn't have the answer to her question. He

wasn't certain what she was asking anymore. He stared at her, at her large eyes that knew more than she said, and more memories flowed over him. He remembered his brother, William—much more than he had before, growing up together, fishing, falling and breaking his leg and being stunned when his brother healed it with nothing more than his hands . . . and then helping William limp home because now *his* leg was broken. No one believed their story at first. Everyone thought they were lying, or at least confused. But they saw how quickly William's leg healed. Some had tried to say it had never been broken at all, but too many had seen the bump on his leg—the broken bone straining against his skin. That was the first time William had ever healed anyone. Drake remembered his brother's wedding and his brother's wife. His father and mother.

He remembered himself, his whole life: the highs, the lows. There were a lot of lows. He remembered the last few years and the loneliness. He had rarely left his stronghold except to reive cattle. He remembered Stephen's death and how he had insisted that Hannah not only make his friend into a blood witch but also turn Luthias into one. He remembered the moment when they had both stood over Luthias's dead body— and it had been dead then—and he had told Hannah to do it.

"What have you done?" Ceara asked again, and this time he knew what she was asking.

The weight on his arm drew his attention. Hannah slept still. Her lashes made dark auburn crescents against her pale cheeks. She was so calm, so peaceful.

Why had he wanted this life . . . or unlife? He remembered everything, but about that, he knew nothing. He feared part of the reason was the woman lying beside him. He had been obsessed with her for more years than he cared to count. First as the reason for Ceara's death, and then as the answer to their problems.

The real question he now asked himself was, Why Hannah? She was not the only one who could do what he'd wanted, what he'd thought he'd needed. Stephen and Deidra were also blood witches, and he had not even considered them. In his mind, it *had* to be her.

Ceara sighed deeply. The breath looked as if it hurt. Her bodice hung limp on her, showing too much of her chest, but there was nothing to see—just bone and rib. It hurt him to look at her. She looked as she had before she had died. The walking dead.

"Why are you here?" he asked.

"I'm just a dream, Drake. A memory."

If this was a dream, he wanted no more of it. He forced himself to wake.

He blinked up at the sky. It was dusk. Hannah slept, looking as if she had barely moved since they'd lain down. Something was wrong. They had not needed sleep before today, and they had not even been tired until after they'd made love. And yet they had inadvertently slept the day away. He had all of his memories back, but even without them he knew that this was how a blood witch operated. Sleep all day, strong and alert at night.

Except that's not what they had been doing.

He leaned over Hannah and shook her. "Hannah, wake up."

Her lashes fluttered, and green eyes gazed back at him. Her expression was soft and sweet. She smiled, and it was unlike any smile she had given him before. Powerful emotion constricted his chest. He recognized it, though he hadn't felt it in a very long while. It frightened him.

She placed a hand against his cheek. Her gaze shifted, taking in the growing dark.

"We slept a long time, didn't we?"

"Aye, we did." He pushed to his feet and held out a hand to help her rise. "So we must be on our way again."

Her expression faltered. Her gaze narrowed on his face, and after a brief hesitation she took his hand and let him pull her to her feet. He readied the horses. The entire time he felt her behind him, watching him in silence. He didn't want to look at her. He couldn't guess what he would see in her face, but it made reluctance sit in his gut like a stone.

When they were riding again she said, her voice emotionless, "You remember."

It was not a question, but he answered it. "Aye."

"Everything?"

"I think so."

"It came to me that way too. In sleep and all at once."

He looked at her. Her face was composed, cool, and he remembered that was who she was most of the time. Which Hannah was the real Hannah? And what was he doing lying with this dangerous woman? But he couldn't forget how he had felt about her those days when his memory had been gone. He had loved her.

He marveled at that thought. He had loved her. He would have died for her, done anything she had asked. And now . . .

Now he was confused. He knew that before she had changed him he had been growing fond of her. Excessively so. But had he loved her?

It was hard to love someone who didn't appear capable of loving back. When his mind had been empty, she had been different. Or she had seemed different.

"Why did we sleep?" Drake asked, changing the subject before she asked something he wasn't ready to answer.

"Because that's what we do. You know that."

"Aye, I do. But we haven't been doing it. Neither of us has slept since we drank the *baobhan sith* blood."

"And you think that has something to do with it?"

He raised a shoulder. "You admitted as much. That you are stronger since you drank it. You couldn't break the lid of the tomb, but I could. You used to be weak during the day, but neither of us has been."

"So what is happening now? What is different?"

"We must drink blood to maintain ourselves. It is the same for a *baobhan sith* who chooses to drink the blood of other *baobhan siths*. In order to maintain these differences, we must replenish the blood."

Hannah's mouth flattened to a displeased line. She looked at him for a long moment, then looked away. He didn't like it any more than she did, but the fact remained—to defeat Luthias, they must be at least as strong as him.

"What? You do not agree?"

"Aye, I do. I've thought as much myself." Her sharp green gaze cut to him. "But it is wrong. Don't you feel it? Everything in me says it is wrong to drink the blood of our brethren."

"You drank it readily enough back at the cemetery."

"I had no choice," she said, and her lips seemed stiff, as if she spoke through her teeth. "I was dying, and it was what *you* brought me. And it felt wrong when I was doing it, but what else was I to do?"

Drake's shoulders tightened with irritation. It was true. Something inside him did recoil from drinking the blood of other *baobhan siths*. But he had done many things he hadn't wanted to do, because they had needed to be done.

"The only way to defeat Luthias is to match him in strength, and the only way to do that is to feed just like he does."

She exhaled loudly and shook her head, looking away.

"Do you disagree?"

"Well, aye. That makes us no better than him. The blood witches we feed on will die. What about being cleverer than he is? Why is it all about strength?"

Drake looked at her incredulously. "How many humans have they killed? What gives them the right? And this is a battle—the strongest army wins."

Hannah shook her head, her mouth twisted bitterly. "I can see the old Drake is back. Warden of the witches . . . or now it is protector of innocent humans. You and Luthias should join forces, since you both apparently have the same goal."

"To destroy my family? I think not."

"You will destroy yourself if you continue on like this."

"What care I?" Drake shouted. "All my memories came back today and I wish to God they had stayed away forever. I cannot go on forever with these things in my head. My wife . . . and now I am with you . . ."

He had not meant it to come out that way, though in truth, he hadn't known precisely what he had meant to say. Nothing kind, certainly. He was angry at her for not being cooperative. He needed her, and she had to be difficult and argumentative.

But that didn't change the fact that what he had said had come out wrong. Her head drew back as if he had swung at her. Her eyes filled with disbelief. Just as suddenly, her shoulders squared and her eyes cooled.

"No one is making you stay with me, Drake. I have tried to send you on your way many times. This is your quest that you have pressed me into. Perhaps the time for us to part ways is now?"

Damn it all.

"Hannah—," Drake started, his tone placating.

"Do not." Her voice was as sharp as a blade, her face stone.

Drake sighed. He saw this spiraling out of control and he was desperate to fix it . . . except he didn't know how.

"You remember your wife and my part in her death

and now the anger is back." Her mouth softened slightly, but not in a release of anger; it was in disappointment. "I had expected this."

"I shouldn't have said that," Drake said, though in truth, he tried hard to remember exactly what he had said. He didn't think he had even completed his thought. Unfortunately she had completed it for him.

"No, it's good that you did. You would be thinking it anyway, and I would wonder, but now I know."

She was granite, her beautiful face carved in stone. For a moment he had almost forgotten what a hard woman she could be, how he had wondered if she'd even had a heart. But he thought he had inadvertently bruised it.

"A truce," Drake said, placating. "We are almost to Creaghaven. Let us discuss strategy when we arrive. Perhaps there is a way to be clever, too."

He did not know if his attempt to pacify her and smooth over their quarrel would work, but she nodded reluctantly. Drake let out the breath he'd been holding and promised himself he would not blurt out any more foolish thoughts for the rest of the trip.

Hannah's heart sickened, as if she had supped on tainted blood and it attacked the very center of her chest. She had done that before, so she knew the pain of bad blood and heartbreak. But this time it was all in her head.

Why had she allowed herself to care for him? She had done so well, protecting herself. But he'd found her vulnerabilities. She couldn't go back and change things, as much as she'd love to, but she could hide it from him. She would die before he knew how much this hurt.

They had traveled a great distance in the past few days, and they found themselves at Creaghaven by midday of their fourth day of travel. She had monitored herself and Drake to see if their special strength had begun to fade, but other than sleeping the day away once, they seemed no different. In fact, the sun had risen, and they'd both been well and able to carry on with no fatigue. She supposed every living thing needed to sleep on occasion—even extraordinary blood witches.

She had pointed this out to Drake, that they were still strong and able to defeat Luthias, but she got nothing more from him on that subject than a grunt and a nod. Now that he had his memory back, she thought they should go after Luthias immediately, before their strength began to fade.

"It's too late," he said. "He knows we are free."

Hannah drew in a quick breath. "How long?"

He shook his head. "I suspected yesterday, but it didn't feel like surprise or discovery. I think he has known for a while . . . perhaps the whole time."

They exchanged a tense look, neither knowing what this meant for them. They couldn't guess where Luthias would come at them next, but come at them he would. So they continued on to Creaghaven, grimly confident that the coming confrontation was no longer in their hands.

When they arrived at Creaghaven, Hannah immediately sensed that something was not right. The stronghold held very little humanity. She smelled no human blood. She could tell by the tight set of Drake's jaw that he sensed it too.

"Perhaps we should go straight to Strathwick," Hannah said when they stood outside the open gates of the outer castle wall. A lone chicken strutted by, stopping periodically to peck at the ground.

He seemed to consider it for a moment, but in the end he gave a tight shake of his head and touched the sides of his horse with his heels. Hannah followed him in, dread a tight knot in her chest.

The first thing Hannah noticed was the lack of humans. There were plenty of animals. Dogs digging through midden piles, pigs sleeping in the shade, chickens strolling and scratching. A horse stood beside a building, head raised to pull at the thatched roof with its teeth. It heard their entrance, shook its mane, and trotted over to them.

Drake dismounted and lay a hand against the horse's withers. "I wish my niece were here to talk to you," he murmured to the horse.

Hannah remained mounted, scanning the courtyard cautiously. She normally sensed humans by their blood, but *baobhan siths* were harder, and these new ones were impossible. Hannah was Luthias's sire. She should be able to sense him.

Her heart fluttered and her chest tightened at the thought of making herself known to him. She tapped her horse and continued to ride into the castle.

She dismounted at the doors to the keep. The thick

wooden double doors stood open, and the interior was dark—no fires or candles could be discerned from the upper windows.

"Where is everyone?" Drake asked in a hushed voice behind her.

Hannah shook her head. "I know not, but I have a bad feeling about this. I think we should go."

"No." Drake brushed past her and entered the keep.

Hannah could see the dark interior clearly; she just did not want to. After a moment she sighed and followed him inside. Drake stood in the center of the room, staring down at the circular fire pit. The ashes were cold. He squatted down and sifted through the gray-and-black powdery dust. After a moment, he folded his forearms over his knees and just stared.

Hannah crossed the room to the screen that hid the door leading into the kitchen. She peeked around it cautiously. At first, the kitchen seemed just as devoid of life as the great hall, and she started to rejoin Drake, but a sound caused her to freeze.

It was not much—a soft scraping, as of a foot being dragged along the floor. Hannah's heart skipped with unease, but she moved deeper into the kitchen. The sound came from the larder. She heard it again; this time it went on longer. *Scrape.* It was probably nothing, she told herself, because she sensed no human blood. But that was what made her uneasy. If it was alive, it wasn't human.

"Hannah?" Drake called, coming into the kitchen.

The sound abruptly stopped.

Hannah put her finger to her lips, then pointed

toward the larder. Drake's brows rose in hopeful surprise. He was beside her in seconds, and they both stood quietly, ears straining to hear anything. But all they heard was silence.

Drake pointed toward the larder and started toward it. Hannah didn't really want to know what was inside. Whatever had happened here was Luthias's doing and would hurt Drake. At the larder door, she snatched at his hand impulsively. He turned to look down at her, one hand on the larder latch.

No words passed between them, but their eyes locked and held. There was still something between them: trust. He trusted her, and that gave her hope that she did not want but couldn't help but hold close in her heart. His hand curved around hers, squeezing.

He turned back to the door and pushed it open. Shelves lined the walls of the larder, which was stocked with sacks and jars. Barrels were stacked against the wall. A man lay on the floor against a barrel, staring up at them fearfully.

Drake's hand tightened, nearly crushing hers. "Jacob?" he said, his voice breaking with disbelief.

"My lord? Is that you?"

Drake released her hand and went to Jacob's side. "What happened, man? Where is everyone?"

Jacob was not a young man, perhaps in his fifties. He was portly, his graying hair sticking out wildly about his face. His plump cheeks looked as if they'd normally been ruddy, but they were currently pale and pasty. Dark circles ringed his eyes.

"He came." Jacob closed his eyes and swallowed

hard, his Adam's apple bobbing, as if speaking was a great strain. "Luthias Forsyth—he came here. We thought he looked for ye, but he knew that ye werena here." He began to cry, the deep sobs jerking his round shoulders.

"You are a blood witch," Drake whispered, apparently just realizing it. Hannah had known all along, otherwise she would have smelled him.

"Aye." Jacob rubbed a grimy sleeve across his eyes. "Some of us ran and others they captured. I do not remember much. I woke strong and hungry . . . I drank blood . . . then afore I even kent who I was, they were feeding on me . . . again." Jacob shook his head, his face twisted in disgust. "And it hurt, oh God—they didna just do it to me, either. They took some with them . . . like slaves."

"Or kine," Hannah said. When Drake looked at her, his forehead creased with deep pain, she added, "For when they need to feed again."

Jacob grabbed at Drake's sleeve. "I'm sorry, my lord. I couldna even think . . . it happened so fast . . . and I've forgotten so much until today . . ."

"It's all right," Drake said, a firm hand on his servant's shoulder. He slid his hand under Jacob's arm and helped him to his feet. "Come on, let's get you somewhere where you can rest."

Hannah walked ahead of him back into the great hall. Blankets were draped over the chairs situated around the fire pits. Hannah gathered several and made a bed for Jacob near one of the pits.

After Drake made Jacob comfortable, they searched

the rest of the castle. They found three more of the inhabitants, but they were dead.

Hannah watched Drake's face carefully the entire time. It had hardened into a mask, his eyes narrowed with one purpose. Revenge.

It was his way, and the blood would make him single-minded in his pursuit of it. There was no room for her. There never really had been.

She knew what she had to do.

"I will get him some blood," Hannah said when they returned to the hall. "And then we will talk."

Chapter 15

*D*rake's skin crawled. He could not sit still. Every time he sat, all he could think about was Luthias, coming into his home and slaughtering his people like livestock. Drake's fists tightened, and he punched the wall again. The stone cracked and his knuckles bled. They would heal. The stone would not. He didn't care. What was a home without its people?

Hannah had propped Jacob up against the wall and fed blood to him from a bowl. Drake did not know where she had gotten the blood—from one of the animals running loose in the bailey, no doubt. But Jacob was not responding—not as Hannah had when Drake had given her the *baobhan sith* blood.

Drake paced the cold, cavernous hall, worry gnawing at his insides. He knew why, or he thought he did. Jacob had already been a *baobhan sith* that last time he'd been fed upon. Therefore it was unlikely that anything but *baobhan sith* blood would make him well again.

Which meant Drake's niece Deidra was no better and possibly much worse.

They could not stay here and just wait to be part

of the slaughter. They must move. He had to act. He continued pacing, his hands flexing and fisting, flexing and fisting, waiting for Hannah to finish so they could have this "talk."

When finally she crossed to him her face was grave. Her gaze remained on Jacob when she said, "He's not improving. I don't understand."

"It has to be *baobhan sith* blood," Drake said. "Nothing else will do."

She raised her palms to show conditional agreement. "Aye, but shouldn't any blood still revive him? He seems no better."

He leaned toward her and hissed, "That is why we have to go. We'll come back for him, but Deidra must still be like this—"

"If she is even alive."

He glared at her and continued, "And Luthias is on his way there. He will kill everything I love. That is his plan. We cannot delay."

Hannah gazed up at him silently. Her chest rose in a deep sigh. "No, Drake, *you* cannot delay. I am not going with you."

Drake's world tilted. He waited for it to steady, for her to give some sign that he had misheard her, but her expression was firm, determined. He stared at her, unwilling to believe she would really defect. "What?"

"This is where we part. I am returning to Edinburgh, where I will take a ship to Italy."

Surely someone had punched him in the chest. It hurt so that he could not speak. She had to see how stunned he was, yet her expression did not change.

When he didn't respond, she said, "You are strong now. Our promises are fulfilled. I wish you luck in your venture."

She studied his mute expression, her brows finally drawing together in a concerned frown. "Have a care, Drake. Do not rush into this recklessly." She placed a hand on his forearm. "I do not wish any harm to befall you."

Her hand on his arm broke his strange paralysis. He jerked his arm away and growled, "Then why are you doing this? I need you." And he meant it, too—more than he'd imagined before she'd dropped this anvil on him. True, he needed her strength and experience, but he also needed her steadiness. She was his counterweight, she kept him steady and smart when he would be foolish. And she comforted him. She made him feel safe, not in a physical way, but she kept the loneliness at bay in a way no other woman had since Ceara.

She dropped her hand and turned away. "I have delayed my own plans long enough—"

"What plans? I stopped you from handing yourself over to a lynch mob. You are alive now because I wished you to be."

Her lips curved in a bittersweet smile. "I do not yet know whether to thank you for that or curse you." She lifted her shoulders as if to dismiss it. "You tell me in eighty years which, aye?"

She turned away, crossing to where Jacob lay. Drake watched her helplessly, not knowing what to say to make her stay and pride not allowing him to try. She didn't even care. Not a bit. So why should he? He would find a way to destroy Luthias without her help.

His gaze turned to the man Hannah knelt beside. If Jacob, Stephen, and Deidra were also to partake of *baobhan sith* blood, perhaps they stood a chance against Luthias. Certainly four was better than the two he had originally planned on. But where to get the *baobhan sith* blood? He would not lower himself to Luthias's methods.

He had been watching Hannah the whole while he'd paced, trying to work it all out in his mind, but his thoughts halted when Hannah took a blade from the ground beside Jacob and sliced it across her own wrist, then held her wrist to Jacob's mouth.

He froze, watching. Jacob sucked weakly at first, then he seized her arm, his eyes closed, ecstatic. He would kill her, suck her dry. Drake couldn't just stand and watch any longer. He flew across the room and knocked Jacob's head from her arm.

"What are you doing?" he shouted, grabbing her shoulders and hauling her to her feet. "Are you trying to kill yourself?" He gave her a shake, furious.

She brought her hands up, knocking his arms away and breaking his hold on her. "Do I seem weak to you? I was giving him a little, enough to revive him so the two of you can be on your way."

Drake's teeth ground together with frustration. He glanced over at Jacob, who was still sitting on the ground but clearly much improved.

She let out a deep sigh. "I'm going now." She stared at Drake for a time, as if she wanted to say something. Finally she placed her palms against his chest, stood on tiptoe, and pressed a soft kiss to his lips. "Good luck, Drake."

"I'll find you," he said suddenly, impulsively. "When this is over, I will come to Italy and find you."

Her head tilted slightly as she gazed up at him, as if she had never seen him before. Her smile was sweet as she turned away and left them in the cavernous, empty great hall. And the light seemed to follow her, leaving him in the dark.

It had been hard to leave him standing there, looking so lost. But Hannah was secure in the knowledge that she had done the right thing. His memory had returned and she had become a thing of suspicion again. His impulsivity and recklessness were also taking over, just as she had feared. Blood intensified a human's strongest traits. A clever man became brilliant. The disenchanted turned morose. Bad became evil. Drake would not be evil, but he might be a danger to himself and others.

Calmer heads were needed, different tactics. Drake would neither hear nor listen though. All he knew was that his family was in danger, because Luthias was after all he loved; therefore he must run in and mindlessly hack away.

That would never work with Luthias. So Hannah would manage this situation herself.

He thought she had left him. She had meant for him to believe that, though it had caused an odd little ache in her chest when he'd looked at her with such shocked disbelief. He would never have agreed with her plan and would have fought her on it. He would have insisted she go with him and fight beside him, unprepared. She would probably have given in to his wishes because she loved him. She knew that now. It was duty that had kept her with him at first. She had helped create the monster. Then it had been justice. Luthias was a cruel bully with nothing better to do than prey on the weak. But in the end it had been love that had kept her with him, and it was love that sent her on a new mission.

But she could not tell him what she was doing or why. If she failed, she could not bear the thought of him altering his plans to wait for her. If his family was murdered because he had delayed on her advice . . . well, she couldn't live with herself. He should carry out his own reckless plan without factoring her into it.

So she had lied and left, and he had let her go. He had seemed hurt at first and she had nearly caved in to that sudden passionate exclamation that he would find her. What did it mean? Was it possible that he truly cared for her, too? She hoped she would find out. But not today. She had remained strong, gathered her meager belongings, and left.

Drake wasn't the only one who'd received a gift of knowledge while they'd slept. Something had happened to Hannah, too, as they'd slumbered in each other's arms. Something unexpected. Her mind had met with Luthias's, and she was fairly sure he had been completely unaware.

She had thought it a dream at first, but it had been too mundane. Luthias had been sitting before a fire, staring at the flames meditatively, lost in thoughts of the past; thoughts of a sister and a mother and a father. The thoughts evoked conflicting feelings in him of fear and sadness and loathing. His thoughts were so fluid and unconscious that Hannah had a difficult time sorting through them, but one thing that stood out was that he had a sister and she was alive. When he thought of her it was with disgust and fear—not fear of her, but fear *for* her. He protected her. And he wondered about her. And overriding it all was intense guilt.

But then, he seemed to realize what he dwelled upon, and shook the thoughts off with great irritation.

Hannah's dreams had drifted on to other things, but the image had remained, so that when she had woken she'd pondered it, wondering if it had just been a dream and finally deciding that no, she had managed to see in his mind without his knowledge.

One thing she had learned in her hundred years of existence was that to win, you had to first understand your opponent. They thought they understood Luthias; that he was simple—a holy man convinced that all witches were evil and therefore intent on their destruction. Well, that was true, but the question was, *why*? She had seen something in his dream—a key to Luthias Forsyth.

Drake would never have agreed. Talking. Investigating. He needed to act, not study. But they were not far from Luthias's childhood home. She had seen that, too.

So she rode through the night, arriving at the little village in the morning. The sky was soft and pink, and the air was damp with dew. Men and women were gathered in a dirt clearing, swinging flails at piles of harvested wheat. Hannah dismounted and walked her horse closer. Children crawled on their hands and knees in another clearing nearby, gathering the grain that had been threshed from the stalk.

Several old women stood nearby, weaving on wooden spools that spun on the ground in front of them. They were yelling directions at the children. Hannah approached the women with a smile.

"Hiv ye lost yer way, miss?" one of them asked. White hair turning yellow was pulled into a long plait. Her wrinkled skin was darkened by the sun and looked onion-skin thin, but her nimble fingers spun and twirled with barely a glance from her watery green eyes.

"No, or at least I do not think so. I am looking for the Forsyth family. I was told they come from this village."

The old woman's spinning paused, as did the spinning of the other women. They all peered at Hannah with new interest.

"Which ones be you asking after? Old Emma Forsyth, she lives alone over by the loch, ever since her husband died nearly ten years past. He got his foot caught in a trap and the wolves got him. Horrible accident, that. Then there's Hercules Forsyth, he's probably with the threshers and his wife, well she be big with child, so she'll be home making ready for the bairn, then there's—"

Seeing that the list of local Forsyths could apparently go on indefinitely, Hannah decided to be specific. "What of Luthias? An older gentleman."

The old woman said nothing at first. She looked at the other women, who gave her nothing; they just stared back, their faces hard and distant.

When she spoke again, the old woman's voice had cooled. "No, ye'll not find Luthias here. He's a great man now, a kirk man. He travels around, or so we hear. He hasna been back this way since he was a verra young man."

"Does he have any family?"

"Why?" the old woman asked, squinting at her suspiciously. "Are you a witch-hunter?"

Hannah let out a short laugh, her palm to her chest. "Me? Have you missed the fact that I am a woman?"

The old woman's brows rose. "Witch-hunters employ many methods to trap witches into confessions."

"Are you a witch?"

The old woman's mouth pursed. "Of course not."

Hannah paused, her mouth curving into a smile. "Are you a Forsyth?"

The old woman's lips pushed together even tighter.

Hannah smiled widened. "You didn't mention that there was a Forsyth standing right here."

The other women gave sidelong looks but were suddenly engrossed in their spinning again.

The old woman's chin rose, and she squared her shoulders. "Aye. I am a Forsyth. Luthias is my brother."

Hannah's smile faded to a resigned line. "Miss Forsyth, I am not a witch-hunter, I vow that to you, nor am I the tool of one. I only want to speak to you about your brother."

"Whatever grief he has caused you and yours is not my doing. I havena seen him in more than thirty years and dinna expect to see him again afore I die."

"I know you haven't." Hannah put a gentle hand on the woman's wrist, and her spinning stopped. The spindle twirled once more and tipped over. "I just need some information about your brother. Nothing more."

The old woman looked at the other women. Again they offered nothing in the way of advice but merely stared back gravely.

Finally she sighed, her shoulders sagging. "My name is Maggie. Let's sit down. My knees are aching."

Chapter 16

$\mathcal{T}$he woman's cottage was small and cramped, stuffed so full of things that there was barely room to move around. She had the normal furniture one would expect in a small cottage—a sturdy wooden table and cabinet, benches and chairs, a heavy wooden bed. But there were other things, things not common in such a rustic setting. The blanket that covered the bed was made of expensive cotton and clearly not from homespun. A hand mirror sat on a small table, along with an ivory comb and pretty ribbons in many colors. Several books on religious themes that looked as if they had never been opened were on a shelf beside a clock.

She offered Hannah a seat on another chair with a silk pillow on the seat. It was rare for a cottar to have one chair, let alone two. Hannah moved the pillow, not wanting to stain it with her travel-worn attire, and sat.

"You have a very nice home, Maggie," Hannah commented, still taking in everything.

"Mmm, isn't it?"

Something about Maggie's tone made Hannah give her an inquiring look. The old woman's mouth pursed into a flat wrinkled line, as if she had tasted something nasty.

"It is not mine," she said finally. "I am . . . holding on to it for someone."

"For whom?"

She let out a small breathy laugh and raised her narrow shoulders in a shrug.

Hannah thought this was curious, but it was not pertinent to her purpose, so she dismissed it.

"You are Luthias Forsyth's sister?"

Maggie inclined her head. "Aye, I am. Though we like to forget about that around here."

"Why?"

"Because he and my father killed nearly every woman in this village some fifty years ago. Including our mother."

The corners of Hannah's mouth turned down. "I am sorry."

"Aye, so am I." She looked away, the loose skin on her throat tightening. "I am sorry to live in a world where men can murder women and not have to pay for their sins."

"Everyone pays for their sins, Maggie. And wherever your father is, he will pay for his."

Maggie's green gaze cut to Hannah, hard and glassy. "My father is dead, thank the Lord. Had he not died, I would not be here now."

"What do you mean?"

"My father was a kirk man. Not a great one like Luthias, but the pastor of our little town. He was a harsh man. There was no kindness in his heart. He saw things one way, the way he believed God wanted this world to turn, and that was the law."

"And how is that?"

Maggie smiled and leaned her head back in memory. "There was no dancing or singing. Everyone should be hard at work from sunrise until sundown and then study the word of God by candlelight. And because he expected others to live by these rules, he set the example in his family. We did not sing or laugh or speak of things that he considered frivolous. So when he 'realized' his wife was a witch, you can imagine how that went."

"His own wife?"

"Aye—well, it didna start with her, you understand. There were others, and as it always goes, once one witch was caught, fingers started pointing. My father, being the pastor, questioned them."

"Without the kirk?"

"No, the assembly helped. No one pointed any fingers at my mother, mind you. Not a single person. He just looked at her one day and became certain. None of the things he claimed that she did were real." Maggie's voice changed, the sardonic tone gone, replaced by disbelief even after so many years. "I dinna ken what she said or did. He thought her cat was a familiar, so he killed it. She cried and cried and called him the evil one, and then he took her away and I never saw her again. He burned her, but I didna attend the burning."

It was an ugly story but not an uncommon one.

"What about Luthias?" Hannah asked. "Did he agree that his mother was a witch?"

Maggie's eyes shifted to the left in recall. "No. I dinna think so. He agreed with my father about the other witches. I remember the two of them discussing the evil things that the women of the village had done. They were so righteous, so full of their own goodness. I hated them. I was a young girl; fifteen and soon to be wed. Luthias was thirteen. He knew nothing about these women; he just took everything our father said and swallowed it whole, as God's word. I didn't know much more, mind ye, but I was fair certain they didn't do all the things my father and brother accused them of." She shook her head, the crevices in her face deepening with sadness, making her look very old. "But that is the way of the witch hunts. Once it starts, it takes on life, becomes a live thing, not just an idea, and a person forgets who their friends are." Her gaze sharpened, grew perceptive. "I think the devil is in the idea."

"Aye, it is," Hannah said. "I have seen much of it over the years."

Maggie smiled indulgently. "You cannot have seen too many years, young as you are."

Hannah smiled back, keeping the cynical smugness that she felt from her expression. "You'd be surprised." She frowned, pursuing the story Maggie had been sharing. "So Luthias was in the thick of the witch hunts, but not when it came to your mother?"

Maggie inhaled deeply. "No, I dinna think he cared overmuch for that." She stared down at her fingers, which toyed with the corner of her arisaid. "I didna protest overmuch either, though I cried every night.

But it was dangerous to protect someone. Even your own mother. So I kept a strong face to my father."

"You were young and afraid. It is understandable."

"I was a coward. I realized then that none of us was safe from my father." She leaned forward, her eyes passionate. "*He was my father.* He was not a kind man or a loving man, but he was my father. I thought he would protect me no matter what."

Hannah sympathized with the woman, she really did, but she wanted to hear more about Luthias. She didn't want to seem rude, though, and she didn't want to insult her—then Maggie might not tell her anything more. So Hannah said, "How were things for you and Luthias after your mother's death?"

Maggie took a deep breath, then let it out, the passion deflating from her eyes as she leaned back in her chair. Her shoulders sagged. "We were odd with each other. I didn't trust Luthias, and he, I think, felt guilty. He did love our mother, and though he had gotten caught up in the blood lust, he had not expected Father to turn on his own wife and kill her. And Father . . . he quieted down for a while. He wasn't even so harsh for a time. So many women had died that some of the men left—went to other villages to bring back new wives. Including my man." Maggie's mouth flattened bitterly. "I guess he decided he didn't want the daughter of a witch for a wife."

Hannah wanted to apologize again for the woman's misfortune, but it was becoming tedious, so she merely made an expression of sympathy.

"Time passed and Father grew fierce again. He

felt that all animals were potential familiars, so he disposed of all of our pets and forbid us to have any animals. This distressed Luthias the most, I think, because he had several beloved dogs. Father was particularly brutal. He smashed their skulls with a club. Luthias was so angry when Father killed them that I thought he would do the same to Father—smash his skull with a club. And I prayed to God that he would. But he never said a word to Father about it." She shook her head, her eyes far away. Then her expression set in grim lines. "One day, Luthias and I found a cat with its leg broken. So we hid it in the woods and tried to nurse it back to health."

She licked her lips and swallowed, her eyes on that long-ago picture in her head.

"I dinna ken how Father found out. Someone might have seen us going to the wood together and mentioned it to him." She shrugged. "I'll never know. We came into the cottage one day and there he sat at the table, the crippled cat before him on the tabletop. We were both terrified. He was so angry. There was no use lying. But Father did not believe Luthias had aught to do with it. He said I was like Mother, that I had used my feminine wiles to trick my own brother into cavorting with the devil—and that the cat was a succubus." She shook her head, looking as confused by it all now as she must have been fifty years before. "None of it made any sense, but it didn't matter. Luthias lapped it up like a dog did milk. He agreed with Father that I was a witch and evil. Then Father said he didn't wish to punish me as he had our mother—I was young and could still be saved—but nevertheless something must be done. He said the devil controlled me through the cat and that Luthias must kill the cat to break the demon's hold over me."

Hannah was appalled at this story and did nothing to hide her horror.

Seeing her expression, Maggie leaned forward eagerly. "So Luthias took the cat out back and drowned it."

"You are certain he drowned it?"

"Aye, I saw it floating in the well water. Father fished it out and disposed of it. Luthias was never the same. Father died not long after and Luthias moved to another village to apprentice with that pastor. I stayed here in this cottage. I haven't seen my brother in fifty years . . . but about thirty years ago, when the witch hunts started around the country . . . I began receiving gifts." She waved her hand, indicating all of the luxurious items stuffed into her small cottage. "I had heard that Luthias was doing well for himself. I have always assumed these things are from him, some way of assuaging his conscience. He knew I had loved pretty things as a lass and Father wouldn't let me have them." She shrugged and sighed. "But that doesn't make sense either, does it, if he still goes about killing women?"

"There are many things men do that make little sense," Hannah said thoughtfully.

"Did this help you?" Maggie asked, eyeing Hannah through narrowed eyes. "Why would you need to ken so much about my brother?"

Hannah considered her options. There were many

ways to use this information, and she didn't know what was safe to reveal to Maggie. People were strange. She seemed to have no love for her brother, but all that could change if she suspected Hannah meant him harm.

Hannah hesitated, then said, "Unlike you, I have seen much of your brother over the past year. And he hasn't changed."

"Still the great witch-hunter, eh?" Maggie sighed. "Who did he hurt? Are you hunting him down to kill him?"

Maggie didn't seem troubled by the possibility that she spoke to someone wanting to murder her own brother. But Hannah supposed that in her place, she wouldn't either.

"It's a long story," Hannah said with a weak smile.

Maggie leaned back and folded her hands on her lap. "Do I look as if I am in a hurry?"

Hannah hesitated. "No . . ."

"Ah, but you are." Maggie's brows lowered thoughtfully. "You came to me for information, and now you are in a rush to use it. But what good are stories about Luthias's childhood?"

"I do not know yet. But he still thinks about you with a certain fond sadness. And he obviously feels remorse for his past misdeeds." Hannah waved a hand at the fine items Luthias showered his sister with. "Have you received anything from him recently?"

Maggie nodded. She pushed herself up from her chair with a grimace and crossed the room to a richly carved wooden trunk. As she threw the lid back she said, "This trunk arrived several years ago. The man who brought it described the sender as a tall, cruel man." She removed a package wrapped in velvet. "That sounds like my brother."

She returned to her chair with the package in her hand. "This came just last week. The man who brought it was very odd . . ." Her face creased in distress. "He was clearly a churchman by his attire, but his eyes . . . they were dead. And he seemed repelled by this." She cupped the package between her palms. "When I opened it, I found his aversion curious . . . as well as the gift."

A fissure of misgiving shivered through Hannah. Luthias had sent one of his brethren to his own sister. It was disturbing.

"What is it?" Hannah asked, eyeing the package cautiously.

Maggie watched her closely. "You seem as fashit as the churchman."

Hannah forced a wooden smile and raised her brows expectantly.

Maggie delicately unwrapped the package. Sitting in the center of the velvet was a wooden rosary. "Curious thing for a Protestant minister to send to—"

Hannah recoiled, standing and stumbling over her chair. It crashed onto its side. Her eyes watered and her belly turned to fire.

"My, my my," Maggie said softly. "What is this?"

The chair creaked as Maggie stood. Panic had Hannah in its claws, crushing her chest so that she couldn't breathe. Maggie moved closer with the rosary, and Hannah shrank away.

Maggie looked down at the rosary with new respect. "I think mayhap my brother finally did right by me. He sent me something to protect me from evil." She peered shrewdly at Hannah. "Is that what you are?"

"No," Hannah cried, then, "aye, aye, I am, but not in the way you think. I mean you no harm, nor do I come here with ill intentions. But I am an evil thing. This body you see is possessed by something foul. It keeps me young and makes me strong, but it is a night dweller and feeds on blood."

Hannah blinked rapidly, trying to look over the rosary to the woman. The intensity of the burning sensation had faded, but she still felt as if she stood too close to a fire. She wanted to look at the rosary, like a child wanting to stare into the sun though it blinded her. It had been so many years since she had seen one; she could not look at them now, their fire scorched her eyes. But she wanted to. She wanted to hold one again.

"If you do not mean evil, then why are you here, asking these questions about my brother?"

"Luthias has changed, too. He is a *baobhan sith,* like me. I believe he sent the rosary to protect you from him."

Maggie stared down at the rosary in her palm, her brows drawn together in consternation. "Why should I believe you?" Her head jerked up. "In fact, that makes no sense at all. My brother was the most devout Christian ever. How could he become evil? I think evil would shrink from him just as you shrink from this rosary." She thrust it toward Hannah.

Hannah jerked back in response. She gritted her

teeth. It was a rosary, for God's sake. Not a torch, or a sword, or even a dag. She was not a good woman, she knew that, but she had not intentionally done evil. She had lived within her bloody nature the best that she could, harming few.

She straightened and faced Maggie. She blinked rapidly, trying to see the rosary, though it seemed all light and caused her eyes to water.

"Your brother hunted a child for twelve years. That child is a woman now. He killed her lover and tried to kill her. He has been punished." Hannah's jaw tightened, and she confessed. "He was punished by me, made to suffer that which he inflicted on so many for so long."

Maggie regarded her thoughtfully. Then suddenly, surprisingly, she wrapped the crucifix in the velvet, hiding it from sight. Hannah let out a shuddering breath. Her limbs nearly gave out, limp. She tipped to the side, letting the wall support her.

"Your justice hasna gone the way you planned, has it now? Else you wouldna be here seeking information from his old sister."

Hannah shook her head. "It hasn't."

Maggie turned and crossed the room. She took a satchel off a hook and walked around the perimeter of the room, dropping things in her bag. "If I ken Luthias, he has managed to twist this curse into a blessing."

"What are you doing?" Hannah asked, an uneasy knot forming in the pit of her belly.

Maggie turned and looked at her in surprise. "I'm coming with you."

Hannah frowned, uncertain how to tell the woman it was not safe for a woman her age and that, moreover, she would slow Hannah down and that was the last thing she needed.

"That's not a good idea," Hannah said. "Your brother is . . . very different than you remember him."

"Oh, I expect he is. But it's been fifty years, and this is the first time I've even known where he was."

Hannah went to the woman and stilled her hands. "This is not a Sunday visit. There will be a fight and people will die. Your brother, I hope. You cannot come."

Maggie's face hardened with stubbornness. But then, without saying another word, she gave in, her shoulders sagging. "You are right." She took the velvet-covered rosary and pressed it into Hannah's hands. "Take this."

Hannah nearly dropped it, afraid it would burn her. But wrapped in the velvet it was no different from any other bauble. "I do not ken what to do with it."

Maggie looked down, her hands still wrapped around Hannah's, trapping the velvet-covered rosary between her palms as if it had been a butterfly that might escape. "Return it to Luthias . . . give it to him, and tell him it is from me."

Chapter 17

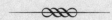

$\mathcal{D}$rake and Jacob rode to Strathwick, stopping only once—for Jacob to feed and regain his strength. He was much improved thanks to the infusion of Hannah's blood, but he was still nowhere near where Drake needed him.

At Strathwick Drake stopped just outside the village. He considered what would happen if he rushed in, hacking away mindlessly, which was what instinct urged him to do. But he restrained himself, relatively sure no good would come of it. He must think it out.

Jacob sat on a stump, waiting for his master to devise a plan. A blood witch he might have become, but he was still Drake's loyal and obedient servant. And not much of a thinker. Whatever was devised, Drake would have to dream up.

He needed Hannah. Her level head, her thoughtfulness. His hands fisted. Soon she'd be on a ship to Italy. He would have to do this without her.

He didn't need her. He had been telling himself that since they had parted ways, and sometimes he believed it. Today he didn't.

Of course it made no difference anymore whether he

entered in the morning or at night. It was all the same to Luthias. Drake paced around the clearing for several more minutes. It was difficult to devise a plan when he did not know where Luthias was. He might not even be at Strathwick. Drake wasted precious time. He could go to the village and inquire there, but again, he did not know if Luthias had already been there. After what he had done at Creaghaven, Drake couldn't take the chance.

There was only one way to uncover the information he needed, short of entering the castle himself.

He closed his eyes and took a deep breath. Luthias had been there sometimes at the edge of his mind. Drake had tried to guard against him, but had no way of knowing if he'd been successful.

It was time to open his mind to Luthias, to see if the link was reciprocal. He let his thoughts drift to the withcpricker, tentative.

Nothing.

He frowned and tried harder, repeating Luthias's name in his head and picturing him. A shock went through him as his mind was seized. Luthias was in a dark room. He stood before a blazing fire, but the rest of the room was in shadows. Luthias's anger generated out around him like a blast of heat from a bonfire. He was furious—beyond furious. Drake's body was held immobile, he couldn't move, couldn't withdraw. He struggled against the anger, trying to perceive where it was that Luthias stood and what made him so angry.

Luthias sharpened suddenly, sensing the intrusion. His mind reached out to meet Drake's. Drake retreated and the connection was severed, the scene fogging.

His head ached. He rubbed his temples, trying to re-create the scene in his head, to see if he had missed something, something that would give him a clue to Luthias's whereabouts. But there was nothing.

"Come," Drake said to Jacob.

He decided to bypass the village, just in case. He had grown up here, had been born in Strathwick. He knew these woods better than he knew his own lands. They kept to the trees, skirting the village, moving deeper into the wood, and then circling around. In one area the wood came right to the edge of the moat. They stopped just inside the trees, and Drake surveyed the castle.

His chest tightened. He sensed the same emptiness that he'd felt at Creaghaven. It was too far for him to smell the blood of inhabitants, but this was more than a smell, this was a sense of desolation. He feared Luthias had already slaughtered everyone and left.

There was only one way to find out for certain.

The moat was not high because of the paucity of rain recently, and Drake knew the best place to cross. There were two ways in and out of the castle. To get to both of them one had to cross the moat, and the only way to cross the moat was the bridge at the front of the castle.

At least, that's the way it appeared.

But William and Drake had created a secret way to cross long ago.

Drake moved to the edge of the water.

"How will we cross?" Jacob asked, surveying the moat dubiously.

Drake didn't answer. He walked along the water's

edge until he spotted the marker they had used: a scarred block of masonry, cracked and pocked and completely out of place with the rest of the relatively unmarred masonry of the castle. That had marked their hidden bridge.

Drake went to the edge of the water and looked over his shoulder at Jacob, who stared back, completely befuddled. Drake brought his leg out in front of him so that it hovered over the water, then leaned forward until his foot hit the water, splashing up a bit before it hit stone.

Jacob blinked and looked up from where Drake's feet disappeared below the surface of the water.

"William and I piled stones here one summer so we could cross the moat secretly." Drake took another wide step forward, hoping the stones were still where they had been. When he was halfway across, he looked back at Jacob, still standing at the water's edge. "Well, come on. Don't just stand there."

Drake leapt from stone to stone until he was on the opposite shore. He turned to watch Jacob's much slower progress.

They circled to the postern door but found that closed and locked. No amount of hammering on the door brought anyone to answer it. Drake didn't say a word, and neither did Jacob. They followed the berm to the front gate. The gates were locked; again, no one came when Drake rang the bell. This didn't surprise him, as he was now close enough to smell blood if there was any: there was no human life within the walls of Strathwick.

His belly knotted. He turned to face the village

across the bridge. There was life there, though not as much as there should have been. Drake couldn't shake the sense that this was some sort of trap, but he didn't know what else to do.

He hit Jacob on the arm, indicating for him to follow. They crossed the bridge and entered the village. All the doors were shut up tight; no animals lolled in the yards, and no glow of lanterns shone from the windows. The wind rushed past them, stirring clothes hanging on a line between two cottages until they snapped angrily.

Drake followed the scent of blood. It led him to a small cottage at the edge of the village. He knew everyone in this village. William had healed most of them at one time or another. This was Lucas MacIlroy's home. He would be in his twenties now. Drake remembered that William had healed Lucas's sister when she'd been a child and his mother a time or two, though it hadn't saved her when her husband had finally hit her hard enough that she never woke.

The last Drake had heard, MacIlroy lived here with his sister, though she was probably married now. Regardless, someone was inside the cottage.

Drake hesitated outside the door, fist raised, wondering if he should bother knocking or just barge in. He decided basic courtesy was still called for, and he knocked.

Some one moved inside. A human would not have discerned the sound, but Drake heard it clearly. No one came to the door. He sighed and pushed on the door. It was secured from the inside. He put some force behind it. The leather hinges snapped as the door swung inward.

Drake quickly scanned the dark interior and spotted a figure crouching behind a table.

"Lucas?" He peered at the young man.

Lucas did nothing at first, remaining crouched, as though he still might be mistaken for a chair or pile of peat. The whites of his impossibly wide eyes glared at Drake. After a moment he eased out from behind the table.

"Good day, my lord."

He was a tall and gangly man, broad-shouldered, but thin, his cheeks hollowed out in a way the women seemed to like. For him to stand up and say "Good day," as if this had been any other day and he hadn't just been cowering on the floor, was as bizarre as the fact that he appeared to be the only human in the village.

"What has happened, Lucas—where is your sister?"

"Ailis? Och, she's marrit. She dinna live here anymore. She marrit Ewan and they had themselves a wean."

Drake let out a short, incredulous laugh. "Aye . . . but *where is she*?"

Lucas licked his lips and swallowed. "I . . . I dinna ken."

"Where is everyone else? Are you the only one in the village? What of the keep? Where is my brother and his family?" Drake's voice rose as his questions went unanswered. Pressure built in his chest as the silence drew out.

Lucas's lips flattened and trembled, as if holding something back with great difficulty. Then he shook his head. "I know not . . . but I'm waiting to see if they come back."

Hands on hips, Drake stared at the young man. A town full of people disappeared and Lucas was just waiting for them to return? Why not look for them?

Drake scanned the room, taking in Jacob, who waited patiently by the door, and seeing nothing apparently amiss. He looked back at Lucas, his eyes narrowed. "If you are waiting for them to return, then why didn't you come to the door when I knocked? What if it was your sister?"

"I was afraid. I dinna ken why they are gone."

"Didn't you say you were waiting for everyone to return?"

Lucas' eyes shifted away, and then back. "Aye, I am . . . but ye surprised me. I didna ken what to do." He blinked rapidly, and Drake could smell his fear— the sharp scent of fresh sweat.

What frightened him, and why was he lying?

"You're not waiting for your sister or any of the villagers to return . . . but you are expecting someone, aren't you?"

Lucas shook his head too quickly. "No, I swear, my lord. I was sleeping and you startled me . . . I was having a bad dream."

Drake scowled doubtfully. "So you hid."

Lucas nodded, eyes wide and jaw tight.

Drake pointed his finger vaguely around the room. "Where were you when everyone disappeared?"

"My lord?" Lucas asked as if he didn't understand the question.

"Did you just wake up one morning and everyone was gone?"

Lucas looked as if he was about to agree with that, then thought better of it and shook his head. "No, I was hunting. When I returned everyone was gone."

"How long were you gone?"

"The day."

"So the entire village . . . and the inhabitants of the keep . . . disappeared in one day."

Lucas nodded.

"And you're just sitting here waiting for them to return?"

Another nod.

Drake rubbed his chin and paced away. He came back. "My brother saved your sister's life. He has helped everyone in this village. And you stand here and lie to me when I could be helping them?"

Lucas's face was wooden, but his eyes seemed desperate and his throat worked from swallowing.

Drake's frustration at the lad's silence was about to boil over. He took an angry step toward him. "Or am I too late already? Are they already dead? *Who was here, Lucas?* Was it Luthias? Did he kill my brother?"

He grabbed the front of Lucas's tunic and lifted the lad off his feet. Lucas's eyes widened, impressed and frightened by this show of strength.

"No—no, my lord. They are not dead. They are fine!"

Drake shook him. "How do you know this?" In his frustration, Drake's incisors came out against his will. But it was the effect he needed to put Lucas over the edge. The lad let out a cry and kicked his legs, struggling to free himself.

"Oh God! Dinna kill me! Prithee, I didna hurt no one. I couldna stop him, there was naught I could do!"

Drake dropped him. Lucas's knees buckled beneath him and he collapsed. He scooted away from Drake like a crab until he was under the table. He peered out at Drake. "You're just like him! Your teeth—you're just like him!"

"Who?" Drake asked, advancing on him. "Who am I just like?"

"Mr. Forsyth, the reverend who fashed after Lord Strathwick's daughter for years. Him—he is changit. He's a beasty—like you, with the teeth."

Drake took a deep calming breath. "I am not just like him and I vow that I will not hurt you." When Lucas still peered up at him in horrified disbelief, Drake squatted down so they were eye level. "I'm here because Luthias wants to kill my niece, me, and my family. You say they are fine. How do you know this?"

"Because I saw them leave, we all did. They left afore Luthias came. The whole castle. They packed up and left. Didna tell us where they were going, but said they would be back when it was safe. They urged everyone in the village to leave as well. Told us to take to the heather and remain hidden."

That sounded like William. He must have known something, or guessed Luthias would head here next. He hadn't told anyone so that the truth couldn't be tortured out of them. There were only a few places William would have gone, though.

Drake's suspicious gaze turned back to Lucas. "Why are you still here? Why did he spare you?"

Lucas's lips pressed together so hard that the skin around them turned white. He shook his head.

Drake tried a different tack. "Why didn't you leave as Lord Strathwick advised?"

Lucas's gaze dropped to the ground. "Me and Ailis, we've got nowhere to go."

"I thought you said she married?"

"Her husband—his folks are dead . . . and well, he didna see the point of leaving. He had animals to take care of and fields to tend. He refused to leave when he didna ken why."

Though in the end it had apparently been a stupid and deadly decision, Drake understood. This was his home. How could he just leave and forsake all the work he'd done because of a supposed threat? Drake could see himself doing the same. Which made him think of Hannah again, with an ache that pierced unexpectedly through his chest. Hannah, who saw to the quick of him and knew his impulsive, reckless nature. If she had been Ailis, she would have *made* him leave. Shamed him into it, most likely.

The bitter sweetness of it lowered his mood further, so that when he asked the next question of Lucas, his voice was unintentionally harsh.

"Did anyone else stay behind?"

Lucas's head bobbed. "About a dozen of us had nowhere to go and didn't fancy sleeping in the open— I've never fancied wolves and fairies—so we stayed behind."

Drake spread his hands wide to indicate the rest of the village. "Well? What happened to the other eleven?"

When Lucas just stared at him as if looking down the throat of a cannon, Drake added, "Are they dead?"

Lucas nodded. His mouth thinned again, and he looked around as if he thought someone other than the three of them were in the room and might overhear. He said, "Not everyone."

Drake waited, but Lucas seemed constrained from speaking. His eyes were red and watery, and his mouth was shut so tightly that Drake thought it might hurt from the pressure.

"I do not know why you hesitate, what threat has been made, but I cannot help you if I do not know what happened, or why."

Lucas nodded, swallowing tightly. "Ailis is alive." The words burst out of him like air from an inflated bladder and the whole of him sagged, as if the words had been all that had held him up. His head hung down, gaze on the floor. "He said he would kill her if I told you . . . but I think he will kill us both anyway."

Drake thought he was probably right, but maybe now Ailis stood a chance. "It's good that you told me."

Lucas shook his head. "No, he will know."

Drake put a firm hand on Lucas's shoulder and squeezed. "No, he won't. I will leave and you can say you told me nothing—or that I never even came—"

"No," Lucas said, his head rising, his prominent cheekbones flushing. "Ye dinna understand at all. H-he tortured everyone left in the village except Ailis and I, trying to force someone to reveal where Lord

Strathwick and his daughter had gone. He knew you were coming. I was to detain you somehow, keep you here until he returned. He said you would know where Lord Strathwick had gone. If you are not here . . ." Lucas fell silent, the red in his cheeks fading.

Drake finished for him. "He will kill Ailis, and if you succeed in detaining me he will set her free."

Lucas nodded.

Drake paced away, his head suddenly throbbing as he tried to devise a way to protect Lucas and Ailis and still destroy Luthias. He had an idea of where William had taken his family. One of his sisters-in-law was a *taibhsear*, a seer, and the other a necromancer. Perhaps one of them had seen something in the future. Perhaps they had seen Luthias coming to kill Deidra and had warned William to leave posthaste, or mayhap Deidra had continued to decline and William had taken her to his wife's family for help. Either way, he would seek help from the same place: the MacDonnells of Lochlaire.

He had hoped for Stephen's help, but it appeared Drake would have to face Luthias alone. A trap or ambush was the only way to win this battle. Luthias might be hard to kill, but not impossible. Drake would have one opportunity to take him by surprise. Something occurred to him, a trick he and his brother had played on each other as children. He smiled suddenly. This would be a surprise Luthias would not forget. In fact, the memory would be his last.

Chapter 18

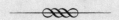

Riding day and night, Hannah traveled as fast as her horse would take her. When she wore one horse out, she slipped into a stable unseen and traded it for a fresh mount. But eventually all things tire, even blood witches, and she was forced to hobble her horse to nap in a secluded patch of heather, hidden amongst stones and brambles. While she slept, she touched minds with Luthias again. It was curious that she kept brushing up against him in her dreams. Never before had another blood witch been so present in her mind. She supposed it was due to their enhanced state. It was unusual and unnerving. Her dreams soon passed beyond Luthias to Drake. She dreamed of his arms and his mouth and his body, beside her, inside her, and she was whole again. She didn't want to wake from this dream but she did, gasping, her body aching.

And froze.

Her skin rippled with awareness. Three men stood around her, leering. A fourth squatted nearby, studying her intently. She thought of them watching her sleep and her belly curdled. There was no sense in wishing they would not see her. That only worked before a blood witch had been spotted.

She was not afraid of them. She had nothing to fear from human men, especially at night. She was irritated that they would delay her. The way they looked at her made her feel unclean. More bullies.

She sat up and gazed around at the men, wide-eyed. "Good day, sirs."

"Good day, sweeting," said the one closest to her. He had a thick black beard, bristly, with streaks of gray running through it. "What misfortune has befallen such a bonny lassy that she is hiding in the bushes?"

"A man pursued me," she said, continuing her blinking gaze of wide-eyed innocence. It was best if they believed her weak and unthreatening. "I have been running . . ." She scrambled to her feet and peered around the men, letting out a sigh of relief when she saw her horse, still hobbled several feet away.

The black-bearded man rose to his feet when she did, keeping his body between her and her horse. The other men closed in, forming a semicircle around her.

"Whot did he want wi' ye?" one of the other men asked. His front teeth were missing and he poked his tongue through the black gap.

She could hear their hearts beating, feel their blood pumping and as they looked at her, their pulses racing. They had mischief on their minds, the kind an ordinary woman might not live through. Good thing she wasn't ordinary.

Their blood was mixed. The black-bearded man's blood was passable, as was the balding one's beside him. But the other two, gap-tooth and his friend, their's was ill. Though they didn't look it, they had diseases of the blood that would kill them both in the near future.

Good riddance.

She thought of influencing the thoughts of the leader, having them desist and leave her alone, but she didn't think the other men would listen. This didn't seem a tight-knit group; it had probably been formed on a whim for some nefarious deed and would disband as soon as it was accomplished.

"I-I think he meant to harm me . . ." She looked at the four men as if just realizing they might have the same thoughts in mind. She clutched at her skirt, balling it in her fist.

" 'Tis not a safe place for a lassie to be on her own." Black-beard came forward and reached out, fingering a lock of her hair that had fallen free from the loose chignon at her neck. "Come here and I'll give you some comfort."

He reminded her of her late husband, a man she had thought of rarely. Sometimes when she slept, the memories returned in a dream, as if no time had passed—his panting breath, his thrusting, sweaty body, when she cried out from the pain he would hit her until she shut her mouth.

Those were the rare moments she cried. But the tears were tears of relief that it had only been a dream.

She hated men like him.

His hand slid from her hair to the front of her shift, fingering one of the ties that held it closed over her breasts. He pulled slowly. The gap-toothed man watched avidly, his tongue darting between the hole in his teeth like a lizard.

Hannah surprised the man by stepping forward, fangs bared and smiling. "I think I am in the mood for some amusement tonight."

He gasped and stumbled backward, crashing into the man behind him. "God's bones," he cried. "It's a monster."

The other men frowned irritably at their leader's bizarre behavior. Their eyes swung back to Hannah, the bloodshot whites glaring at her. She grabbed the front of black-beard's plaid and yanked him to his feet. "You think I am weak. That you can take what you want from a woman because she cannot fight back?" She threw him. He hit a rock and rolled to the ground. As she suspected, the rest of the men gawked for nearly a full minute, then scattered like insects from a flame.

She didn't know where they'd gone, but they had deserted their leader. Left him for her. He lay on the ground, groaning and struggling to stand.

She jerked him up. "Look at me."

"No, no, Lord, I swear, from now on—no more drinking or women or—"

"Stop your blubbering and look at me," she growled.

The man sobbed some more, his nose leaking into his beard. He opened his eyes and looked at her.

"It will be fine," she soothed. "Fash no more."

And he immediately calmed, gazing at her with blank eyes. It was almost a pity that this part was painless for a human; he deserved a little pain.

"Come closer."

When she left him, he was still alive. He would have a terrible headache and feel weak and sluggish for a sennight, but no real harm done. And Hannah felt better, though she noticed that as the night faded, some of her strength and sharp senses slipped away with the dark. They did not disappear, but they were not what they had been before.

It was inevitable, she supposed, and there was no help for it. She did not intend to start feeding on other blood witches.

When she stopped again, it was at a good-sized village. Her horse was exhausted and needed a longer rest than she could give it. She left it to wander into the village where someone would find it and keep it, then slipped into a stable near the edge of the village to steal a fresh horse.

She stood alone in the dark, dusty stable, surveying the small selection of mounts, not particularly pleased with any of them. They were all ponies or nags.

The door opened behind her.

Hannah whirled around, her heart in her throat. She had heard nothing, not a sound. She was rarely caught unawares, and now it had happened twice in a short span of time. Her mind reflexively projected *Do not see me.* But her mind could not influence the person who stood just inside the door.

Luthias Forsyth had found her. Dressed all in black breeches and doublet, just like a lowlander. He didn't even try to blend in.

He was alone.

"How did you find me?" she asked.

"It was easy. You think you are ever vigilant, but your mind drifts, and when it does, I am there."

Hannah's mind rejected this, but the proof stood before her. She had not felt him in her mind. Not once.

"So you've found me," she said with feigned boredom. "What now? I thought it was Drake you wanted, not me."

Luthias smiled. "You are right, though you will not go unpunished. For now, you are merely a means to an end."

Hannah rolled her eyes. "Revenge. Surely that is sin? It falls under pride, eh?"

"Pride? No, justice. God's justice." His lips curled slightly in disgust. "You and Drake are naught but the devil's puppets."

Hannah's heart picked up its pace at the mention of Drake. "If that is true, then how are you any different?" Before he could answer, she rushed on. "I am a waste of your time, anyway. Drake and I have parted ways. I cannot help you."

"Lover's quarrel?" he said with mocking sympathy.

"Aye—but at least my heart, dead as it is, has known love." As the words came out of her mouth, that dead heart she spoke of fluttered to life. She did love him, more than she thought possible. This new knowledge made her bold. "What love have you given or received?"

A muscle beside Luthias's eye twitched. A thin, strained smile pulled at the corners of his mouth.

"Where, pray tell, are you traveling with such haste that you have worn a horse out?"

"To the coast. To Ireland." It was as good a place as any.

Luthias raised a dubious brow. "Why would you do that?"

"I am Irish. My real name is Aedammair and it is time to return to my homeland, since Scotland has brought me nothing but misery."

He turned partway toward the door. "Well, then I won't stop you from your journey."

"Good," Hannah said as if she believed him. She returned to inspecting the horses. Her heart beat into the silence, willing him to leave, knowing he would not.

He paused and put his hand to his mouth, as if just remembering something. "But first, I'll ask you to accompany me on a short trip. It's not far out of your way and it will give you a chance to say good-bye to an old friend."

"I have no friends."

"Doubtless that is true, but you do not believe that." He was directly behind her.

She whirled, surprised, as she had heard nothing. Her arm rose instinctively to knock him across the room. He caught her arm and held it immobile between them. She could not move or pull from his grasp. His grip was painful, crushing. She gritted her teeth.

"Do not make me force you," he warned, his brows lowered. "It is distasteful to me and undignified for you."

"Then let me go."

He released her and took a single step back.

They were headed in the same direction anyway, to the same person—not that she had a choice. She sighed, as if he were merely an irritation, rather than a threat to her life, but inside she quivered with fear.

"I'll need a horse." She turned back to the horses, her heart thudding in her throat. She tried to think of what to do, how to escape, but her mind was blank.

"I have one ready for you." He pushed the stable door open and waved his hand with a gentlemanly flourish, urging her to leave.

There was no other option but surrender.

It was a strange group that Hannah traveled with. She didn't know quite what to make of them. Luthias rode in the center and kept her close behind him. He didn't appear to pay attention to her, but apparently that was an illusion. He was aware of everything. A handful of churchmen stayed close behind her and there were others, perhaps a dozen riders in all. Hannah deduced that nearly all of them were blood witches and some held against their will. She did not know if they were Drake's people. There was a girl near the front with long dark blond hair in a flat plait down her back. She turned repeatedly to steal glances at Hannah. Her heart was the only human heart in the group.

After the incident in the stable, Hannah examined her thoughts and now recognized Luthias in her head. How had she not sensed him earlier? He was in the back of her mind all of the time, listening like a moth fluttering about a lantern. She had not recognized him because there had always been something else in her head. She did not understand what exactly made a *baobhan sith* stronger and longer-lived, but it was not merely the consumption of blood. If that was all there was to it, any human could drink blood and transform themselves. The fact that a human had to die and drink the blood of another *baobhan sith* to complete the transformation was significant. In death, one left the earthly plane and went elsewhere. Hannah didn't remember her own death, but she wondered if she'd brought something with her when she'd returned to her body. Something unholy that lived inside her, keeping her body young and strong.

Hannah had wondered this before, but the thought had been so disturbing that she'd put it from her mind and reasoned that she was no different than she had been as a human. That illusion wasn't entirely true, however. Eighty years later she was very different, but that came with living long. The early years she had been the same person, but with an overriding urge to drink human blood, an urge that had waned over the years. Perhaps because Hannah had not been depraved to begin with, mayhap whatever she had brought back from the dead with her had little power over her. But in someone such as Luthias, who had already been evil, it could dig in its heels. It seemed an insane theory, and yet how did one explain holy objects causing such fear and pain?

That thing had been in Hannah's head for eighty years, so long that she had grown accustomed to ignoring it. So when Luthias had begun slinking around in her thoughts, she had paid no attention.

Now she was paying for that oversight.

When they stopped, Hannah got to see the reason for the large entourage. Luthias's blood witches were clothed in black, just like Luthias—the attire of a Protestant man of God. They forcibly removed a blood witch from the clustered group of them, then fed on him until he was dead.

Hannah's stomach soured, and she had to look away. Some of the other blood witches averted their eyes as well, their faces taut with fear. Others stared with open horror as if unable to look away. Still another wept. Hannah was kept apart from them.

During the feeding, the blond human was very vocal. She called them evil and monsters and swore that she would take them to hell with her. She mentioned "Harry" several times, saying he waited for them and would sup on the shriveled black things in their chests that substituted for hearts. She did not cry or seem distraught. She was icy cool and clearly held together by her hate. She reminded Hannah of herself.

Luthias's men did not appear to like her or her diatribe, judging by the scowls she received, but none of them touched or spoke to her. Luthias preserved the woman for some purpose, just as he preserved Hannah. Luthias seemed to think she meant enough to Drake that Drake would endanger himself for her preservation.

Her heart skipped with both fear and a sinking pleasure. Could she really mean so much to Drake?

Even if it was true, she did not wish to be Luthias's tool.

She put her hand to her chest, feeling the bulge of the rosary. Though it did not touch her skin, it felt warm through the material of her clothing.

What an odd thing she had become.

Hannah looked skyward, wondering if God even cared about the fight between good and evil when it happened between the damned.

Chapter 19

It had taken the rest of the day for Drake to locate all of the materials he needed. He and Lucas spent the evening in construction while Jacob kept watch. It was a long shot perhaps, and Drake's timing had to be perfect, but he thought it might work. He had to do something. He couldn't just sit here and wait for Luthias. His biggest challenge was to keep a wall around his mind. If Luthias had expected him to come here, surely he would also be poking around in Drake's head, trying to discover what he was doing. He wished he understood the mind connection a blood witch had with its sire. He knew it was there, felt at times that there was more than himself knocking around in his head. It was unnerving, but it remained a mystery.

Minutes stretched into hours and hours into days. They waited inside Lucas's cottage for two endless days. Lucas slept some. Drake did not. He sat by the fire, thinking about Hannah in Italy, and seeing her hair in the flames.

He missed her. Far more than he had expected to. There were so many things he missed. Talking to her, looking at her, the way she looked at him as if he was addled when he made little jests about being dead. She never laughed, yet he knew she was amused. Though her face would remain composed, her eyes would dance. He loved her eyes.

He had been wrong about her. She was not a cold, dead thing. She was a woman who'd been hurt so often and so deeply that all she had left was her pride. And she clung to it like flotsam from a shipwreck.

He would find her when this was over. He had to destroy their tormentor so he could find her in Italy and they could both be at peace. He imagined the look on her face when she realized he wasn't like any of the others and that he wasn't going anywhere.

It was that image that sustained him as he waited for the confrontation in which he was outnumbered. He had to be like Hannah this time and use strategy rather than brawn.

Lucas snored softly on the bed and Drake stood near the window at the side of the cottage when he heard them at the door. Jacob was at the next cottage a dozen feet away. He was to come in from behind once the trap was sprung.

Drake assumed his station near the door and took the dangling rope with both hands. Now that the moment was at hand, calm fell over him. There was only one definite way to kill a blood witch. Hannah had taught him that.

Beheading.

There was no knock. The door pushed open, sighing softly on its leather hinges. Lucas woke with a snort and a cough and sat up blearily. Drake's fingers tightened around the rope.

"Lucas?" a female voice said.

A small woman stepped in the door. Drake's fingers squeezed reflexively but didn't pull. He looked at the woman and thought, *Do not see me.* She did not even look his way.

A thick dark blond braid swung at her waist as she rushed across the room to her brother.

Ailis. Drake refocused on the door, glad that at least Lucas's sister was out of harm's way.

Drake's heart beat into the intervening seconds as he waited for the next person to enter. He heard the *swish* of fabric, saw the tip of a boot. He yanked.

Ailis turned as the hush of a curved blade sliced through the air. Her hand thrust out. "No!" she screamed.

Drake's heart leapt into his throat, but it was too late; the blade was loose. He saw the gleam of dark copper hair shine at him, and his breath caught hard in his chest. The blade finished its arc with a thunk.

Drake couldn't move, couldn't think. *Jesus God, he didn't. He couldn't have.* And then with a start, the air rushed back into him so hard and fast that it hurt. Luthias and Hannah were on the floor. The man who had entered behind them bore the effects of Drake's trap. His decapitated body toppled over.

Two blood witches behind them snatched at the torso, dragging it outside.

Drake put a shaking hand to the wall before he fell over. His legs were weak with relief. Hannah's hair fell over her face. She looked up at him from her crouched position on the floor, green eyes visible between wisps of copper. Even odder was the arm that covered her protectively, the arm that had clearly pulled her to safety at the last moment.

Luthias.

Hannah crouched in the dust and dirty rushes on the floor of the cottage, trying to collect her bearings. Drake stood across the room with a long piece of hemp rope in one hand and the other braced against the dirt and stone wall. His face was colorless, as if he'd seen a ghost. Ailis stared, stock-still, mouth hanging open.

Luthias came to himself much quicker. He stood and shut the door on the grotesque feeding frenzy just outside. It had been a trap. Drake had set a trap for Luthias and it had nearly worked.

But Luthias had known. Hannah had thought it odd when he had sent Ailis in first, unescorted. Odder still when he'd pushed Hannah through in front of him. And oddest, when he'd pulled her to the ground, shielding her with his arm. And though some of it was now explained—he had somehow known Drake had set this trap for him—she still could hardly believe he had protected her.

But she was a tool—and apparently a valuable one. She was useless to him without a head.

Hannah straightened, her eyes still on Drake. He had not looked away from her for even a second. His jaw was rigid, and after a moment he pushed it out and exhaled as if he'd been holding his breath.

"I thought I would find you here," Luthias said. His gaze cut to Lucas and Ailis. "You did well. You may take your sister and leave."

Ailis's head whipped around to look at her brother. "You helped him?" Her voice oozed disbelief.

Hannah had not had much opportunity to speak with Ailis on the remainder of the journey, but she had managed to exchange a few words with her and had discovered that she was from Strathwick and did not know why she was being held prisoner. She was a spirited girl, and Hannah liked her. From what she had gathered, these monstrous things—Hannah could not bring herself to call them blood witches, since they were some new abomination and she would not group herself among them—had turned her husband into a blood witch and then killed him. Ailis had not told her this. Hannah had surmised it from the foul things Ailis had yelled at Luthias and his brethren at every opportunity until they'd gagged her.

For a woman who had just been through what Ailis had, it was obvious she had a spine of steel and she was about to give her brother a taste of metal.

Lucas stared at her, mouth unhinged but completely silent.

"You're as vile as they are," she said. "I would rather die than have my life spared because you aided such . . . such . . ." She turned and locked eyes on Luthias. "*Swine.*"

Luthias opened his mouth to speak, but Ailis wasn't finished.

"Nay, I wilna insult the swine in such a manner."

"Ailis," Lucas warned, finding his voice and giving his sister a harsh look. He took her arm. "Let's just leave."

She flung his arm off. "No! He killed Harry. And then he killed him again." Her face was so red that her lips turned white at the edges. "It's unnatural for a woman to have to watch her man die twice and not be able to do a damn thing."

Lucas put his palms together beneath his chin. "Ailis, I pray you, just come with me."

"You should listen to your brother," Luthias warned, "and take your wicked unwomanly tongue out of here afore I change my mind."

Before Ailis could respond, Drake found himself. "I have succeeded then."

Luthias turned on him, his eyes gray ice. "What are you blathering about?"

Drake came closer, his lips curved into a humorless smile. "I meant to change you into that which you loathed, and I did better than I ever dreamed. Except you are not truly what you hate—you have become what you believe a witch to be. A monstrous thing that murders for no reason. No witch I ken fits that description."

Luthias glared at him, his chin high. "You do not even understand what I am, so you cannot judge." He opened the door, his gaze fixing on Ailis and Lucas. "Get out or you will share your husband's fate."

Lucas grabbed his sister's arm and dragged her from the cottage. She gave Hannah an almost apologetic look on her way out. When they were gone, two of Luthias's brethren entered and shut the door.

Hannah felt Drake's gaze on her again, and when she met it, he gave her a quizzical frown. She didn't need to see his thoughts to know what he asked with that look. What had happened? Hadn't she been going to Italy?

She managed a slight shrug.

Luthias crossed to the center of the room. He stood between the two of them. His eyes were on Drake. "You know where your brother and his family are." It was not a question.

"I have not spoken with William—"

"Let us not equivocate!" Luthias's voice was harsh. "I did not ask if you had spoken to him or if he had told you. I said that you *know*. And you do. But, being a blood witch, there is little I can do to you that would make you reveal anything. We are, I've found, astonishingly resilient to the more . . . painful forms of persuasion."

Hannah knew he'd found that out the hard way. For six months Drake had made sure Luthias was hunted and tortured. He'd managed to live through every moment.

"So," Luthias said, waving a hand in Hannah's direction, "I brought along your female thing."

Hannah looked at him with amusement. Female thing? She should be insulted, but rather she found it absurd. She felt the velvet-wrapped crucifix pressed against her heart. She had placed it in her bodice to keep it safe and hidden and had not removed it since being in Luthias's custody.

"You can watch her suffer until you decide to tell me."

"You don't already know?" Drake asked. "You knew

about the trap. Surely you know everything else that runs through my mind, because I strove to hide it."

Luthias tilted his head slightly. "Is that what you think?" His lips thinned thoughtfully. "Perhaps I shouldn't tell you, but methinks you will figure it out anyway. It's not you I can read—but Jacob. He is an empty vessel. Everything he thinks floats around in that gourd for all to see."

Drake's jaw went rigid. He was angry with himself. Hannah could tell by the way his eyes narrowed and his gaze turned inward. It wasn't Drake's fault Jacob was a fool. Even Hannah had told the man to guard his thoughts, but Drake nevertheless took responsibility for it.

Luthias held out a hand to Hannah, directing her to a chair near the fire. "Have a seat." He smiled, his teeth yellowed and sharp. "It's been awhile since I've encouraged anyone to talk."

Encouraged. A pretty word for torture. His encouragement was the reason that Stephen Ross had become a blood witch. Luthias had encouraged him to death. With a hammer.

Hannah's heart quickened, afraid. It would take more than a hammer to kill her, but there were worse things than death and Drake giving up his family to save her was one of them.

She took the seat. Drake swallowed hard, watching her. He seemed poised to act, but he looked as if he couldn't quite decide what to do.

"You have me," he said. "What do you need with the others?"

Luthias raised his brows "It was not good enough for you—why should it be for me?" He leaned forward slightly, eyes glinting like dirty ice. "Justice, aye? It must be properly served."

Drake's lips thinned and his teeth showed momentarily. He *had* hounded Luthias for a very long time. He *had* denied Luthias the escape of death. And he *had* done it all in the name of justice.

His anguished gaze cut to Hannah.

"Remember," she said, holding his gaze, "I have lived a very long time. Longer than it is right or natural for any human to live."

Drake's mouth hardened and he exhaled loudly through his nose several times, like a bull blowing in fury.

Peace, Drake, Hannah soothed him in her mind. He was about to do something reckless and foolish, and she wasn't worth it. Besides, she hadn't yet pulled out her ace—giving Luthias Maggie's gift.

Luthias looked from Hannah to Drake's forbidding expression with a smirk of indulgence. "Aye, Hannah, but it is unlikely the women in his family will whore themselves as you do."

Drake started across the room, his hands fisted and ready to fly. The other two blood witches intercepted him several feet from Luthias.

"There will be a reckoning," Drake said, straining against his captors, his face flushed with passion.

"Like the last one?" Luthias slowly bent his neck to one side, ear nearly touching his shoulder, then he bent it the other way, proving the break in his neck to be completely healed. "Give up. The Lord protects me and favors me. All that you do only makes me stronger."

There was unfortunately some truth to what Luthias said, enough truth that Hannah wondered if she was the one seeing the world skewed. Could Luthias be in the right? The blood had turned Luthias into a monster. Human life had become cattle to him and nothing was too heinous for him to do if it brought him closer to his goal. What God rewarded this?

The weight of the rosary in her bodice pressed into her heart. It seemed to burn through the velvet against her chest. *Not my God.*

Luthias circled Hannah's chair. He stopped beside her and stooped, removing a blade from his boot. He grasped Hannah by the wrist and held her hand up.

"I have many questions about what a blood witch is capable of. Questions I have not yet had time to explore. There will be time for that later. But for now, my question is this. If the only way to kill a blood witch is to behead or burn them, and they heal from all other wounds . . . what about the loss of an appendage?" Using his own fingers, he separated Hannah's little finger from her others. "If I cut this finger off, what will happen? Will it grow back?"

He brought the blade to her finger. Hannah couldn't deny that she felt a spark of fear. It wouldn't grow back. Unlike humans, who often died from loss of limbs, blood witches did not. But they didn't grow them back, either. She knew this because she had known *baobhan siths* who were missing entire arms.

The blade pierced her flesh. It stung and burned. It

was just a sliver; he did not press hard. Blood dripped down her finger, sliding down her hand to her wrist.

Drake watched, his face flushing again.

Hannah did not know how to gauge the right moment to reveal what she knew. She had not even known how she would use her knowledge, but now seemed like a good time to distract Luthias, before Drake did something stupid.

"Is this what you did to your mother?" Hannah asked, looking up at Luthias.

He jerked, slicing her finger deeper. Hannah hissed. Drake lurched forward, but the blood witches held him fast. The pain was searing, but it was over quickly.

He pulled the knife away. Though he did not step away from her or release her hand, he leaned back slightly, putting distance between them.

"What did you say?"

"I asked if you tortured your mother. Did your father give you that pleasure?"

His mouth opened. Then it closed. She had never seen him speechless. He stared down at her, thin lips parting again but no words issuing forth, his eyes so wide they bulged.

She leaned closer and gave him a look of confidence. "Did you enjoy it?"

He thrust her hand away from him as if she were a viper and stepped away.

Hannah turned in her chair to face him. "Maybe you enjoyed it a little more than was right for a lad to enjoy his mother."

"Hold!" he screamed, blade pointing at her now, as

if warding her off. "Do not speak such vileness to me. How do you know this?"

Hannah smiled. "You think you are the only one who can crawl inside a mind and look around?" She shook her head, making a clucking noise. "And the filth I saw in that mind of yours. Are you certain it is a reward God is giving you?"

"Silence!"

"Why?" She stood, emboldened by his agitation, wanting to capitalize on it before he became rational. "Why do you get to spew forth your sermons while we shut up and listen? Was that what your father did? Preach while you lapped it all up, only to bock it up as if it were your own?"

He backhanded her. Hannah brought her arm up to block him, but he still sent her reeling backward. He was so very strong. He came at her, grabbing her by the hair and flinging her against the wall.

"Silence, vile witch, silence your evil mouth."

Hannah huddled on the ground as if wounded. She reached into her bodice and pulled out the rosary. He had her by the hair again and yanked her to her feet. She managed to unwrap the rosary. When she was on her feet she held it up before him, grasping it by the velvet cloth.

"Your sister sent you a gift."

He looked at it blankly for a second, then his eyes widened. Before he uttered a sound, Hannah thrust it at his face.

He screamed and released her immediately. He tried to rush backward, to put some space between them, but Drake was there. His captors were on the floor and he was free.

Before Drake could grab Luthias, Hannah brought the rosary up at him again. Both Luthias and Drake cringed from it and even Hannah blinked rapidly, her eyes watering so that she couldn't see.

Luthias broke away and rushed to the door. Drake grabbed him, swinging him back. Luthias swung out wildly, breaking Drake's hold. He made it to the door. Hannah and Drake pursued, but when they got to the open doorway they were confronted with the rest of his blood witches.

Surrounded by his brethren, Luthias turned to face them. This would not end today. He looked as if he might rally the troops and fight, but Hannah held up the rosary again. They shrank backward.

Luthias regained some of his composure. He smoothed his hands over his graying hair. He tried to look at them, probably to give some parting remark, but he could not look at the rosary.

Finally he signaled to his blood witches, and they mounted up and left the village.

When they were out of sight, Hannah let her hand drop to her side, exhausted suddenly. She carefully wrapped the rosary back in the velvet and stuffed it in her bodice. She turned to look up at Drake. He stared down at her, his expression inscrutable.

"Well," she said, "at least now we know he hasn't gotten to your family. There's that, right?"

He nodded. His mouth was a thin line, his jaw tight. The scar stood out a stark white against his dark skin.

She tilted her head. "Are you fashed with me?"

"Why would I be angry? You saved us both."

"Because I lied to you."

He raised a brow. "Did you? I wasn't aware of your lie."

"I never meant to go to Edinburgh. I went to see Luthias's sister."

He rubbed a hand over his face. "And she told you all of that." He laughed ruefully and shook his head. "You were never in his head at all."

Hannah smiled.

"God's bones, you are a conniver." He closed his eyes, letting his head fall back with a tired moan. "What would I do without you, aye?"

Hannah dared to hope that he would never find out.

Chapter 20

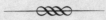

$\mathcal{D}$rake was overwhelmed by Hannah. So much so that after a day of travel he had hardly uttered a word. Words had sounded inadequate in his mind. He had wanted to hear all about Luthias's sister, and most of all, how she had devised such an idea. He would never have thought of such a thing. And if someone had offered up such a plan while strategizing, he would have dismissed it as a waste of time. She must have known that, must have known he would have fought her on it. She knew him too well.

They had only one horse. Hannah rode behind him, her arms around his waist, her head resting on his back. And they were silent. They had somehow gone beyond words, and there was much discomfort in that for Drake.

More than discomfort—bigger, stronger. Fear. Fear so profound that it circled his heart like a vise, crushing it every time he thought of losing her.

Because he loved her.

He had been struggling with that knowledge since his memory had returned. Doubting it, rejecting it, fearing it. But when he'd let that blade loose and spotted her the second before it had arced down over the doorway, his heart had died. And when he'd seen she had lived, that Luthias had preserved her, he had been overcome, unable to speak or think. No doubt Luthias had sensed that and had used it.

He couldn't bear it if he lost her. He had lost his wife; he *could not* lose Hannah. He would not allow it. But she knew him so very well. He would have to be as clever as she had been when she had convinced him that she was leaving him to continue her journey to Italy. He had not doubted her for a second. There must be no doubt in her mind.

All of these feelings made words stick in his throat. He still digested all that had happened and all that had changed. It was wonderful to have her back with him, pressed all along his back. They could have stopped and lifted another horse for her, but Drake had not wanted to. He wanted to keep her close to him for as long as he was able. She didn't complain.

They were again traveling by night and resting by day. The great strength that feeding on another blood witch had imparted was nearly gone. They were no longer a match for Luthias. He had taken Jacob, too. Probably to feed on. His strength grew while theirs dwindled.

Drake had more to lose than ever before. There was no stopping Luthias, no defeating him. There was the possibility of escape. It was something he had never considered before, to run and hide. But everything had changed.

Drake's newly formed plan included going to his family and urging them to leave Scotland, to go far away. They were no longer the most important things in his world. He had another precious thing to preserve.

They lay together in the ruins of a Highland abbey, hidden from the sun in an alcove with no roof, but still drenched in shadows. He was surprised they were able to enter it, but Hannah pointed out that it was a ruin, the ground no longer consecrated.

She slept immediately and deeply, but Drake's mind remained alert in spite of the lethargy that stole over his body. Every noise shot tension through his muscles. He was hyperaware, imagining he heard riders in the distance or Luthias whispering in his mind. He did not know if it was real.

To distract himself, he thought about the godly people who had once lived in these walls and the reason they had abandoned it. Because men like Luthias had said that what they had believed was wrong.

Drake himself did not have a strong preference one way or the other. He had been raised, as most Highland youths were, to believe in Catholicism in private but to declare oneself a Protestant outwardly. Drake had never debated with others or himself who was right. He knew there was a God and that was really all that mattered.

But the rosary changed things.

Hannah's bodice drew his gaze. He remembered when she had revealed it; it had seemed so bright that he could not see, like a sun. Luthias had acted as if a torch had been thrust in his face. Drake closed his eyes and wrapped his arm around Hannah. She didn't stir. He pulled her body closer, so that her back molded all along his front, and he sighed as exquisite desire rocked through him. He wanted her, even when he was so tired that he could barely move.

They slept that way until night came. When he woke, his arms were empty and Hannah was gone. His heart jerked and he sat up quickly—had the noises been real? Had Luthias found them? The tension drained away when he spotted her, safe.

She had built a fire about ten feet away. She sat beside it, watching him thoughtfully. Drake joined her, studying her expression, but it was cool and smooth, showing nothing of what she felt.

"Are you cold?" he asked.

She raised a brow. "Are you?"

Drake shook his head. "I do not feel cold or hot anymore."

"Either do I. But I like the light. I like to watch the flames. It helps me think."

Drake had been thinking of how he would tell her, what he would do to make this clean and quick. The only way was to hold his tongue until he had her in a place where she could not easily find him—and more importantly, where Luthias could not easily find her.

"What do you think about?" he asked.

"What to do about Luthias."

"And?" he asked, trying not to appear too eager. He would like to hear any idea she had before they parted.

"The rosary." She placed a hand on her chest, her fingers forming around the outline of the rosary hidden there. "There must be some way to use it, or some other holy object."

Drake rubbed a hand over his jaw as he considered this. "Aye, but will we not injure ourselves in the process? The rosary had the same effect on us as it did on Luthias. It might not even be possible to carry out such a plan."

Her mouth flattened and she lifted a shoulder in grudging agreement.

"And," he added, raising his palm, "Luthias knows we have it now. He may be guarding against us using it again."

Hannah stared thoughtfully into the flames. "I cannot help but remember the old story about the blood witch."

"Which one was that?"

She smiled at the fire. It was a wistful smile, full of bittersweet memories. "My mother told me." She glanced at him, smiling ruefully. "It was how she connived my sisters and I into working. She would tell us stories as we went about our tasks—often, we were so eager to hear her stories, we couldn't wait to do our chores."

Drake laughed at the image she brought to mind. It was hard to imagine Hannah as a bairn, but it delighted him to see that there had been some happiness and contentment in her life, even if it had been more than a century ago.

"I remember she told me this one when milking the cows. I had asked her about faeries, if they had stolen our milk during the night and she had said no, but if ye dinna watch yerself the blood witches'll come for ye."

Drake smiled as her voice took on an Irish lilt with an elaborate roll of her "r." She talked about herself very rarely, and when she did, it was with much probing on his part, so he was almost afraid to breathe, lest he break the spell.

"We lived near a forest and my mother filled me with stories of faeries and wolves and brownies to keep me from wandering into the wood, but the stories never worked. In fact they only served to ignite my interest. I often went into the woods looking for brownies." She laughed and covered her mouth in a girlish way that made Drake smile. "I had the idea that they would make wonderful pets. So I would go into the wood with salt to throw on birds."

Drake frowned and tilted his head in confusion. "Salt?"

"Aye, my mother told me brownies disguise themselves as birds and if you throw salt on them they revert to their natural form."

Drake laughed out loud and shook his head. "Did it work?"

Hannah rolled her eyes. "Not for lack of trying. I never did get near enough to throw salt on a bird. When I got my arse tanned for spilling her precious salt, I decided brownies were too difficult to bother with." She shook her head and sighed. "But she did finally find an effective deterrent."

Drake leaned on his hand, moving closer to her. If she noticed, she made no indication.

"The *baobhan sith* was a beautiful woman. She was part animal, with deer hooves for feet. She wore such a beautiful long flowing gown that strangers couldn't see them."

"Hooves?" Drake said, sitting up and taking her foot

that was nearest to him. She wore a cork-soled leather shoe, appropriate for travel, though he remembered that on her island she had preferred to go barefoot. "Is that what is beneath these shoes?"

She gave a halfhearted tug of her foot, but he held fast. He pulled off her shoe and tossed it aside, then tugged on her hose, dragging it off her leg. She watched him with a slight smile on her face that grew when he caressed her bare foot. It was small and soft.

"No hooves here."

She shrugged. "It's just a story."

"What else did your mother tell you about us?"

"She said the *baobhan sith* slept in a hole in the ground all day. She came out at night to hunt. She was attracted by the scent of fresh blood, so her prey was often hunters, as they tend to have fresh kills with them or blood on their clothes. She said that they usually live in groups but the one in our wood was a lone blood witch."

Drake watched and listened, all the while caressing her foot and her smooth, shapely calf. She seemed to enjoy it. He wanted to soak her in, to listen and watch her, to hold onto this moment in case it was the last sweet one he had of her.

"She said our witch was deceitful. She could change into any animal she wished to lure her prey. She might turn into a deer to lure a hunter, or a kitten to lure a child." Hannah laughed, shaking her head. "There was a time I was afraid of every animal I saw after dark, wondering if it was the *baobhan sith*." Hannah touched her teeth briefly. "She never mentioned the fangs, though. She said they had sharp claws and they would tear open their victim's flesh and drink their blood. I do not think she ever really saw one. We are rare, you know, though of late it may not seem so."

She fell silent, gazing into the fire with a slight frown.

"Anything else?" Drake prompted, reaching for her other foot and removing her shoe and stocking. She looked down at him with a quizzical brow but did not protest.

"I'm thinking . . . which is rather hard when you do that."

"It is?" He grinned and slid his hand farther up her skirts.

She caught his hand through her skirts and frowned severely. "Do you want to hear the story or not?"

He sighed but confined his wandering hands to her feet.

She looked upward for a moment to gather her thoughts. "My mother said if I saw the blood witch to guard my thoughts carefully, as she would know what was in my mind. She said the witch would perform a dance that would entrance me and I would follow her to her lair without even knowing what had happened."

She looked down at Drake and shrugged. "That's all I remember."

"Huh." Drake pondered her story while stroking her feet. "I tend to think that most of such stories are told to entertain or to frighten children, but I wonder, do you really think you had a *baobhan sith* living in your woods?"

"It certainly sounds like it. True, we have no hooves,

and I've never danced to entrance prey, but the rest of it is pretty accurate." She sat up straight so suddenly that she yanked her foot from his hands. "God's blood, I cannot believe I did not think of this before."

"What?" Drake asked, catching her excitement.

She slid off the stone so that she knelt beside him. "There was a well in the wood, a holy place. You could not drink from it if you were a liar or else it would kill you. The priest did baptisms there. My mother told me that if I ever found myself in the wood after dark with the *baobhan sith* to run there. She said to cover myself in the water from the well because then I would be vile to her and she would not touch me."

Drake caught her shoulders. "Holy water. By God, Hannah, you are remarkable."

She smiled up at him, her head tilted back, gazing up at him with complete openness, utter beauty. She had never looked at him so. Never. She was unguarded, giving him everything in her joy. He imagined her again as a child. There must have been a time when she had been like this always until the ugliness of life had forced her to armor herself. He wanted her to be like that again. Instead, he would soon crush her joy.

The reminder of what he would have to do to her in a few days deflated his excitement. When he found her again—if he lived to—her armor would be thicker than ever. This beautiful smile would be even harder to coax out of her.

It made him angry—angry at fate and himself and at Luthias for forcing him to hurt her again. But it was preferable to her death. He would not lose her. He would not go through the agony of losing a loved one and trying to pick up the shattered pieces of his life and somehow muddle on. He would not do it again, not ever.

He felt this so fiercely when he looked at her glowing smile that it must have shown on his face. Her smile faded, though the openness did not dim from her eyes. She tilted her head to study his expression.

"What is it?" she asked.

It was on the tip of his tongue to tell her that he loved her. He loved everything about her, and he hoped that she never looked at him any differently than she did at this moment. But if he did that, what he had to do would never work; she would never cooperate.

So instead of saying anything, he kissed her. She twined her arms around his neck and gave back as good as she got. It was a long kiss in which he conveyed all the things he could not say—that he didn't want to live without her.

He tumbled her backward onto the ground, needing to possess her, to make her his one last time. He pushed her skirts up and she undid his belt. Her eyes shone with pleasure and eagerness and he kissed her again, his tongue tasting her deeply. He buried himself in her and she cried out, her body gripping him beautifully, instantly, so that he groaned at the pleasure it gave him. Her legs wrapped around him. He was home here, with her, in her. He made love to her hard and fast, and she scratched him with her nails as she cried out.

When he was spent, he lay atop her, breathing hard while she stroked her hands over his hair, her fingers combing through it, her nails skimming his scalp so that he shivered. He could lie like this forever, joined with her, so close he didn't know where she ended and where he began.

"Drake?" she said, her voice soft and uncharacteristically hesitant.

"Aye?" He rubbed his chin against the silken skin of her shoulder, then kissed it.

"I am with you still because I cannot imagine being anywhere else. I love you, and however much time I have left in this life, I want to spend it with you."

These were not welcome words. Oh, his heart leapt to hear her admission, but then sank like a bitter stone. He could not acknowledge them or return them. And now, he feared that what he meant to do would wound her so deeply that even when it was over, she would not love him anymore.

It was a chance he had to take. She was a smart woman. Perhaps she would understand why he did it. After all, she had done something similar to him.

He stood, rebuckling his pants. She pushed her skirt down but did not rise from where she lay on the ground. He could feel her gaze on him, though he could not look at her. If he looked at her, she would see his duplicity.

She just stared at him, as if in shock, as if she couldn't believe that he had no response to what she had said.

He felt like a clod. He turned away from her, away from the light of the fire lest she see his shame and said, "We should leave."

Chapter 21

The next few hours of their journey were a daze for Hannah. She felt as if a horse had kicked her in the head and scrambled her brains. What had happened beside the fire?

She had lived a hundred years and had learned many things, the most important being that life was like a card game and everyone wanted the pot. It was imperative to always guard her hand. And she had been so good at it. She had elevated inscrutability to an art.

Drake had shattered that. A facade a century in the making had been destroyed by a single man. She was thankful that she rode behind him so he could not see her expression. She tried to compose her face into the look of cool composure she had mastered, but it felt foreign to her, and she became convinced, as the hours passed, that she was not making that expression at all but a wooden grimace, a horrible mask that displayed her pain for the world to see. She couldn't fathom anymore how to arrange her features into that insouciant smirk.

It terrified her.

With Drake she had finally let it all go, had thrown away the mask and given herself to him fully.

He had crushed it under his heel like an insect and walked away.

She didn't know how to show nonchalance to such a thing. She had been hurt before by a man, but she had not loved him, and she had certainly not told him anything that might have led him to think she had been. She had retained her pride in that affair even though she had died inside.

She had no pride left, no dignity. Drake had stripped them away. The worst part, she thought as she stared at the back of his head, was that he didn't care. He was oblivious to the woman silently falling to pieces behind him.

She wondered, with an insidious sliver of suspicion, if this hadn't been his plan all along. Was this his great revenge for what she had denied his wife all those years ago? He would make Hannah fall in love and then show her how it felt to lose it all.

But no, surely he was not capable of such cruelty. She leaned slightly to the side and searched his profile in the moonlight, desperate for some sign of the man who had looked down at her a few hours ago as if she were the sun and had finally given him light.

Her eyes shut as her throat thickened. She wanted to lay her forehead against his back, but she wouldn't allow herself. What poetic drivel her mind spun. *The sun.* She was as much a fool as she'd ever been. Apparently even one hundred years wasn't long enough to learn that men had no hearts and would say anything to lie between a woman's thighs.

He broke the silence abruptly. "What might be the most effective use of holy water?"

She blinked dully at the back of his head. Her mind couldn't quite grasp why he spoke to her about holy water.

When she didn't respond, he turned his head and asked again. "Holy water. What would be a way to use it against Luthias?"

He expected her to think about this now? Her mind was a quagmire. Like most men, he was oblivious to her pain. Their mission was to save his family from Luthias, and strategy was important.

She shook her head. "I know not."

He frowned, apparently expecting more.

She shrugged and averted her eyes. Looking at him caused a confusing mixture of anger and misery to bloat her heart.

"You seem fashed by something," he said. His tone conveyed curiosity. He made an observation; he didn't care. Again she felt as if she were in a bad dream. As if this was some strange nightmare-Drake.

Fashed. He thought she was merely fashed? She wanted to scream at him, but it was not in her nature. She worked hard to create a tone of blandness.

"I know not what you mean."

He frowned into the night for a moment, then shrugged and faced forward again. "I'll think of something, I suppose."

They did not speak for the rest of the night. Hannah had not paid attention to where they traveled, but now she realized they headed southwest and had been traveling in that direction for some time. They had left behind the heather and mountains and entered a forest of oak. The trees towered above them, their branches spread out like canopies. The deeper they penetrated the forest the darker it grew. It felt as if a cold wet cloth had been slapped over her face, so moist was the air. The ground was uneven with lichen and moss-covered rocks and roots thrusting up through the ground.

They dismounted to walk the horse.

"Where are we?" she asked. She walked beside the horse and Drake led it, on the opposite side of the beast.

He glanced at her over the horse's withers, his brows lowered in consternation. When he didn't answer she said, "I asked you a question."

"Aye, and I heard it. I just do not know if I should tell you."

"What?" She stopped, drawing back in surprise. Had the faeries taken off with her Drake and replaced him with this evil thing she traveled with? Since when was she not privy to their plans?

Drake stopped, too, and came around to the other side of the horse to face her. He tapped a finger to his temple. "Luthias is in your head. I cannot chance him picking that information out of your mind whilst you are unaware."

Despite the logic in his statement she was offended. "Well, I am not stupid. We are heading southwest. Your family must be at the coast. Ardnamurchan?"

Drake scowled, eyes narrowed. She must be close.

He started walking again but didn't answer. Hannah's irritation expanded. She was growing weary of his quicksilver moods. What had she done, anyway, but save his sorry arse time and again? Surely she deserved better than this.

Though the sun was hidden from them in the forest, their bodies knew when it rose. Drake said, "We'll be there tonight. We'll rest here until evening."

Hannah lay on her blanket and turned her back to him, staring at the leafy liverwort in front of her. He lay behind her and put his hand on her hip. Her teeth snapped together. His hand moved, stroking over her hip. She knew that touch. It meant his blood quickened and he wanted to lie with her. His hand felt good. It always felt good when he touched her, but she was angry. Did he really think she would lie with him after the way he had treated her? Did he think she was his whore?

In that moment her suspicions began to solidify. This was some kind of revenge. However, she wasn't sure he even knew he was doing it. Being with her this way was a betrayal of his wife. He had hated her for so long, and now he needed her and lusted after her. He couldn't have it both ways.

His hand put pressure on the front of her hip, trying to draw her back toward his body.

She wondered how she should handle this. How she would go about rejecting him and making him as miserable as she was. A smile pulled at the corners of her mouth as she waited for him to kiss her or try to roll her over. She would make sure he understood that she was not to be dandled like some village trull. She waited, increasingly impatient as time passed and he did little more than stroke her hip at intermittent intervals.

Finally his hand stopped moving altogether. And after a long while she realized it was because he was asleep. She jerked around. His hand fell away. His eyes were closed and he breathed deeply.

She was so angry that tears burned at the corners of her eyes. What was the matter with her? Tears? Over a man? She slammed her impotent fist down onto the loamy ground. She could not believe she had done it again. One hundred years old and she had fallen for another bastard.

Drake woke that evening to find Hannah curled into a ball not far from him. He tried to be quiet so as not to wake her until they were ready to leave. He had felt her confusion and anger yesterday. It had emanated off her like heat from a fire.

He was saddling the horse when she said, "Planning to sneak away while I slept?"

Her voice was emotionless. Flat. He recognized it. It was the same voice she had used when he had first came to her little island to fulfill his promise and she had released him from it. He didn't like that tone.

Playing this part was excruciating for Drake, but there was nothing else he could do. If she believed even the slightest bit that what he did was out of love for her, she would fight him on it. He didn't have time to start an argument he knew he couldn't win. She was the cleverer of the two of them. Even this idea he'd gotten from her. His family didn't have time for him to be anything less than convincing, either.

"Sneak away? Is that what you thought I was doing?" He chuckled, as if she were a foolish child. "Just letting you sleep. No sense us both being up for a one-man job."

She sat up, shaking twigs from her red hair. "I am hungry," she said. "Perhaps we should find sustenance before we set out."

"You go on. I'll wait here for you."

She still sat on the ground, her legs curled beneath her. She turned her head to stare at him. Her gaze probed him, hard. And he felt her in his head. She did not speak or convey any thoughts. No, it felt more like fingers, flipping through a book. She was looking for something.

He closed himself off, like a portcullis slamming down. He was irritated now. "What the hell was that?" He had not known she could do that to him.

"What was what?" she asked innocently, standing and working her hair into a plait. He watched her, fascinated by her slim white fingers working the auburn silk. Fine a sight as it was, it didn't make him forget her intrusion.

"You, in my head. You've never done that before." She had always respected his thoughts. Always.

And it dawned on him, like a fist to his chest. She didn't respect him anymore.

His ruse was an unmitigated success.

Funny, the victory tasted sour.

And it troubled him, how fragile her heart was—that it had taken him one night to destroy what it had taken weeks for them to build.

She tied her plait off with a piece of string she had removed from the sleeve of her gown. "I don't know what you're talking about." She tossed her braid over her shoulder. "Perhaps we can steal a horse for me. Riding behind you is uncomfortable."

It shouldn't have stung as much as it did. "We're almost there."

She placed her fists on her hips. "And we won't need horses when we get there?"

"No." He gave her an enigmatic look and mounted the horse. He brought it around to where she stood and held his arm out. Her lips flattened with disdain, but she had little choice but to take his hand and let him swing her up onto the back of the horse. She gripped the edge of the saddle rather than touch him.

Drake sighed and tapped the horse's sides.

They left the forest a few hours later and entered a morass. He left Hannah mounted and picked their way along the treacherous ground. It was difficult to tell without close inspection what was solid ground and what wasn't. The narrow strips of land were feathered with tall reeds that concealed sucking mud. And beneath the surface of the algae-covered water there was more of the treacherous sucking mud, the kind that never let go.

As he picked their way along the trail he found himself ruminating on the last person she had turned into a blood witch. The one she had mentioned briefly.

He asked, "So whatever happened to the person you healed, eh? You never did say."

She didn't answer, so he looked over his shoulder. She stared at him, her eyes icy.

He raised a brow in surprise. "That bad, aye?"

She lifted a shoulder, her mouth twisting in an uncaring smile. "He got bored."

He. Jealousy twisted Drake's gut. He faced forward. "He just left one day?"

"Aye. He was dying . . . I had taken a fancy to him when he was human, and when he grew ill . . . I decided I wasn't ready to give up his company. So I changed him . . . and became ill myself because of his dirty blood."

Drake didn't want to know what had happened next. He had long since stopped being angry about Ceara's death. But this . . . this made him ashamed he had been angry at all.

"He stayed a few days . . . out of guilt, I suppose. Then the ennui set in. Or that's what he said. He had all this power, all of this life, and he couldn't do anything but sit and nurse me. He reasoned that since I am a *baobhan sith*, I would heal whether he was there or not. So he left."

Damn.

Drake wondered where this man was now. If Drake ever happened to cross paths with him, he would not live to see the morning. He wanted to say something comforting. He wanted to apologize and tell her he understood now. That he had forgiven her a long time ago, but that seemed so small-minded and petty. There was nothing to forgive.

He couldn't say any of it. He had to be callous and cold and as ugly as her last human pet had been so that she would not want to follow him, so that she would hate him and be glad to be quit of him.

So intent was he on his thoughts that he made a misstep and his foot splashed into the water . . . and sunk. He tried to jerk it back out, but the mud sucked at it and he stumbled, his other foot joining it. The horse must have sensed Drake's panic, because it whinnied and reared back, yanking the bridle from his fingers. Drake tipped, off balance, and fell to his knees.

"Damn it!" He managed to stand, but he had sunk into the mud all the way to his knees. The horse shook its head and backed away.

"Bring her closer," Drake said. "And throw me the reins. She can drag me out."

Hannah stared down at him. It occurred to him then that perhaps his plan had not been a good one. Why would this woman help him? The last man she had played God with had left her to suffer alone. She had to sense that he was no better and would probably abandon her too.

Damn, damn, damn.

"Hannah," he said again, trying to mask his worry and keep his voice calm and reasonable.

Still no expression from her, no response. In his mind he saw her leaving and him sinking into the morass. Except he was a *baobhan sith* and he would not die. He would be stuck in it forever, the muck pouring into his mouth and eyes and ears and trapping him as surely as the tomb had.

She would not.

It flashed through his mind that had their positions been reversed, if she had treated him so poorly, he would have left her. Because that's what he did—that's what he had lived for all these years. He had thought of it as justice, but it was just base and unsavory revenge.

She tapped the horse's sides. It shook its head and reared onto its forehooves. She made a hissing sound and tapped it harder. It stepped forward, its eyes rolling. She threw the reins to Drake.

He took the leather straps in his hand and looked up at her, his throat strangely thick. She was beautiful, like some fierce Viking woman staring down at him with the slate clouds of the gathering storm hiding the night stars behind her.

"Wrap them around your wrists," she said.

He wrapped the leather tightly around one wrist and gripped the reins with both hands. He nodded to her.

She pulled back on the horse's mane. "Back."

The horse backed up, dragging Drake. It felt as if his legs were being crushed, as if the sludge that had him trapped clamped down harder, refusing to give up its prize so easily.

"Back," Hannah said, pulling.

The horse pulled harder, and, with a sucking sound, Drake was free. The horse dragged him a few feet before coming to a stop and shaking its head irritably.

Drake unraveled his hand from the reins and stood. He looked down at himself. The lower half of his body was caked with sludge that would harden and make travel uncomfortable. As soon as he found a loch he'd rinse himself off.

"I should pay better attention to where we're stepping, aye? It would have been bad had the horse stepped in it, too."

It went against everything inside him not to thank her. But clods didn't thank people. They acted as if it was their due, or they took credit for it. He didn't think for a second that she hadn't noticed, either. Her eyes narrowed and the corners of her mouth curved slightly. Her eyes were empty.

"I guess you'd better."

He turned to lead the way through the morass again. A sensation of insects crawled along his shoulders, as if the skin was puckering. He imagined it was from her eyes, ramming daggers into his back.

They emerged from the morass and rode around the edge of a loch. Drake mounted the horse again, forcing Hannah to ride behind him. She held onto the saddle. Before them spread a vast open field of wildflowers. The full moon cast a glow over the flower heads bobbing in the gentle breeze. He smelled salt. The sea. Though it was not in sight, his senses picked it up miles away.

It was still dark when they arrived at the coastal village. It was a large village, and there were villagers out even though it was the middle of the night. The village had no wall, but two men were posted at the end of the road a mile out. They sat on the ground, a lantern and a draughts board between them. They got to their feet as Hannah and Drake approached.

One man came forward and caught their horse's bridle. He wore a belted plaid with no shirt or shoes. His hair was long and red, as was his beard. "Gude e'en. 'Tis late to be out traveling."

Drake inclined his head. "Aye it is, but we're in a hurry."

"Are ye now? Whot business brings ye rushing here?"

"We're just passing through. We're here for the crossing."

The man studied him for a long moment, then peered around him at Hannah. He looked over at his companion, who gave a nod and a shrug. He released the bridle. "Go on with ye then and have a safe crossing."

When they were further down the road, Hannah asked, "Crossing? Where is your brother—on Mull?"

"I told you, I cannot tell you that."

She huffed with exasperation. "You jest? We're about to make a crossing and you will not tell me where to?"

"We're not leaving till the morning."

"What?" she said incredulously. "But we'll sleep through it!"

"Aye, but I'm doubting they're ferrying travelers across at night."

She couldn't argue with that and fell silent. He could almost hear her glowering. Drake knew how hard she slept; in fact, that was the linchpin of his plan.

Most of the village was shut up tight, but several

men walked the street, all dressed similarly to the men on the road, in plaids without shirt or shoes. They stared suspiciously but continued on their way.

When the village ran into the sea, Drake detoured and took them to where jagged slabs of black rock thrust up through the pebbly ground. He dismounted.

Hannah slid off the horse. Without a word, she wandered to the water's edge, where she stood, arms folded under her breasts, gripping her elbows.

This was one of the hardest things he had ever done, and he had done some pretty difficult things. His chest ached dully. She would hate him when she woke. She would curse his name.

But she would be alive. That knowledge renewed his resolve. She was worth preserving.

He sat down with his back against a rock and watched her. She stood motionless for nearly an hour. Her hair had slipped out of her thick plait, and the breeze picked it up to float locks of it around her shoulders.

And he imagined her doing this on some distant shore where no one knew what she was. Where maybe she could start over, live like a human woman and not be hunted. He wished for all these things for her, but he knew wishes were not enough. They never had been.

Chapter 22

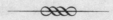

The sun rose on the horizon. A glowing pink ball, spreading rippling rainbows of orange and pink out over the water. It was beautiful. But the growing light brought with it waves of lethargy. Hannah missed the day. Over the years she had grown accustomed to being a night creature. Then the *baobhan sith* blood had given her back the day and reminded her of all she had been missing. She sat down in the sand and rested her head on her knees.

Drake was beside her. "Come. Let's get a boat."

She looked up at him. He looked tired, too, though not as exhausted as she felt. He held a hand out to her, to help her stand, but she got to her feet under her own power. She did have to let him pull her up on the back of the horse, though. She longed to rest her head against his back, but she would not give in to the urge.

Some blood witches could function quite well during the day. They had no special gifts, but they were able to stay awake and function. They seemed melancholic to most, dragging themselves through the daylight hours, but Hannah was not one of them. At least most of the time. She had forced herself to stay awake at times, but usually the siren call of sleep was too strong to resist.

This morning her head felt like ballast, wobbling around on a thin piece of wire that was about to droop under the weight at any moment. They rode along that way, Hannah swaying behind Drake, back into the village. The only thing Hannah focused on was trying to stay upright on the horse.

She was startled when Drake dismounted and his hands spanned her waist, lifting her down. He put his arm around her and she didn't protest; she didn't have the strength to.

He led her about the docks, asking the different captains where they were sailing. Most of them were off to Mull or some other island. He didn't pay for passage until a short bald man said he was headed to Ireland.

Ireland. That surprised her. Drake led her to a small rowboat, where one of the sailors rowed them out to the galleon.

She asked, "Ireland? Your family is in Ireland?"

He didn't answer, but nodded his head at the sailor.

How absurd! She couldn't believe he was still worried that Luthias was in her head. Hannah was almost positive that Luthias was not poking around her mind, but if he was, she was on her way to a ship headed for Ireland. The secret was out whether Drake said it aloud or not.

It was a good-sized galleon, a big wooden tub with multiple levels. The water lapped the sides periodically, exposing barnacle-covered wood beneath the waterline. When they reached the ship, they climbed a rope ladder to the top deck.

The top deck was half open to the elements and half enclosed, lined with several doors. Drake led her to one of them and pushed the door open. "Only the captain and his officers have their own quarters, but I bribed the captain to make two of them bunk together."

It was a tiny room, hardly more than a clothespress, and windowless. It contained a hammock with a blanket folded inside it, a little shelf with a basin and ewer fitted into it, and some hooks on the wall.

"There's only one hammock," Hannah observed with a yawn. Even if she wasn't angry with him it would be impractical and uncomfortable for the two of them to share a hammock.

"Aye." He nodded, looking around with his hands on his hips. He no longer looked tired, but he did seem a bit anxious. "You get some rest, I'll see about finding another one."

Hannah didn't argue. She needed his help to get into the hammock, but once she was in, it cradled her like a cocoon. Drake covered her and tucked the blanket around her, his fingers lingering. Tenderness now? What was it with this man's shifting moods?

She opened her eyes and frowned up at him. He gazed back at her, tight-lipped, almost regretful. The moment their eyes met, however, his face changed, wiped clean and cool. She knew that look, and it confused her. It was what she did: cleared all traces of emotion from her face, like chalk from a slate. Why would he do that?

She yawned.

He turned away. "Get some sleep. I'll be back."

She did as he said and sunk into the dark comfort of sleep. She would think about it tomorrow.

Drake waited until the ship was ready to sail. He paid the captain extra to see Hannah safe to an inn in Ireland, and then he checked to make sure she was fast asleep. She slept deeply, her breathing shallow and her dark red lashes fanned against her cheeks.

He forced himself to leave the ship with the last rowboat, then stood on the shore and watched as the ship set out to the open sea. He couldn't bear to imagine what she would think when she woke and found him gone. But she would be safe, and that was all that really mattered.

He was exhausted, but he didn't want to stay the night in this village. He returned to the beach and found a shallow, secluded cave to sleep in.

He woke at night, strong again, and set out for the MacDonnells of Lochlaire. He was fairly certain that's where his family had gone. It would be a few days' ride, but Drake did not intend to stop for sleep.

The ride was lonely without Hannah, as if some great void had been created by her absence and everything was empty and hollow. He thought of her being hungry, and he cursed himself for not making sure she had fed.

He rode on through the next day, nearly passing out in the saddle a few times. But he could not sleep; he didn't have time. Now that he was no longer strong from the *baobhan sith* blood, he found that Luthias was in his head, especially during the day. It had been so easy to wall off his thoughts before, but now he felt Luthias calling to him, trying to home in on him. He fought it, and it depleted him. Thankfully the night fell, reviving him, and he was better able to block Luthias so long as he remained vigilant. In the wee hours of the morning he rode through the mountain pass and found himself looking down over the glen of Lochlaire.

The Lochlaire MacDonnells were a powerful clan. The MacDonnells had died a few years back, and Glen Laire had passed to his grandson, Sir Philip Kilpatrick and Isobel MacDonnell's son. The MacDonnells were all witches—Isobel who lived at Lochlaire and her sisters Gillian and Rose. The MacDonell family had strong ties to many clans, so there were a number of places William could have taken Deidra to hide her. But this was the place where they always returned— the center of MacDonell power.

As his horse picked its way down the mountainside, Drake noticed a crowd gathering on the south side of the loch. Several boats left the water gate—the only way in and out of Lochlaire, as it sat on an island in the center of the loch. The castle was nearly impenetrable and strategically sound. They could see anyone who entered the glen long before they were ever close to the loch. Drake hoped that his family was here, as it would be difficult, if not impossible, for Luthias to get at them.

The entourage from the castle met him halfway across the glen. Drake recognized the leader of the group right away; Sir Philip Kilpatrick. Drake reined in and waited. There was no welcoming wave, and the severe set of Sir Philip's expression did not relent. He was a big man with hard eyes.

"Drake MacKay," Sir Philip said, halting before him and visually inspecting him to assess his potential threat. "What brings you to Lochlaire?"

"My brother."

Sir Philip's brow arched, and he exchanged a look with the enormous red-haired man beside him. The red-haired man gazed back, expressionless.

Sir Philip cocked his head quizzically. "Why would you assume he was here?"

Drake was growing tired again, and he was weary of this cycle. He needed to be better again, stronger—at least until this was over.

"Where else would William go?"

Sir Philip shrugged. "There are many places."

Drake nodded. "Aye, there are, and one of them is your stronghold, Sgor Dubh. Since you are obviously not there, something has happened to make the family rally together. And when they rally, they invariably come here."

Sir Philip's eyes narrowed. "Lady Kincreag says you died."

Drake frowned and looked down at himself. "No, I am here before you, alive."

"Aye, but she said she saw you in spirit, and as ye ken, she only sees the dead."

Sir Philip's words stirred a shadowy image in Drake's memory of when he had died, before he had awakened in a blood lust. He had seen Gillian, the Countess of Kincreag. She was the sister who spoke with the dead. There had been a dollhouse and a boy.

"Is that all Lady Kincreag told you? Did she and I speak?"

Sir Philip looked at the red-haired man again, and this time he nodded. Drake guessed they were trying to make certain he had not been compromised somehow. If he was a blood witch, who controlled him? Luthias was in his head now, telling him he couldn't hide forever, that his blood flowed in Drake's veins and it called to him. And suddenly Drake wondered if it was true. Had he become Luthias's puppet? Had he led Luthias to them without realizing it?

Sir Philip watched Drake closely and apparently saw or sensed Drake's sudden unease. "Aye, the countess said ye spoke. She also said that you had become one of them."

Drake's gaze sharpened. "One of *who*? Creatures like Stephen and Deidra, is that what you mean?"

Sir Philip shook his head. "No, I mean like that female leech ye consort with. The one who turned Luthias Forsyth from a mere parasite into a demon. And I meant Luthias as well."

Drake's fists clenched. The skin tightened around his eyes and mouth. "If you're asking me if I am here with evil intent, my answer is no. But if you're asking if I am in league with the woman who made Luthias what he is today, then aye, I am. She did it at *my* urging, not knowing anything about Luthias. And when she did it, I was as human as you are. So if you want to blame someone for that, blame me."

Sir Philip's measuring gaze turned appreciative. After a moment he nodded decisively. "Come, Drake. Your brother has been waiting for you."

Chapter 23

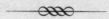

*H*annah woke to the gentle rocking and creaking of the ship. There were no windows in the tiny chamber, but Hannah's sharp eyes saw everything—the peg on the wall where Drake had hung her arisaid, the shelf with the basin and ewer.

Another thing she noticed immediately was that she was alone in the room. She swung herself out of the hammock. It was the only hammock in the room. Drake must not have been successful in finding another one. He probably slept elsewhere.

She left the cabin to find him. She knew it wasn't safe for a woman to wander a ship full of men at night, but she had nothing to fear from human men.

Her first stop was the main deck. Sailors slept curled up on straw mats. One man sat awake next to a lantern. His gaze fixed on her, but he didn't say a word. Hannah climbed down to the mid-deck. Cannons lined up on both sides of the ship. Ballast rested in gutters along both outer walls. Sailors also slept down here, as well as other paying passengers whose funds could not afford something more private. Here passengers slept in both hammocks and on straw mats. Two lanterns were lit, one at either end of the open deck; just like on the top deck, a man sat with his back against the wall. On a wooden ship no flame was ever left unmonitored.

This sailor appeared a bit more approachable than the one on the top deck. He blinked his bloodshot eyes blearily, his chin resting on his fist as he stared listlessly into the darkness.

"Good evening, sir. I am looking for my companion. He was not in our quarters when I woke, and I wonder if you've seen him."

The man sat up straight. "Whot's he look like?"

"Tall, black hair and blue eyes—" Her hand touched her cheek. "He has a scar on his jaw. He is wearing a leather jack and trews."

He shook his head. "No, but I saw a man like that afore we set sail. He didna stay on board, though. He left."

That could not have been Drake. Hannah thanked the man and continued her search. Animals and supplies were on the next level. More passengers slept down here among the goats and chickens.

The beginnings of unease made Hannah queasy. As she climbed back up to the foredeck, it occurred to her that perhaps he had bunked with one of the officers or the captain. She didn't want to disturb them at night, so she sat by the railing and gazed out at the night sea. She was in no hurry to talk to him, though her mind continued to dwell on the tender way he had tucked the blanket around her. He was such a confusing man.

She waited, lost in thoughts. And waited. The longer she waited, the tighter the tension bunched in her chest. It had been dark for some time. He would not still be asleep. Something was wrong. She stood, restless, and turned.

The captain stood a few feet behind her. She almost let out a shriek of surprise, but she managed to contain it. The captain was not human. She could not smell his blood, nor could she sense his heart flow. That surprised her. In her time as a blood witch she'd encountered another maybe once a decade, but it had happened. A sea captain was an interesting profession for one to pursue. She supposed it gave him an endless supply of human blood, captive on his ship.

She inclined her head. "Good evening, Captain."

"Good evening to you, miss. Are you finding my ship comfortable?" He was an older gentleman, completely bald, his head scarred and shiny and sun-reddened.

"I am, but I was wondering where my companion has gone off to—the man who bought us passage."

The captain's brow shot up in surprise and Hannah's belly sank like an anchor. It had been there, in the back of her mind, though she had refused to let the ugly thought press to the forefront of her mind.

"Your man . . . he left. He did not sail with the ship." He peered at her closely. "I didn't realize you didn't ken."

Hannah had no words. Her heart seemed to stop, then knock painfully at her ribs. She stared at the captain, waiting for him to slap his thigh and confess it was all a big jest, then Drake would pop out from behind the coil of rope.

Of course that did not happen.

The captain put a hand out, as if to catch her in case she fell. "Do you need to sit down, miss?"

Hannah shook her head. "Uh . . . no. I'm just going back to my quarters."

"I'll escort you."

He walked beside her the short distance to her quarters. Hannah tried to maintain composure until they reached the room. Her insides were crumbling, her shattered thoughts fighting to come together and make sense of the captain's revelation. At the door, she thanked him and tried to close the door, but he held it open with his hand.

"Your man left a message that I was to convey in private." He looked over his shoulder.

She knew it! She knew he wouldn't just abandon her. The relief that washed over her nearly made her weak. She opened the door wider. He slipped in and closed the door behind him.

"Why did he leave?" she asked, eager for his information.

The captain walked closer. "He asked me to take care of you, pretty lassie. He wanted to make sure you were safe."

He put a hand on her upper arm. She looked down at his hand, perplexed. Did he know what she was? He had to.

"Get your hand off me."

He did not remove his hand. "Come, lassie, it's not often I chance to meet another one of us, especially one so bonny. I dinna fancy the human women—I smell their blood and ken they're only good for one thing. But you . . ." He raised his hand to touch a lock of loose hair. "It's just the two of us on this ship. It'll make the time go by faster."

He grabbed her other arm and pulled her up against him. Hannah shoved him away. It was nothing like fighting off a human man—with a human, there was no fight. The captain was as strong as she was. He came back at her with a leer, as if the fight only excited him. Becoming a *baobhan sith* did not stop one from being a rapist, but for Hannah, it did stop her from being a victim.

He pushed her against the wall, tearing at her clothing. She hit him hard enough to draw blood. He kept at her, ripping her bodice. Hannah felt no fear—only anger that he thought he could just take what he wanted without her consent, and revulsion at his groping hands. He would never make such a mistake again. She threw him off again, and he slammed into the opposite wall.

His eyes narrowed and he came back for more. She could smell his blood now that it flowed outside his body. It was *baobhan sith*, forbidden. She should be repulsed, and she always had been in the past. There was still a part of her that rejected it. But the smell reminded her of the last time, and when he came at her again, she opened her arms to him. He growled with triumph as he shoved his hands under her skirt.

She sunk her fangs into his exposed neck. It was such a surprise that he cried out and didn't even fight at first. He soon gained his bearings and grabbed her arms and head, struggling to extricate her. He broke her hold on him. He reeled away from her, losing his balance because of the ship's wallowing.

He gaped at her, his hand on his bleeding neck. It was unthinkable what she had done, and he couldn't seem to digest it.

"What are you?" he breathed.

Hannah had the taste of his blood in her mouth. She took advantage of his shock to go after him. No longer interested in rape, he scrambled for the door, fumbling with the door latch as Hannah grabbed his shoulder and whirled him back around.

"Stupid man," she said, "to think I would just let you violate me." She bit at him again, and again he fought at her, but she was stronger than him now. His blood flowed through her, and she was able to restrain him.

She did not wish to kill him or even render him unable to function, so she stopped before he was insensible and backed away.

He slumped against the wall, staring at her, aghast. "What are you?" he gasped again, both hands clasped over the wound in his neck.

What was she? The question troubled her. She wiped her mouth self-consciously, then stopped herself. *He* was the one who had tried to take advantage of the situation, not she. Was she supposed to just let him? She refused to allow a man to beat her down. *That's* what she was.

She tossed her hair back over her shoulder and said, "I am what happens when men like you think you can control me."

"What do you want? Are you going to kill me?"

"Mayhap." She took the few steps it required to bring her right in front of him. He cowered. "So long as you do as I say, I will harm you no more. But if you refuse to comply, or say a word to anyone else on the ship about this incident, I *will* kill you."

He nodded quickly. "Aye, aye, what do you want?"

"Turn this ship around and take me back to Scotland."

He hesitated, his eyes darting right and left. "I . . . uh . . . I cannot do that."

Hannah grabbed his shirt and lifted him. "You're the captain. You can do whatever you want."

"T-there are schedules to be kept," he stammered, heels knocking against the wall. "Shipments that are e-expected."

"Then they will be late."

He held her gaze for a long moment, apparently seeing that she meant what she said. He nodded weakly. "Aye, aye. I'll turn her around."

She stepped away from him to let him leave. When she followed him out the door, he looked back at her, alarmed.

"What is it?" His voice had taken on a whining quality that Hannah already found annoying.

"You and I will not be separated the rest of this journey. Unlike you, I do not need sleep. Not anymore."

And she didn't. The intoxicating strength was back. Hannah felt alive and capable of anything.

The captain closed his eyes and swallowed, his Adam's apple bobbing. He nodded, then led her out of the cabin.

Drake found his niece much the way he'd left her—listless and pale, lying in bed like a stalk that would snap in the wind. Her face was small and white among the riot of black curls.

"I know what will cure her," Drake said as he stood over her bed. His eyes burned and his arms and legs were lead weights, dragging him down. He wanted to sleep, but they needed to hear this first. There was much information to impart.

"You're certain?" William asked, his mouth a flat, dubious line. Drake's brother would remember all of the failed attempts to cure Ceara. Every time Drake had heard of some magical cure, he'd been certain that *this time* it would be the real thing.

"This is different," Drake said. "This is real and Deidra will be fine."

This caused a small uproar of joy in the room, and Stephen, who sat beside his wife on the bed, took her in his arms and hugged her. She smiled weakly, but with such deep affection that Drake's heart ached with loss.

"Well, what is this cure?" Rose asked. She stood beside William. They were the only two who weren't bursting with happiness, though they did appear hopeful.

Drake rubbed a hand over his lips, wondering how much was necessary to share. "Deidra must do what was done to her. She must feed on another blood witch."

At this revelation Stephen turned to his wife and held out his wrist. "Of course. I cannot believe it never occurred to me."

Deidra pushed his hand away with a small scowl.

"No," Drake said. "It cannot be you, Stephen."

Stephen swung around, brows drawn together. "Why not? I am a blood witch. What is wrong with my blood?"

"Nothing. And it would work . . . but then you would be just as Deidra is now." Drake shook his head. "The two of you would only end up passing this illness back and forth."

"So another *baobhan sith* must die or become an invalid for Deidra to be well again?"

The question came from behind them. Drake turned. It was the earl of Kincreag. He had been leaning against the wall, in the shadows. Lurking, as Drake saw it. He blended with the shadows well. He was tall and dark—his skin, his hair, his eyes. He looked like a corsair, and rumor had it he had been fathered by one. He was a shadowy and taciturn man, not given to speaking unless what he had to say was of import. This was important.

Drake nodded, hands on hips. "That's the way it works."

Lord Kincreag stood over the bed, looking down at Deidra, black brows knit together in contemplation. "Where do you plan to get a blood witch? Until Stephen and Deidra, I have never known such a thing existed."

"Luthias," Drake said, drawing every eye in the room to him. "He is the obvious one. He did this to her. We want him dead."

Deidra's eyes widened, and she shook her head.

Everyone started talking at once. "You would bring him here?" "Look at what he did to Deidra and Stephen!" "We cannot fight him. He is a monster."

"Listen to me!" Drake raised his voice to be heard above the others. "He is coming. He will find us. You have two choices: to run or to fight." He looked at his niece, his resolve wavering. He had meant to come here, warn them, give them all of the information he had . . . and then leave. Return to Hannah and make sure she was safe. But looking at his niece, so small and weak, made him reconsider. This was *his* fault, *his* fight. Luthias was after his family as revenge on Drake. How could he abandon them?

"How do we fight him?" Deidra asked. "He is too strong. He . . . he was able to kill the animals with his bare hands."

"There is something that even Luthias fears." Drake pinned both Deidra and Stephen with a hard stare. "Something that you and I fear as well."

They gazed back at him blankly, and Drake guessed they had not yet had cause to discover that holy objects were offensive.

"Recall you the story of the *baobhan siths* and how they attacked and killed the men . . . all except one, who had a crucifix."

"I thought it was iron," Lady Kincreag said, moving beside her husband, a vertical frown line between her dark brows. "Horseshoes or some such."

Drake shrugged. "Iron doesn't bother me. But a rosary does."

Deidra looked at Stephen, aghast. "Is this true? Why is this?"

Stephen didn't seem nearly as concerned as his wife. He placed an absent hand over hers and asked, "What does this mean to us?"

"It means that we have a weapon with which to

fight him." Drake paced to keep his body awake. His mind was alert and racing in spite of the lethargy in his limbs. "Hannah suggested holy water."

"Throw it on him?" Sir Philip asked.

Drake nodded. "Aye, that's good. But also, we'll douse the humans in it and give them a crucifix, to keep you safe."

"Where will we get all of this holy water?" Isobel asked, speaking for the first time. She had been busy with a wean, but now she passed him off to her husband, Sir Philip, who settled the tiny babe in the crook of his arm.

Drake realized suddenly that he would never have one of those. He had lost his chance for children, and so had Hannah. When Ceara had been alive he had very much wanted children, and though that wish had not gone away entirely, he found it did not matter so much, as long as he and Hannah were together.

"I cannot stay," he said abruptly. They all stared back at him with confusion. "I sent Hannah to safety, but Luthias has found her before. I fear there is no safe place."

"He cannot be in two places at the same time," William said. "Who does he want? Hannah or us?"

"Both." He began pacing again, sick from the need to expose everything. "It's me. This is his revenge for the vengeful way I punished him. It is not enough to kill me. I must suffer as he did. He wants to kill everything I love. All of you. Hannah." His pacing stopped. "You have all the information I have. I can do no more here."

"What about the holy water?" Isobel asked again. "Where do we get such a large amount?"

"Do you not have a priest hidden around here somewhere?"

"There hasn't been one since Father died," Lady Kincreag said. "There is a friar who travels about, pretending to be a Protestant pastor . . . but we never know when he will be here."

Damnit. And like that, Drake and Hannah's plan was useless.

"We do have holy objects," Philip said and motioned to someone. The large red-bearded man stepped forward. "Fergus, gather up all of Alan's old papist idolatry."

"Good." Drake nodded and paced faster. "Send someone into the village and instruct them how to protect themselves—surely they all have a rosary hidden away—then locate a priest to bless some water." He crossed to the bed and sat at his niece's side. She gazed up at him sadly.

Drake remembered what Hannah had done for Jacob before she had left them back at Creaghaven. It had not made her ill, and Jacob had been much improved. Drake reached into his boot and pulled out his dag. He slashed it across his wrist.

Deidra recoiled and Stephen said, his voice urgent, "What are you doing?"

"Drink." He held his wrist to Deidra's face.

She twisted her head away.

William was beside him, trying to pull Drake's arm away. "Stop it, Drake. You told us that will make you ill."

"Just a wee bit will make her feel better—get her

out of this bed at least—and not cause me any harm."

"Then let me," Stephen said, brandishing his own knife.

"Aye, you can—but just a bit. With a bit from both of us, she should improve."

Deidra shook her head, pulling the covers up over her mouth. "I cannot, Uncle."

Stephen yanked the sheet down and took her face between his palms. "You must. I need you for this. *We* need you."

She stared into his eyes, then nodded. Stephen sat back and Drake offered his wrist again. This time Deidra took it, hesitantly, and sucked. Drake was surprised by her control. After less than a minute she turned her head away, swiping the back of her hand across her mouth. "There."

Drake stood. Rose appeared beside him with a fresh white bandage, which she wrapped around his wrist.

Stephen promptly sliced his own wrist and pressed it to Deidra's mouth. She looked like she wanted to fight him, but again, she sucked briefly and turned her face away.

She seemed to slowly become conscious of everyone watching her, waiting. Drake saw the change, saw the slight color bloom in her cheeks, the dullness fade from her large blue eyes.

"I feel better," she said and seemed surprised. She pushed the covers back and stood. She immediately plopped back down on the bed and closed her eyes. "Mayhap not."

"Take it slow," Drake said. "It will take a bit. But

you will feel better." He turned to his brother. "Now I must go."

William followed him out the door. "How will you know where she is?" he asked when the door was shut behind them.

"I sent her to Ireland. I'll start there."

"Are you sure she stayed? I thought she had plans to go elsewhere—to Italy."

Drake shrugged. "I'll find her. If Luthias is after her, I cannot leave her to face him alone." His brother's brow furrowed with concern. Drake grinned and punched him in the shoulder. "Don't worry. If I pass a priest, I'll send him your way."

William shook his head and sighed. They were walking down to the water gate when a man-at-arms burst through the doors of the great hall and rushed past them, straight to the great chamber where Sir Philip and Deidra were.

William and Drake exchanged a look. Drake's belly sank. He wanted to leave now, to get in a boat and row before he heard the news. But he could not—he had to know.

They returned to the chamber. The man stood before Sir Philip, gesturing wildly. Sir Philip nodded and sent him away, then gave Drake a sour look and asked, "I dinna suppose you found a priest out there?"

"What is it?" Drake asked, dread twisting his gut tight. "Who's here?"

Sir Philip strode past them, his face set with purpose. "Luthias Forsyth. Who else?"

Chapter 24

Hannah loved the day power. Loved to be in the sunlight, wide awake and full of energy. Mostly she loved how human it made her feel. She had left the ship and the captain behind yesterday and had covered more ground than would have been possible had she been a mere blood witch. There must be a name for what she was now. She was better. She was *more*.

She had thought a great deal on that short sail back to Scotland. She had been angry that Drake had abandoned her. She had been hurt by his cruelty and rejection. Until she had thought about it.

His abandonment of her made little sense. He needed her. Even if he didn't care for her the way she cared for him, he would be a fool to send her away. When she had questioned the captain further, he had admitted that Drake had given him extra coin to see her someplace safe.

That was what was true.

He'd seen her to safety and had gone into this alone. He had done exactly what she had done to him at Creaghaven, because he'd known that if he had told her that he wanted to take her someplace safe, away from the coming battle, she would have scoffed at him and reminded him that he needed her.

His need for her aid had been overridden by something else.

Love?

Hannah dared to hope. The Drake of their last days together had not been *her* Drake. It had not even been the same Drake who had been angry with her over his wife's death. It had been a facade, and she had fallen for it. Temporarily.

But now she rode. She did not know where Drake had gone. But she knew where Luthias was headed, and that's who she followed.

She had found, after drinking the captain's blood, that she could summon Luthias up at will. It should have been like this all along, as she was his sire, but he had been far stronger than she had been, and she had not recognized his presence. Once alerted, she was quickly catching on. To find Drake, she needed only to find Luthias, and that she could do.

She would need supplies. She stopped at an old kirk and stood a dozen feet away. Fear and revulsion billowed up inside of her, and it angered her. *She* was not afraid of this kirk. She had done evil things, but she had not done them until this thing had started sharing her body. *It* feared the kirk. She was tired of being ruled by its fear and hungers. For eighty years, it had dictated her life. Today she would take back some control.

She strode to the kirk, trying to feel the confidence that she displayed outwardly, but her heart fluttered madly in her chest. A tall stone cross stood outside the church, the knotwork carvings faded by time and the elements. Her skin crawled knowing it was there. She could not look directly at it, though she wanted to. There would be time for that later.

She stopped just outside the open kirk door.

"Hello?" she called.

Her eyes could not penetrate the shadows inside. No candles lit the interior, yet she sensed a heartbeat and blood flowing. Someone was here.

She glared at the slate floor on the other side of the threshold. She wanted to step in, to place her foot on the floor, but her legs wouldn't work. She was rooted to the spot just outside the door. She wanted to go inside. She *needed* to go inside. She needed to know that she wasn't an evil thing.

"Hello?" she called out helplessly, scanning the interior, or at least what she could see from the doorway. Normally her vision was sharp in the darkness, but she could discern nothing through the gloom inside the kirk.

She bit her lip, trying to force her leg over the threshold, but it felt like there was a barrier that she couldn't pass through.

"Come in, child," a voice said from within the kirk.

Hannah gasped. The voice came from a few feet away, yet she saw nothing.

"Where are you?" she asked. "Why do you stay in the dark?"

There was a long pause, and she wondered if he had gone away. Then the voice said, "I am not in the dark. There are candles lit all around me."

Hannah's heart slowed to a frightening, heavy

throb. Candles were lit, but all was dark to her. Her eyes burned. She was damned. God did not want her in His holy place. He would not give her aid. Her legs trembled and gave way. She fell to her knees, overcome by what she had become.

She had stayed away from kirks since she had been transformed into a *baobhan sith.* She hadn't really known why at first; it had been instinctual—probably the demon in her. But as the decades had passed, she had realized they always seemed dark, in the shadows. They never had before: It was *her, she* was the one filled with darkness, kept outside of the light.

She clasped her hands beneath her chin and stared into the darkness of the kirk. "I have done some evil things that I am sorry for. But Lord, do not forsake me; it is not myself I come for, but others who need your help, others more deserving."

Her pleas were answered with silence. Not even the voice from within responded to her prayer. Her head fell forward, her chin hitting her chest.

A gentle hand touched the crown of her head. Hannah looked up. A man in a rough dun robe stood in the doorway. His head was completely bald and shiny, ruddy from the sun. He had a full black beard, and pale lines crinkled his eyes from smiling in the sun.

And he touched her. She had not been touched by any holy man except Luthias, and she guessed that did not count, infested as he was with demons.

"Why can you not come inside?" the priest asked.

"There is a demon inside me that blinds me and holds me back."

His brows drew together with concern. "Then we shall cast the demon out."

Hannah shook her head. "I am afraid if it is gone, I will die."

The priest gazed down at her sadly. "Is your life not death now, sharing it with a demon?"

Hannah dropped her gaze. She didn't know. It used to be so, but now she felt alive again when she was with Drake. She did not want to die, and she knew in her soul that without the other, she could not exist.

"I want to master it," she said, unable to look at him. "I do not want to be ruled by it."

He removed his hand from her head and held it out to her where she could see it. "Take my hand and stand up."

Hannah hesitated, afraid to touch him. But his hand on her head had not caused her any pain. She placed her hand in his and let him raise her to her feet.

"How long has it been since your last confession?"

Hannah didn't want to tell him. That thing inside her didn't want her to speak, so she blurted it out. "It has been more than a lifetime."

He stared at her with probing blue eyes, as if searching for the truth.

She said, impulsively, "Shrive me, Father."

He nodded slowly and brought his hand up between them. She turned her face away. Her entire body trembled in anticipation. Her hand rose and made the sign of the cross over her head and heart. "In the name of the Father, and of the Son, and of the Holy Spirit. Bless me, Father, for I have sinned." That was such an understatement that she hesitated, unable to give voice to the decades of sin bubbling up through her, desperate for an outlet.

As if sensing that she was overwhelmed, he said, "Peace, child. He does not expect you to remember all of them. Confess what you remember. He trusts that you regret the rest."

The tightness in her chest eased and she said, "I am guilty of pride . . . I have turned those in need away to protect myself."

The priest was silent for a moment, then said, "I think that might be envy, actually. Did you gain pleasure by turning those in need away?"

Hannah shook her head vigorously. "No, Father."

"Would giving aid have caused you harm?"

Hannah hesitated. "Aye."

"Then that is not such a great sin."

Hannah's eyes closed. A weight lifted from her shoulders. But there was more.

"I have lied . . . many times over. I could not possibly remember them all."

"Are you truly sorry for these untruths?"

Hannah again hesitated. She could not remember all of the ways she had equivocated over the years, but the most recent ones included her lie to Drake in order to investigate Luthias's sister, and to the men who had planned to rape a woman alone and had instead met with a monster.

Hannah's head hung low, the weight returning. "Of the most recent ones . . . no."

He made a thoughtful noise, then said, "Go on."

"I have lain with a man who is not my husband."

"Do you have a husband?"

"Nay, he is many years dead."

"Does this man have a wife?"

Hannah shook her head, then remembered his hand up between them, hiding her face from him, and said, "No."

"What else?"

Hannah knew she should have said her worst offenses first, but the worst, in truth, had happened so long ago that it seemed another person had done it. But this was confession, and she was determined to do it properly.

"I have killed."

The priest's hand held up between them faltered, but steadied. "Indeed. How many people have you killed?"

"One. A man."

"And was your life in danger had you done otherwise?"

Hannah's head sank further. "Nay . . . not at the time."

"So this man had threatened your life previously?"

Hannah swallowed hard and nodded. "Aye . . . many times. It was an act of revenge, and I am heartily sorry for this sin of my past life." And she was. So many years later that Gareth would have been ashes anyway. She wished she had not revenged herself on him all those years ago, but she could not take it back, could not do it over.

"Is that all?" the priest asked.

"No, Father . . . I am a *baobhan sith*, and blood is my sustenance."

This time the priest's hand dropped, and he gaped at her. Her brows rose apologetically.

He raised his hand between them quickly. "Do you lie to me now, child?" His voice shook slightly.

"No, Father, I would that I did. Do not fear me. I do not feed on human blood . . . often . . . and I do not kill humans."

He was silent for so long that Hannah turned her head toward the priest's hand. "Father? Do you think I lie?"

"No . . . no . . . My whole life I have never seen a *baobhan sith*, and now, in the past two days, you are the second."

Hannah grabbed the priest's wrist, pulling his hand down so she could see his face. "What?"

"Wait!" He twisted his arm out of her hand. "Let us finish first."

Impatient, Hannah turned her head away and quickly said the words—they rose from her memory, last spoken eighty years ago, "Oh my God, I am heartily sorry for having offended You and I detest all my sins, because I dread the loss of heaven and the pains of hell. But most of all because I have offended You, my God, who are all good and deserving of all my love. I firmly resolve with the help of Your grace, to confess my sins, to do penance, and to amend my life. Amen."

The priest dropped his hand and looked at her reproachfully for rushing through it. "Your penance is to give aid to three people in need, no matter the inconvenience or hurt to you—so long as it is not mortal."

Hannah nodded eagerly. "Aye, Father."

"And you must marry this man before you lie with him again."

Hannah didn't nod so eagerly this time, but she said, "Aye, Father."

He raised his brows expectantly, and Hannah dropped to her knees as he blessed her and said the prayer of absolution over her.

When she stood, she asked, "Who was the other blood witch you have seen?"

He rubbed a hand over his eyes, suddenly old and weary. "It was a minister . . . or some perversion of one." He gave her a sheepish look. "We all equivocate, child, and as a papist in Scotland, I must do it often. But this man . . . he knew . . . and he wanted what you have forsaken."

"Your blood?" Hannah asked.

"Aye, and like you, he could not enter the kirk, so I stayed there until he left . . . which was a very long time."

"He is why I am here. He is going to murder an entire clan—to drink their blood until they are dead."

The priest blanched.

"I am here to stop him. I need holy water, Father. Can you give me some?"

The priest nodded. "Of course I can, but will the water not bring harm to you?"

"Aye . . . well, I know not about the water, but other holy objects have hurt me . . . burned me."

The priest eyed her thoughtfully and said, "Let us test it."

Hannah's breath snagged, afraid, but the priest either didn't notice or didn't care. He disappeared inside the kirk and returned a few minutes later with a small wooden bowl filled with water. He brought it to Hannah.

She did not touch it but stared at it apprehensively. It did not affect her in the same way that the crucifix and the kirk did. It looked like water. Innocuous.

Her hands curled into fists. No sense drawing this out. She quickly dipped a finger in the water. It did not take long for the pain to shoot through her. Her finger was on fire, burning. She yanked it out, gasping and cradling her hand to her chest. She tried not to whimper.

The priest was beside her with his hand on her shoulder. "What is it? What happened?"

"It burned my finger."

"Let me see."

She wanted to stick it in her mouth and suck on it, but she held her finger out for his inspection. He set the bowl aside and took her hand by the wrist. He turned it right and left. Hannah quickly realized that her finger didn't hurt anymore and peered with him.

Her finger was red, as from a scald, but as they both watched, the redness faded until the finger was entirely unmarred. A blood witch healed quickly, but not that quickly. She pulled her hand away from him and inspected it closer. Not a mark or even redness. She looked at the priest in amazement.

He raised his brows with a slight bemused smile.

"How can it be?" she gasped.

The priest shook his head slowly. "I know not, but the Lord favors your cause, methinks. This is a sign."

Hannah smiled back, wondering if she had finally found a way to end Luthias's reign of hell.

Chapter 25

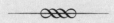

In theory, Lochlaire was impenetrable. But this theory depended heavily on whether or not the attackers were human. Their current foe was not. The sun streamed through waterlogged slate clouds as Drake watched Luthias and his men overrun the small village of Lochlaire. Drake was tired, his limbs heavy and his head thick. Sir Philip's men had not had the opportunity to warn the villagers, and none of them had any defense to mount against the intruders.

They had an excellent view of everything from the castle walls. Many of the villagers escaped to the wooded mountains that surrounded the northern side of the glen; others were not so lucky. Luthias, however, did not seem intent on murder. He wanted to get into Lochlaire. Sir Philip was not stupid; he had all of the boats brought into Lochlaire so that no one could come to the castle unless they were rowed over by castle inhabitants. But there were boats hidden in the village, because every scenario could not be anticipated.

Luthias knew they watched and even waved at them once. Drake ground his teeth. He couldn't wait to kill him.

Deidra had improved dramatically from the small amount of blood Drake and Stephen had shared with her. She stood beside Drake, staring solemnly down at Luthias.

"I hate him with everything inside of me. I cannot help myself. He is the scourge of all our happiness. God cannot love him."

Deidra had suffered more than anyone at Luthias's hands, and now Drake had brought him back into her life. With a sinking sickness in his belly, he watched as Luthias exited one of the larger cottages, followed by two of his blood witches dragging a boat.

Sir Philip swore and paced away from the embrasure where he had been watching, but he immediately paced back and stared downward, his hand braced against the wall, his face granite.

"At least he did not find all of them," he said under his breath.

"There are more?" Drake asked.

"Two more." He nodded with his chin. "And the dock there—it can be used as a raft. Those rain poles double as oars to push the raft."

This was Drake's fault. Every bit of it. If only he had left Luthias dead, none of this would be happening. If anyone should go down there and sacrifice themselves, it should be Drake. Unfortunately, Drake was the one person Luthias wanted alive. At least until he was finished killing everyone Drake cared about.

Luthias and his men found the two other boats, but it was still not enough to carry all of his men over. Sir Philip had a lot of men, too, and though a blood witch was strong—and these were exceptionally strong—they were not invincible. Without a head, a blood witch would die. Their greater number had to give them some advantage. A group of men-at-arms with enough determined hacking could surely cut one blood witch down. But there was more than one.

In fact, Luthias had managed to gather a dozen of them.

"Archers, ready," Sir Philip instructed. The archers all along the wall notched their arrows. When Luthias was within strike distance, they let loose a blanket of arrows. The men in the boats held up their arms and ducked their heads to shield themselves. The arrows all bounced off them, leaving them unscathed.

"They must be wearing some kind of mail beneath their clothing," Drake said. He left the wall, climbing down the ladder and descending into the tunnels that led to the water entrance. Sir Philip and the other men were close behind.

The women had been hidden in a secret room and given all of the holy items. None of the men believed they would stay there, however. Some had suggested pushing a bed or clothespress on top of the trapdoor, but there were too many problems with that idea: If all the men were killed, the women would be trapped with no way out. But more likely, Luthias would see the oddly placed piece of furniture and sense the women's blood. The best they could do was leave a few men outside the door to keep the women from interfering.

The water gate was locked down. Despite the way Luthias and his blood witches deflected the arrows, the

gate should still keep them out. None of Sir Philip's
men were entirely convinced it would, however.

They waited, swords drawn, muscles tensed and
ready. The slice of oars through water was heard, but
there was no other sound. The blood witches were
completely silent. Drake's chest drew tight, anticipation making him hyperaware of every single sound.

The bow of a boat hit the metal of the portcullis.
Drake could see them between the bars of the gate.
Luthias came to the fore and grabbed the bars in both
hands, gazing at them between the bars.

"You really thought this would keep us out?"

Lord Kincreag and Sir Philip shot Drake an alarmed
look. Drake realized that until this moment, they had
not truly understood how vulnerable they were. Drake
glanced at Stephen, and their eyes locked with the
grim reality of it. He knew. Only he could.

The metal bars of the water gate were crosshatch.
Luthias gestured to the other two boats and they
rowed right up to the gate on either side of Luthias.
He and a blood witch from each boat came forward to
grip the horizontal bars just below their waists.

As they lifted, cords of muscle stood out on their
necks with the effort. The gate creaked in protest. The
creaking turned to a groan, and the groan turned to a
scream of metal. A sharp crack like a gunshot signaled
the chains that operated the gate snapping. The gate rose.

Sir Philip no longer stood with his sword at the
ready. It had dropped to his side; in disbelief, he stared
at Luthias holding up the portcullis. The two boats
with Luthias's men passed beneath the open gate while

he held it up. Then support of the gate was passed back as Luthias's vessel rowed beneath it. When his boat just cleared it, the gate was released and crashed down into the water.

Drake and the men on the water dock all exchanged a look of unrest.

They were trapped.

The first thing that Hannah noticed when she and the priest arrived at Lochlaire was that there was no way to surprise Luthias. Their approach could be seen clearly from the castle walls, but oddly, no one came to meet them. It wasn't until they reached the loch and the stable beside it that they encountered any opposition.

Two of Luthias's blood witches lurked outside the stable. They rushed at Hannah and the priest.

"Your rosary, Father," Hannah said, reaching into her bodice and removing hers. She believed that it would not hurt her, that for some reason God had favored her in this fight. Nevertheless she still *felt* the pain, so she held the rosary as she had before, with the velvet wrapped around her hand. She squinted through the blinding light.

The blood witches drew back, shielding their eyes. Hannah and the priest raced to the dock, but there were no boats. They searched the shore of the loch for some means to get them to Lochlaire. There was nothing.

Hannah looked to the village. Boats were probably hidden there. The village had appeared deserted when they'd arrived, and she had felt very little human life radiating from it. But now she not only felt but also saw a human. He stood on the opposite shore. The priest saw him the very moment Hannah did, and said, "Look!"

The man looked from the two blood witches to Hannah and the priest. He cupped his hands around his mouth and yelled, "The dock—it's a raft."

The blood witches took off after him. The man ran, disappearing among the cottages. Hannah hoped he made it to safety.

The priest dropped to his knees at the edge of the dock. The wood hooked onto spikes driven into the dirt and covered by weeds. Hannah grabbed one of the rain poles stuck into the water beside the dock for measuring the water level and pulled it up out of the ground. She beat at the wood with it until it splintered and broke off the hooks. She did the same thing to the other side.

The blood witches returned alone. The priest thrust his rosary out. He pulled another large cross from his robes. "Stay away, foul demons!"

Hannah pushed them off, using the rain pole. There was another one a dozen feet away. She pushed the raft toward it. They were far enough from shore to stow their idolatry. The moment they did, the blood witches began shedding their clothing.

"They're going to swim," Hannah said.

The priest set his stick down and pulled out a small pouch. He sprinkled salt into his palm, then tossed it into the water. He held his hands out over the water. "I exorcise thee in the name of God the Father almighty, and in the name of Jesus Christ His Son, our Lord, and in the power of the Holy Ghost, that you may be able to put to flight all the power of the enemy."

He was making the entire loch holy. Hannah looked around her in creeping horror. Despite the priest's demonstration back at the kirk, her skin still twitched at the sight of all that holy water stretching out around her. Dipping a finger in holy water was one thing, but falling in? She didn't want to test it.

The priest went on shouting his blessing. The blood witches stopped undressing and backed away from the water.

The priest dropped his arms and head suddenly. A sheen of sweat coated his bald head. He grabbed the other pole, dunked it into the water, and pushed, helping Hannah move the raft along faster.

"So this entire loch is holy water?" Hannah asked.

"More or less," the priest replied.

"More or less . . . ?"

He lifted a shoulder in a halfhearted shrug. "When water is made holy, the water should be pure, which this loch is not. And for a body of water this size I really should have used more salt. But it doesn't matter."

Hannah gaped at him. "What do you mean? Of course it matters. If it isn't holy, it will never work."

The priest shook his head and chuckled softly as he thrust his pole along the bottom of the loch. "Do ye not understand, child? God favors us. It is holy enough for our purposes." He gestured to the shore, where indeed the blood witches now gave the loch wide berth.

Hannah hoped it was holy enough. They reached

the water gate. Hannah peered through the bars. The stone water dock was devoid of human life. But there was plenty of death. Several bodies littered the dock.

"He's inside," Hannah whispered. She did not know how to get through the portcullis, nor did she know of another way inside. She gripped the bars and stared through, her muscles tense, heart racing. There must be another way in. There had to be.

"We'll have to go under," the priest said, throwing off his robe. He wore a thin linen shirt and trews beneath.

"Swim?" Hannah stared at the water, heart hitching. "You blessed the water." Her voice raised an octave.

The priest gave her a reproachful look. "Remember the bowl? The Lord protects you."

On some level Hannah understood that, but more of her, the part that ruled her, believed the water would boil her alive. She had heard of other blood witches being drowned in holy water. It was not a pleasant death. She hadn't perspired in eighty years, but her palms were now clammy.

"Hannah."

She looked at the priest. He waited for her solemnly. She swallowed her fear, or at least stuffed it down. *The Lord protected her*. She didn't really believe that. Why would the Lord protect her? She was a dead thing, evil. But it was the only way in, and giving up was not an option.

She unhooked her bodice and untied her kirtle, removing them both. She handed the priest her velvet-covered rosary. "Hold this for me until we're on the other side."

He raised a reproachful brow but took it from her and dropped it over his neck so that it tinked against his.

She tucked her shift up between her legs and tied it so that she was bare from the knees down. She took a deep, shoulder-shrugging breath. "I'm ready."

The priest put a hand on her shoulder. "You *are* ready."

She nodded, his words giving her an extra measure of courage.

"I'll go first," he said, walking to the edge of the raft. "You're the one with all the power. Don't leave me down there alone."

He was gone before she could reply. She stared at the rippling waves that shuddered outward from the place where he had dove.

This was it. She tried to see it as water, nothing more. *Just water. Just water. Just water.*

She took a deep breath, closed her eyes, and forced her fear-rigid muscles to dive in.

It burned. This time it was her whole body, and the skin was searing off. She tried to scream. Water flowed into her mouth and nose. Her flesh burned off her bones; she boiled. The thing inside her screamed long and loud and constant, so that Hannah couldn't think.

She floated upward, limp. She could see the gate below her. The priest gripped the bars and gazed up at her, eyes wide with alarm. She had brought him with her so that everyone she cared about wouldn't die, so Luthias wouldn't win.

She was still alive. Her skin burned, but she was not

dead. The thing in her squealed and writhed, but it grew tired.

Hannah kicked out with her feet and cut through the water with her arms, moving rapidly to the gate. Something had happened to the gate. The jagged spikes on the bottom had come down to rest against the rocky bottom of the loch. But the bottom of the loch was deeper than the gate reached, so boulders had been piled into a wall.

Now the wall was crumbling. The spikes along the bottom had pierced several boulders, splitting them.

Hannah pulled at the boulders, making a hole for them to swim through. The priest had resurfaced for air but was beside her again. When Hannah had moved enough boulders for him to slip through, she gestured for him to go. He had just wiggled through the hole when the stones beneath the gate shifted and the gate slipped. Hannah grabbed it, bracing her feet against the shifting boulders.

The priest twisted and made it through to the other side, but not before a plume of red bloomed around his leg. Hannah's heart seized. Something was wrong with the gate. The chains that lifted and lowered it must have snapped. The metal shrieked inhumanly as it tipped back, toward Hannah. If the ground below her feet had been stable, she could have stopped it, but the boulders continued to fall and crumble beneath her. All Hannah could think about was being trapped beneath this metal gate for eternity.

She had to get through before it fell on her. She heaved upward and shot beneath it, feet first. Boulders tumbled down with her, beating her back and shoulders. A large one came down on her back. Though she twisted, it sunk her to the bottom, where it was joined by more, pummeling her arms and back and head.

When the chaos came to an end, she found herself on her back, staring upward into a murk of water filled with dirt and sediment. She was fairly sure the gate was not on top of her, but her legs were trapped. She tried to move them, and the rocks shifted.

She was not human. This would not keep her down. She pushed at the boulders until they rolled off and she was able to pull her leg free.

She was kicking the last of it off when the priest appeared, crucifixes floating up around his face. He grabbed smaller rocks, moving them aside.

He took her hand, and together they swam upward. Hannah was stronger and faster and dragged him until they broke the surface, gasping for air. Hannah did not need to breathe, but she did anyway. It was just the way the body worked. Her body began to relax as her chest deflated.

They climbed the stone stairs leading out of the water to the dock. The priest had a gash on his leg. Hannah smelled the blood seeping from it.

"Can you walk?" she asked.

"Aye, I am fine."

Hannah nodded and started back up the stairs.

"Wait," the priest said, his voice hushed and urgent.

Hannah turned.

"You are whole, child. Your skin is as smooth as the day you were born. You did not burn up—in fact, you do not even seem to be in pain."

Hannah blinked and sagged back against the stone wall behind her. He was right. When she had begun fighting with the gate, she had forgotten. Even the demon that had screamed in her mind had been silenced by the urgency.

"This loch has been your baptismal. God has forgiven your sins."

The leaden heaviness that had lain across Hannah's heart lifted, leaving her light, buoyant. "Thank you, Father."

He nodded briskly. "Dinna thank me. This was your doing. Now, let's go meet our fate."

The fight had gone better than Drake had expected. Since he had expected to die within minutes, the fact that he still lived and fought was remarkable. Drake's only objective was to kill Luthias. He would leave the rest to the others. And though many men-at-arms had been lost, they had a good strategy, as effective as could be expected, considering what they were up against. As the blood witches climbed to the dock, a handful of men-at-arms rushed the foremost *baobhan sith.* Strong as they were, they could not anticipate an attack from all sides. The men-at-arms hacked and hacked until they cut one down, making sure to take the head.

Effective as this strategy was, it wasn't nearly enough. Far more men-at-arms died than blood witches.

They had managed to lead them away from the women, to the top of the keep. Drake charged at Luthias, swinging his sword, but Luthias blocked him every time, his strokes so strong that they sometimes knocked Drake off balance. He noted that Sir Philip and Lord Kincreag formed a shield around Drake's brother, which Drake had asked them to do. William was needed for the fight, but he would be needed even more to heal the survivors. They could not afford to lose him.

There was little room to fight at the top of the keep. Stephen and Drake had maneuvered Luhias and two other blood witches up here. The others were still below. They had trapped several in a room, but that would not hold them for long.

Drake renewed his attack, his sword clanging against Luhias's hard enough to send sparks flying. He went for the neck every time. And Luhias returned the favor.

"You cannot win," Luhias said, smiling, his incisors gleaming. "It is almost daylight, and then this will be over."

He was right. That sent black anger through Drake's limbs, giving him a burst of strength. He came at Luhias from the side, his swing so powerful that it knocked Luhias back against the embrasure. He caught himself, his eyes widening in surprise. But his face immediately hardened.

Drake braced himself for the new assault when a familiar voice brought them both up short.

"Luhias! I am here!"

Luhias's head swiveled around. Deidra stood on the outer curtain wall, waving her arms at him.

"Come and get me!"

Stephen swore somewhere behind Drake.

Drake tried to take advantage of Luthias's surprise, but the blood witch ducked away so quickly that Drake's sword cut through air and hit the stone. The shock reverberated up his arm.

Luthias smiled at Drake, wicked with promise. "It's hard to pass up such an invitation. I think I will go get her."

Drake swung savagely, wanting to wipe that evil smirk away forever. Luthias leapt aside. He was at the ladder leading back inside the keep in seconds, and then he was gone. Drake tried to follow, but one of the blood witches locked swords with him.

This new development lit a fire under Stephen. In a few bold strokes he cut a blood witch down and divested him of his head. Drake took the other one, slashing him down equally quick.

They both dove down the narrow curving stairs, racing after Luthias. Sir Philip and William still had the blood witches trapped in a room, but the door splintered from their swords hacking at it. Lord Kincreag was nowhere to be found. Drake feared the worst.

He didn't have time to ask for help, but as he raced by, a series of crashes originated from the room where the blood witches were trapped. It sounded as if a dozen bowls had been smashed on the ground.

The blood witches' assault on the door stopped abruptly. Seconds later they were screaming and beating on the door—this time with fists, not swords.

Sir Philip, William, and his men all stood back, staring at the door in astonishment. Wisps of smoke curled up from under it.

Lord Kincreag raced around the corner with two men, his long black hair falling free of the leather thong that normally held it back. "Did they stop?" No one had to answer that—the unholy screams told the story.

When the others looked at him, he grinned. "Greek fire. I threw them in through the arrow loops." He shrugged when they stared at him, amazed. The arrow loops were slits in the wall and at least fifteen feet from the nearest place to throw. "You learn things on the Barbary coast."

Drake continued down the stairs, confident the others could handle whatever remained when Lord Kincreag's Greek fire died out.

Out in the courtyard Drake spotted Luthias. He was already on the curtain wall, chasing Deidra, who had reached the corner bastion. She jerked frantically at the door, trying to open it. Stephen appeared from the staircase near the gatehouse and followed.

Drake sprinted across the courtyard, running to the opposite side so he could head Luthias and Deidra off from the other direction. He was climbing the staircase when he heard a scream from above. His heart jammed into his throat as he cleared the wall walk.

He raced for the bastion. The door flew open and Deidra stumbled out, falling to her knees. Before she could get to her feet, Luthias was there. He jerked her up, and when she fought him, he hit her.

Stephen appeared, a mace in his right hand and an ax in his left. "I will have your head if you touch her."

It was enough of a distraction. Deidra rammed an elbow to Luthias's throat and twisted away. Luthias snatched at her, but Stephen was there, swinging his ax. Luthias blocked the strike and dealt Stephen such a blow to the chest that he flew back over the wall, landing on his back in the courtyard.

"Stephen!" Deidra screamed.

She raced for the stairs. Luthias was after her, but he pulled up short, and Deidra made her escape. Drake raised his sword and ran at Luthias's back, only to stop, as Luthias had, when he saw Hannah.

Her wet hair hung like copper yarn around her shoulders. A thin wet shift billowed around her, leaving little to imagination where it hugged her breasts. Had she swum over? She had no weapons that he could see. Something was balled into her fist, but it was far too small to be a weapon.

His heart squeezed, so that he could hardly breathe at the sight of her. Why was she here? She was supposed to be safely hidden.

Luthias looked over his shoulder and smiled. He knew Hannah was even better than Dee-dee. He grabbed Hannah, bringing his sword up to her throat. She seemed strangely blank, detached, his puppet.

"She'll be the first," Luthias sneered. "Then I will kill all of the others while you watch. You will not be able to do a thing."

Like hell he'd watch. Drake raised his sword, preparing to race forward, but found he couldn't move. He was rooted to the spot.

Luthias laughed maniacally. "I've been in your head since the beginning, lad. You've been my puppet."

Drake struggled to move forward, to lift his sword.

But just as Hannah had once controlled him with her mind, Luthias now held him back.

As Drake fought against himself to *move*, he noticed smoke rising from Luthias and Hannah. It threaded upward in ribbons from where their bodies touched.

Luthias noticed it and thrust Hannah an arm's length away from him. "What . . . ?"

"I swam through holy water to bring you this." Her hand opened and the rosary unfurled, dangling from her fingers.

Drake wanted to turn his face away, but he could not, as Luthias still held him. The light from the rosary blinded him and he blinked, his eyes watering. It surrounded Hannah, covering her in light.

"You're covered in holy water. . . ." Luthias turned his head to the side, bringing a hand up, his mouth opening and closing. "How can this be?"

"I've been baptized. And I'm here to give you this." She stepped forward and threw the rosary, high and wide.

Luthias's concentration broke. Drake was free. The rosary spun, falling in a loop over Luthias's head and hooking on his ear.

He shrieked, an inhuman cry of an animal in pain, and he clawed at the rosary. Drake ran forward, bending to snag up the ax Stephen had dropped. He swung it with every ounce of strength he possessed. It landed with a thunk across Luthias's neck, separating head from body.

His torso hit the wall walk with a thunk.

Drake stood there, ax in hand, panting from the exertion.

Hannah stared up at him, a strange little smile on her face.

"My God, woman, what are you doing here?"

One perfect copper brow arched. "I came to help. And you're welcome."

He dropped the ax and closed the distance between them, snagging her wrist, and pulling her hard into his arms.

He kissed her, her mouth breathing life into his, her body filling the emptiness. Her arms twined around him.

"I missed you," he said against her neck.

She felt warm against him, so warm her skin burned into his. And then he realized she *was* burning him.

He stepped back, releasing her. "Holy water? You're really drenched in holy water?"

She nodded, that odd little smile on her face again. "Well, blessed water. Which is close enough, apparently."

"How is that possible? Why does it burn me, but not harm you? And the rosary . . . ?" Drake turned to look at Luthias's decapitated head, the rosary still tangled around the ear.

Hannah shook her head, her gaze on Drake. "I know not. But I am pretty sure Luthias was not doing God's work."

Drake touched her damp hair, which was hot, as if lit from a fire within. He snatched his hand away and shook his head in amazement. "I love you."

Her little smile grew wider. "I know."

Chapter 26

Hannah did not know how or why she had been able to swim through blessed water or hold a rosary in her bare hand. Whatever spirit had entered her and made it possible left her when the water dried.

But it had been in her and it could never have entered her if she were truly evil. She might share her body with a demon, but she supposed everyone had their own demons that made them do things they weren't particularly proud of.

Stephen was fine. A little sore, but he was a *baobhan sith*, after all. Once the remaining blood witches in the village realized Luthias was dead, they fled. And the villagers, hearing the glen was safe, returned to their homes.

Hannah agreed to stay to help dispose of the *baobhan sith* bodies properly and to be there in case any of the blood witches reappeared. With Luthias gone, the Highlands would be a much safer place for the Mac-Kays and the MacDonnells.

Hannah wondered what would happen next. It was Sir Philip who had asked her to stay, not Drake. In fact, since Drake's declaration of love on the wall walk, he'd hardly spoken to her.

Of course it had been day, and he had slept. She was full of *baobhan sith* blood and needed no sleep, so she helped the humans burn the corpses. Still, when dark fell, Drake did not come to her.

She thought about seeking him out but decided that the next gesture was his to make. She had come back after he had abandoned her. Now it was time for him to explain himself. It didn't matter that she knew why he'd done it and understood. Her heart needed to hear it from him.

She went down to the water dock and stared into the water. Was it still blessed? She was afraid to dip her finger in and check. The priest was in the village, counseling those who had lost loved ones, so she could not ask him.

The water lapped against the stone. She stepped closer, right to the edge, and looked down. She saw herself in the water, reflected like glass, except the color was wrong, green and gray.

A figure appeared beside her.

Drake.

Her heart snagged, but she did not turn around.

"Are you angry with me?" he asked.

A sad smile tugged at the corners of her mouth. "No."

He looked at her in the water. The soft lapping waves obscured his eyes, but she could tell that his gaze was on her. "The way I behaved . . . I was a clod, I know . . . but I wanted you to be safe, to stay safe. So I had to make you believe I was a clod."

"I have lived a very long time, Drake. I do not care to do it alone any longer."

He moved closer, though he did not touch her. "You are different now. Are you still a blood witch?" He seemed hesitant, worried.

She tilted her head slightly. "Aye, of course I am."

"But the blessed water . . . the rosary."

"I know not. Perhaps I was an instrument of God. I was shriven. I placed my fate in His hands. Mayhap that is all we can do?"

He took her shoulders and pulled her back against him. Hannah closed her eyes, reveling in the feel of his solid chest against her back. "You confessed? What sins have you to confess?"

Hannah laughed softly, melting back into him and leaning her head against his shoulder. "So many I could not remember them all."

"Anything about me?"

"Certainly."

When she didn't elaborate, he squeezed her shoulders, then slid his arms down around her waist. His mouth was at her ear, tickling the down along her neck. "Well?"

"I told him I had lain with a man who was not my husband."

"And what was your penance?"

Hannah tilted her head thoughtfully, inadvertently giving him full access to her neck, which he took advantage of. His tongue slid along her skin and she shivered.

"He did not give a different penance for each of my sins, but one penance for them all. He also told me that I was not to lay with a man unless he was my husband." She shrugged. "I suppose that is my penance?"

His arms tightened around her. "You jest?"

"Nay."

"Damn," he breathed against her neck. He released her and took her hand, pulling her toward the stairs. "Get in the boat. We're going to the village to find your priest."

Hannah laughed and pulled back so that he had to drag her along. When he turned to look at her, her smile faded. "Are you sure, Drake? Forever is a very long time."

He gave her a heart-stopping smile. "Not nearly long enough."

Discover the darker side of desire.

Pick up a bestselling paranormal romance from Pocket Books!

Kresley Cole
Dark Deeds at Night's Edge
The Immortals After Dark Series

A vampire shunned by his own kind is driven to the edge of madness….where he discovers the ultimate desire.

Jen Holling
My Immortal Protector

Deep in the Scottish Highlands, a reluctant witch is willing to do anything to give up her powers—until she meets the one man who may give her a reason to use them.

Marta Acosta
Happy Hour at Casa Dracula

Come for a drink….Stay for a bite.

Gwyn Cready
Tumbling Through Time

She was a total control freak—until a magical pair of killer heels sends her back in time—and into the arms of the wrong man!